Helmuth Graf von Moltke

Essays, Speeches, and Memoirs of Field-Marshal Count Helmuth von

Moltke

Vol. 2

Helmuth Graf von Moltke

Essays, Speeches, and Memoirs of Field-Marshal Count Helmuth von Moltke
Vol. 2

ISBN/EAN: 9783337383985

Printed in Europe, USA, Canada, Australia, Japan

Cover: Foto ©Raphael Reischuk / pixelio.de

More available books at **www.hansebooks.com**

ESSAYS, SPEECHES,

AND

MEMOIRS

OF

FIELD-MARSHAL

COUNT HELMUTH VON MOLTKE

THE ESSAYS TRANSLATED BY
CHARLES FLINT McCLUMPHA,
Ph.D.; THE SPEECHES, BY MAJOR
C. BARTER, D.A.A.G.; AND THE
MEMOIRS, BY MARY HERMS

IN TWO VOLUMES

VOL. II.

NEW YORK

HARPER & BROTHERS, FRANKLIN SQUARE

1893

TABLE OF CONTENTS.

VOL. II.

On the 24th February, 1867, King William opened the first German parliamentary assembly, the Reichstag of the North German Confederation—such an assembly as had not for centuries, to quote the words of the Speech from the Throne, rallied round a German ruler.

The campaign of 1866, fortunate beyond precedent in its results, had made it possible to build up on the ruins of the old German Confederation a new German constitution which at any rate assured to the majority of the nation a unity which it had so long and so passionately striven to attain, and which at the same time offered a guarantee for the hopeful development, in the future, of a State organization which would comprise the whole nation. The election to this first Reichstag of a number of the most highly esteemed of those generals to whose leadership the successful issue of the war was chiefly due appeared as an act of grateful homage on the part of the nation. That the name of the Chief of the General Staff, General von Moltke, should be included in this roll was a matter of course. Three different constituencies (Memel-Heydekrug, Fürstenthum, Bitterfeld-Delitzsch) gave him their votes. He also stood at that time as one of the candidates for Berlin, but was defeated by his opponent, Wiggers. "I can forgive the town of Berlin, if I fail," were the words which, on the 28th January, 1867, he wrote to his brother Adolphus.

Moltke represented the same constituency (Memel-Heydekrug) uninterruptedly until his death, and seldom was absent from a debate, save when, as in 1870-71, he was in the field. From the year 1881 he regularly opened the parliamentary sessions in the capacity of "doyen" President. In the beginning of 1872 the confidence reposed in him by his Imperial master led to his translation to the House of Lords [1] (Herrenhaus), to the legislative labours of which he devoted himself with no less zeal. He appeared in the Reichstag for the last time two days before his death, and his last journey in life—it was on the 24th April, 1891, the day of his death, and but a few hours before it—was from the House of Lords to his private residence. His unwearying devotion to duty marked his political life as it did all his acts. No representative was more conscientious than he in his attendance in the Reichstag, and no other member of the House was more zealous in his desire to master, in all their bearings, the questions under debate.[2]

Moltke well understood how to secure a position of high consideration in both Houses, and but few possessed in the same high degree the power of compelling the attention of an assembly. As he rises to speak the House assumes at once a changed aspect, deep stillness settles on the whole hall, and from all sides members press round for fear of losing any of his words. Adversaries and admirers follow with equal attention utterances the weighty import of which none dare gainsay. What he proposes is in all cases so appropriate, so exactly fitted to the occasion, so transparently and unequivocally clear, yet withal so simple and noble in form, that it never fails of its effect, and gives opponents food for thought, even when it does not convince them. Moltke's speeches were never marred by those unrepressed and bitter personal observations

[1] A Prussian, not an Imperial assembly.—[Note by Translator.]
[2] Recollections of a follower of his party.

which so frequently prejudicially affect our parliamentary life. What he says has always to do with the thing in hand. His lofty reserve absolutely forbade any disparaging criticism of persons. There is no doubt that a man possessed of such clearness of understanding and fulness of knowledge must have formed thoroughly matured, and certainly most interesting, conclusions, even on subjects not immediately connected with his profession, yet, with the exception of the occasions when he spoke on the first Socialistic Bill and on that relating to the introduction of a Standard Time, he was careful to restrict his participation in debate to questions of a military nature, or to those political subjects which were inevitably allied to them. He always strove earnestly to demonstrate the inseparable connection which exists between the interests of the army and those of the State and nation.[1] It cannot, however, be said that he was merely a technical adviser of the House in military matters. His utterances on such matters frequently disclosed views on internal and external political questions which never failed to produce a marked impression, and which reveal the field-marshal in the character of the politician who is striving to throw a clear light on the highest aims of statesmanship.

That Moltke was governed by staunch conservative sentiments and by unswerving loyalty to the constitution can surprise no one. Nothing seems to indicate, however, that he ever associated himself with that current of thought which, at least in his earlier days, moved many to look upon any constitutional system as only a temporary makeshift, which, sooner or later, should necessarily be compelled to make way for the establishment of a rigid autocracy. Having once accepted the responsibilities resting on a representative of the people, he formed too high an opinion of the

---

[1] *In memoriam* Speech by Councillor Ernst Curtius in the Academy on the 2nd July, 1892. Compare " Essays, Memoirs, and Speeches of Field-Marshal Count Helmuth von Moltke," vol. ii.

duties which had devolved upon him to admit such thoughts as these into his mind. In this respect the debates relating to the Constitution of the North-German Confederation, at the outset of his parliamentary career, made a deep impression upon him, as appears from various letters written in 1867 and 1868. We single out more especially the letter which he addressed to his brother Adolphus on 10th March, 1867, and in which we read: "The debates in the Reichstag consume a terrible amount of time, but they are in the highest degree interesting now that the preliminary business of the House and the electoral revisions are at length over. Orations of great talent are undoubtedly heard in this assembly, but side by side with these are speeches of no power, the conventional utterances of those who speak only for the sake of speaking. It seems as though even the more enlightened spirits amongst those who represent the minor States brought with them only their more circumscribed field of vision. . . . Thus I have listened with great interest to Waldeck, who, with views which are liberal, republican almost, and decidedly antagonistic to the principle of the autonomy of the States, opposes the Government proposals. The speeches of Braun, from Saxony, of Miquel from Osnabrück, and of Wagner, in support of the proposition, were listened to in absolute silence, and twice did Bismarck reply with truly statesmanlike orations. I am collecting the stenographed reports of the debate . . . . you should read them some time; they are well worth the trouble. I have already, after only a two-days' general discussion, acquired the conviction that the defeat of the 'Constitution Bill' is an impossibility. The Opposition can do no more than attack isolated clauses. As it cannot damage the Bill as a whole, it is obliged to attack it in its details."

It cannot be said that Moltke often rose to address the Houses. The number of his speeches was not

great, as he himself remarks, and those that he made
were certainly not long. He spoke altogether on forty-
one occasions in the twenty-one years during which he
was a member of the Reichstag, and in the Upper
House he delivered three orations. The absence of
length in his speeches is, however, richly compensated
for by their weight and intrinsic value, and meet it is
that they should be recorded not only as hitherto, in
stenographed reports for the historian or the politician,
but in a form which shall be accessible to the people at
large. Often we have only brief observations, yet, even
so, they are almost invariably of lasting value in
connection with the question in hand. These shorter
utterances, where they deal with a separate subject and
are not supplementary or complementary to some
more important speech, relate in the main to special
technical military questions, which have been brought
forward, as a rule, with the object of improving the
defensive power of the country and its armed forces.
In this respect the speeches dealing with the " Baltic
and North Sea Canal," and with the construction of a
ship-canal between the Rhine and the lower Ems,
occupy a prominent position. Of not less interest are
the opinions expressed by Moltke with regard to the
railway system of Germany and the employment and
utilization of railways in war—opinions which are all the
more interesting when regard is had to the fact that
Moltke was the first of the great commanders of modern
times to appreciate the full importance of this weighty
factor in war, and to take full advantage of it. The
German army was the first to possess a technically
trained railway corps. At great reviews it was Moltke's
custom to place himself at the head of this corps, and
to lead it in the march-past before the Emperor.
Whenever the question of railways came to the front,
the occasion always found him ready to intervene,
either to award unqualified praise to the officials of the
railway and postal branches for the extraordinary

success attending their efforts in the last war, or else to offer his opinion when the debate had relation to special technical railway affairs or to the construction of new railway lines. To these matters belong the interesting opinions which he expressed in connection with the remodelling of fortresses generally, and of Cologne and Strasburg in particular.

The energy which Moltke displayed when advocating the improvement of the standing defences of the country and its defensive power was equalled by the fervent zeal with which he supported all measures, even of comparatively narrow scope, which had the welfare of the army in view. We note especially his utterances regarding punishments by arrest, barracks and officers' mess establishments, commissariat duties in peace and war, the food supply of the German army of occupation in France, and the use to which the savings hereby effected should be put. He demanded, with much emphasis, an improvement in the position of officers as regards pension, and he resisted with great energy, as well as with success, the proposal to cancel the exemption of officers from local taxation. In all cases he argued from the standpoint of justice, and it was chiefly owing to his efforts that an understanding favourable to the general interests of the army was finally arrived at in Parliament.

It is needless to insist on the importance of Moltke's speeches advocating the reorganization of the army on a German, instead of a Prussian, basis. They speak for themselves. Their influence extends far beyond the limits of their parliamentary effect. They belong to history, and must, whether considered from the point of view of the soldier or from that of the statesman, ever remain unforgotten, so long as the German army and the German nation exist, and so long as a record survives of the unexampled difficulties which characterized the successful founding of the German Constitution and its first development. They afford significant and incontrovertible evidence of the critical position in which Germany finds herself placed with regard to her Western, and, during the last decade, also with regard to her Eastern neighbour. The argument upon which he laid so much stress, that the maintenance of peace was endangered not by the ambition of rulers but by the impulse of nations, gave his utterances unanswerable force.

When, in 1888, Moltke retired from the office of Chief of the General Staff, it did not enter his mind to resign also, on the score of great age, his position [1] as first military adviser to the nation. This position he gave up only with his last breath. His words of advice will neither be lost nor forgotten. They form an invaluable heritage for our nation.

To the speeches which Moltke uttered in the Imperial Reichstag and in the Prussian House of Lords are added four drafts of speeches which were found amongst his papers after his death. Of these, three had been written for the Customs Parliament (Zollparlament), and one for the North-German Reichstag. The former have to do with the relations existing at that time (beginning of 1868) between the North-German Confederation and the States of Southern Germany. They are directed against the influences and tendencies, so full of discord and prejudice, which at that time moved a section of South Germans to oppose Prussia, and which found their expression in more or less despicable agitations and movements. They define clearly and in a temperate spirit the attitude which Moltke considered should, under these circumstances, be taken up with regard to the South Germans.

Nothing marks more emphatically the growth of the national sentiment than the fact that these prejudices have now, in the case of the vast majority of the South Germans, been completely overcome. These drafts are

---

[1] Moltke was President of the National Defence Committee (Landes-Vertheidigungs Commission).—[Note by Translator.]

in the highest degree remarkable and noteworthy, as enabling one to form a just estimate of the events occurring between 1866 and 1870. They throw a bright light on the views and opinions which after the war of 1866 governed men's minds with reference to the great German Question, and they are not less significant as indications of the way in which Moltke, from the commencement of his parliamentary career, faced his task as a member of Parliament.

For this reason we place these drafts of speeches at the beginning of our collection, whilst we introduce the fourth draft, which has reference to the debate in the North-German Reichstag on the "Public Debts of the Confederation Bill," with a speech actually delivered by Moltke on this subject.

DRAFTS OF SPEECHES
IN THE "CUSTOMS PARLIAMENT"
(ZOLLPARLAMENT).

INTRODUCTION.

AMONGST the papers left behind by Moltke were found four autograph drafts of speeches which were never delivered. These papers bear the superscription, " Customs Parliament " (Zollparlament), although the last draft, which appears to have been added later, was doubtless intended for the North-German Reichstag. They all date from the first half of 1868, the second year of Moltke's political life.

The leading thoughts expressed in these papers must have occupied Moltke's most earnest attention, even before the session, for in a letter dated 24th January, 1868, we find passages which are reproduced almost word for word in the drafts themselves. Of the three drafts written for the " Customs Parliament," two are so similar in form, and indeed in language, that one may be fairly regarded as an amended copy of the other. This assumption is further borne out by references in the second draft to certain points contained in the first. We have, therefore, to deal only with one speech, which we give according to the second version, but for the sake of completeness, we introduce those passages of the first draft which, on the authority of notes in the later draft, we know that Moltke wished transferred to it.

The speeches are directed against the adoption of an Address from the " Customs Parliament " to the King of Prussia, a motion which was, on the 7th May, 1868, negatived on a simple division, by 186 votes to 150.

As regards the third draft, which is given in this work as the second, it is not quite clear with what object the speech was prepared. As, however, mention is made in the first few lines of the "Customs Parliament," it is not unreasonable to conjecture that it represents the subsequent revision of a speech which Moltke originally intended to deliver before this special assembly. Whilst in the other drafts the Address is directly dealt with, reference is made at the end of this one to a projected law which is specially welcome as representing a "portion of a combined building plan agreed to by all." He had in his speech stated that the "Offensive and Defensive Alliance" (Schutz-und Trutzbundniss) and the "Customs Union" (Zollver-band) formed the foundations of this new German building. It is possible that Moltke intended to express himself in this sense in the event of a general debate on the new Customs Tariff. For the rest the draft contains sentences and opinions extracted from the first drafts, and in one place a passage from them is directly referred to.

We can do no more than conjecture why Moltke did not avail himself of an opportunity to deliver these carefully prepared speeches from the tribune of the "Customs Parliament." It may have been that he was influenced by the consideration that, in view of the advisability of sparing South German susceptibilities, at that time so strongly marked, it would be politic not to extend too widely, in the "Customs Parliament," the scope of discussion on weighty political questions. It seems to us, however, more reasonable to suppose that the intention to deliver these speeches was not the leading thought which moved Moltke to prepare them, but that he was governed by the particular motive which is disclosed throughout all his literary work. He wished, by putting them on paper, to bring order and clearness into his thoughts. "It was such a very distinctive feature of his genius to mould and remould his thoughts, until they attained the most concise and complete form possible, that he considered it a positive pleasure to remodel them on paper. The publication of his literary efforts appears to have been ever the intention lying farthest from his thoughts, and on the occasions when he thus gave them to the world, he was always moved, not by self-interest, but by the belief that they might be useful." In any case these drafts prove to us in how great a degree Moltke was filled with the sense of the importance of his parliamentary duties.

"CUSTOMS PARLIAMENT" (ZOLLPARLAMENT).

I.

I rise to speak against the Address, not because I am opposed to the wishes which it expresses, but because I believe that this Address is here out of place.

A change in the relation, established by treaty, of the South-German States to the North-German Confederation can be effected, in my opinion, only in one of two ways: either by war, which brushes aside existing compacts and substitutes others which are more suitable to the existing order of things, or by a general understanding.

I admit that by the latter method little can be effected in Germany.

However much German unity may have been extolled by word or pen, and however much it may have been sung and toasted, it is certain that no reality has as yet been called into existence.

The opportunities of uniting, which the Almighty has offered to the German nation at intervals of centuries, have never been seized, for the reason that each State views itself as the only possible central point of the union. Each wishes to pursue a different course, and one, therefore, impossible of realization.

Any real unity which has hitherto been attained is
due to the compulsion which Prussia, in gentler or
rougher form, has exercised through her commercial
policy, her diplomacy or her sword.

Prussia's reward has been a rich harvest of hate and
enmity. Party passion especially has, quite recently,
caused Prussia to be held up, in South Germany, to
suspicion, contempt and ridicule. I do not believe that
these efforts have prevailed with the educated portion
of the nation, and I am of opinion that a certain number
of the South German representatives will carry away
with them a more favourable impression than this of
Prussia, " the great barracks."

Each State is entitled to exalt its own characteristics.
Allow us, therefore, to hold ours in esteem. We see in
our military institutions, which certainly are prominent,
a school which trains the people to order and exactness,
to loyalty and obedience, but we impose our institutions
on no one but ourselves. I ask you, what steps has the
North German Confederation taken, since the conclusion of peace, to constrain the South German States to
abandon their individuality, their self-reliance or, if you
prefer the term, their independence? Certainly it is
desirable that a *rapprochement* should be effected in
the domain of military affairs. There exists at the
present time a Defensive and Offensive Alliance. This
is an imperfect form of mutual assistance.[1] A defensive
and offensive alliance is worth no more than the means
which each side possesses for offensive or defensive
action. I am not referring to the fact that North
Germany possesses the greater war strength; that is a
matter of course; but then we maintain an army,
you only furnish contingents, we have a War-Lord

---

[1] In the manuscript, the following note is here to be found,
" The experiences of the year 1866." The remarks referring to
them are contained in the first sketch, from which we have transferred them to this place.

(Kriegsherr), you have a Commander-in-chief. The difference is a great one, as the year 1866 proved.

The conduct of the war by South Germany has been severely censured and its leaders have been held responsible for its non-success. The vanity of nations ever demands a scape-goat in the event of an unsuccessful campaign. But for him all would have gone well. But, gentlemen, the South-German leaders are not, in the main, to blame for the ill-success of the war. Nor are the South-German troops, who fought everywhere with bravery, responsible for it. Conflicting interests amongst the populations of South Germany made it possible for 46,000 Prussians, homogeneous in their organization and energetically led, to take the offensive against an enemy 100,000 strong, and to push forward from the Eider to the Yaxt. They had placed in the hand of their commander a weapon of most excellent steel, but it was composed of separate pieces.

This is the difference between an army possessing unity of purpose and a coalition. With the best of wills these States of South Germany can at present offer nothing more than a coalition, whilst all around us we see only great compact armies. We, too, therefore desire internal fusion, but we desire it less in the interest of North Germany, or of Prussia, than in that of Germany generally, and in yours more particularly. The North does not need to constrain the South ; it can await the time when the necessity of circumstances shall bring the South to us. No sooner does a cloud appear on the political horizon than the necessity at once arises. It is true that with the disappearance of this cloud vanishes all inclination to establish any of those permanent institutions which would enable the North to assist, and which would actually even make such assistance unnecessary. The utility of the institutions which have proved valuable in Prussia is generally recognized, but a hope is entertained that the burdens which they necessarily entail may be avoided. Yet these are burdens which Prussia has borne alone for 50 years without succumbing, and to the existence of which we owe it, that to-day we can all meet together in this hall, deputies from the South, as well as from the North. And this vacillation is a charge that lies not only or altogether against the governments of States, but lies especially against their Representative Assemblies.

You have in principle adopted universal military service for three years, but in practice the weakness of your "cadres" and the large number of recruits which will have to be incorporated will compel you to adopt a system of service for two years, a period which will, from financial considerations, be further reduced to one year, as before.

That the North desires union with the South is well known, and no Address is necessary to emphasize this fact. What is wanted is the establishment of intimate understanding between the Government and the representatives of the people in each individual State of South Germany, and this, gentlemen from South Germany, appears to me, to be a domestic matter, which you can surely settle at home. An address, here, in the "Customs Parliament," proceeding only from a section of the popular representation, and without the sanction of the several governments, can lead to no practical result, but must of necessity be the cause of party strife. Treaties cannot be abrogated by one party alone. Only bring us to union, and no fear of possible external complications shall hinder your admission to that place in the confederation to which you are by right entitled and to which duty calls you. Nothing could more greatly conduce to complete union than a blow from without, a shock which would once more set in action the interrupted process of crystallization.

Our neighbours know right well (even those who assume ignorance) that Germany does not wish for conquest. When they act as though they feared an attack by us, it may be assumed that defence is not their aim ; they have some ulterior purpose in view. They know well that we have no aggressive design ; they know just as well that we shall not suffer any interference as regards our internal affairs.

Should peaceable times, therefore, be in store for us, it is not too much to hope that there may be a gradual drawing together. Even now a strong impulse is making itself increasingly felt, not a material compulsion, but that compulsion which common sense and self-interest exert on human life.

I anticipate the gravitation of the South to the North, because of its patriotism, as well as because we offer the higher price. We maintain an army, you only contingents ; we have a War-Lord, you only a Commander-in-chief. We offer you what we have purchased with our blood, and which no power on earth shall again wrest from us, we offer you what without us, you can never achieve—a Fatherland !

II.

I do not desire that the discussion in this House, should strengthen the extraordinary delusion existing in the minds of our countrymen from the South, that we have nothing of greater importance to do here than to win them over to us. Their deputies of the " Customs Parliament" (Zollparlament), could have informed them how far this is from the truth. The delusion exists, nevertheless.

Prussia has, by prowess in war, made a unified Germany a possibility. This is surely no reason, however, even if it be not desired to turn this possibility to account, why we should be daily held up to hatred and scorn in South Germany, both at large public gatherings and in the papers.

I can find no other cause for this peculiar phenomenon, than the fear—the anxiety, lest some day we should suddenly invade their country, curtail the rights of their Princes, and interfere with the freedom of the people of each State.

The year 1866 did not complete the work of German unity. It might have been expected that what remained to be done would have been effected by statesmanlike wisdom and German patriotism.

It appears that in some places, the terms autonomy and sovereignty have been confused with each other. In patriotism the German stands far behind the Frenchman or the Englishman, behind the Pole or the Dane. In Esthonia, the German becomes a good Russian, in Alsace a good Frenchman, in America an ardent Yankee; only in Germany will he not be a German; he will not even be a Coburg-Gothaer, but only a Gothaer, or a Coburger.

Three centuries have passed since the days of Charles V., and now again Fate confronts us with the question : "Will you, German men, who through internal discord have lost Lorraine and Burgundy, Alsace, Switzerland and the Netherlands, will you combine to preserve through all futurity, the large, though curtailed, heritage which yet belongs to you ?" What reply will you make ?

For fifty years German unity has been extolled in prose, in verse, in song, and in toasts. Rifle meetings have been held, and public speeches made, in honour of German unity, but still there has been no union. You want unity, but you will not make use of the proffered means—Prussia. You wish to adopt some other means, that is to say each one desires to attain it by his own particular, and therefore impossible, method.[1] You think it enough to say that, perhaps, under certain conditions, you will, at a later date, consent to unity.

Gentlemen, this appears to me a complete misconception of the real state of affairs. If the South

---

[1] See the letter referred to above, of January 24th, 1868.

imagines that it can stand without the North, be it so. We are accustomed to rely on our own strength.

Two national bonds have hitherto linked together Germans of all races: the "Customs Union" (Zollverband), which is not, we hope, disadvantageous to the South, and the "offensive and defensive Alliance," (Schutz-und-Trutz-Bündniss). With reference to the latter, I beg to draw attention to the fact that whilst we gain some help by the adhesion of Southern Germany, we also give help, and that we give more help than we get. I do not wish to lay stress on the fact that we in the North can put forth a tenfold greater power against the enemies of Germany, nor that we still bear, for the sake of Germany as a whole, too great a proportion of the military burden, nor that the fortresses of South Germany are to this day still armed with our guns.

The North, however, maintains a compact army under its "War-Lord;" the South furnishes merely contingents. The South, however excellent its intentions, can offer nothing better than a coalition, and the South knows best what this word represents.

A coalition is admirable, so long as all the interests of the various members are identical. But if the achievement of the great common object should happen to be dependent on the self-sacrifice of one of the members, then I, for one, would no longer count upon the efficacy of the coalition. One of the factors which most contributed to the successful issue of the last war, was the determination of His Majesty the King of Prussia to denude the Rhine Province of all troops, except the garrisons of the fortresses, in order that he might bring into the field, at the decisive point, forces equal to those of the enemy. Allow, for a moment, that the Rhine Provinces and Westphalia constituted at the time an independent Grand Duchy. Do you believe, that, even under an offensive and defensive alliance, it would have been possible to prevail upon this State to despatch its army to Bohemia? And yet, had it not done this, we should have been weaker at Königgrätz by 66,000 men.

The game is not an even one—we wager different stakes. The North offers that which Prussia has purchased with blood, that which no power on earth shall ever, if it be God's will, again tear from us, that which the South can never without us possess—a Fatherland, a real, great and powerful Germany. This, gentlemen, we are already. Abroad, beyond the sea, we are respected, perhaps dreaded, or even hated—though without cause—but it is only in Germany that we are despised and ridiculed.

Well do I know that this mental blindness is to be found only amongst the masses, who are not capable of forming a correct judgment; yet even towards them we do not act as if the association were indispensable to them, but rather as if it were so to us.

Under the influence of the "Customs Union," and under the protection of the League, the South Germans may continue a while to sulk apart, until the first internal or external shock exposes the weakness of this condition of affairs. If, believing that they can find better friends than their North German countrymen, they refuse to share our labours, we shall persevere in them notwithstanding.

Let us build our house strongly and firmly, for it may have to defy the storm. Let us so build it that, when they seek us, we shall be able to admit them, not as strangers or as guests, but as co-tenants in their own right. They must not, however, then exact of us that we should pull down that which already stands completed, in order that it may be built up again according to their taste.

It is for this reason that the Bill now before us is so welcome. It forms a portion of a building plan in the creation of which all have collaborated.

SPEECHES IN THE REICHSTAG AND IN THE PRUSSIAN HOUSE OF LORDS (HERRENHAUS).

I. COMMUNICATIONS.

CANALS—POSTS AND RAILWAYS—LAND DEFENCES. NORTH SEA—BALTIC CANAL.

Debate on the Naval Estimates.

Sitting of the Reichstag, 17th June, 1868.

It would certainly be desirable that we should possess more harbours, and efforts have been made to give effect to the wish, but I should like to remark that the cost of the harbour at Jasmunder Bodden alone, if the fortification works be included, is estimated at thirty millions.[1] I cannot, therefore, but think that we have already devoted too much attention to harbours, which are so expensive that nothing is left for the construction of the navy which is to protect them. With regard to the canal I should like to lay before you a statement of facts. I do not doubt that the so-called Königshafen is an excellent harbour, although the entrance channel is difficult of navigation, but no connection exists between Romöe and the mainland, and the construction of the works necessary for the establishment of such connection across the flats, over which the tide ebbs and flows four times daily, would involve very great expense.

As regards the Flensburg canal, I was struck by the peculiar physical configuration of the land when we occupied Schleswig in 1864, and I therefore entered into a close examination of it. The high ridge which divides the peninsula runs up almost to the east coast, and slopes steeply down towards the harbour of Flensburg. From the Bay of Flensburg a valley tends

---

[1] In thalers,—equivalent to 3*s.* each.—[Note by Translator.]

westwards, up which, at a distance of not more than 1500 paces, may be found the sources of the streams which flow towards the North Sea. It would be natural, therefore, to suppose that a canal could here be constructed in the most favourable direction for ship navigation. I have, however, had levelling surveys made of the heights, by a trustworthy land-surveyor with theodolites, in two directions, and have ascertained that the height of the lowest point is 121 feet above the level of the sea. I must add, that no water is available for the feeding of the canal, and further, that a canal constructed with locks would obstruct navigation. You must therefore imagine a ditch, which would have to be $120+23$ feet deep, and over 600 feet wide. To excavate a ditch of these dimensions, for a distance of a couple of thousand feet or so, would be an expensive, though feasible, project; but the most serious objection to it consists in the fact that from the summit of the ridge the slope to the North Sea is so gradual that for a further six miles the canal would require a depth of $90+32$ feet. The construction of this canal would, therefore, be far more expensive than that of the one proposed at a cost of 30 millions (thalers), which has, moreover, the additional advantage of connecting two harbours, one of which, Kiel, has already been fortified, while the other, on the lower Elbe, must, in any case, be provided with defensive works. I therefore hold that the construction of a canal leading from Flensburg is impracticable.

Sitting of the Reichstag, 23rd June, 1873.

Gentlemen,—I shall not prolong the discussion much, but I think it may be of some advantage to reduce to reasonable proportions the very great expectations which have been based on the realization of the North Sea—Baltic Canal project. This I do unwillingly, because the scheme is one which clearly has advantages of a military nature to recommend it. I, myself, as early as the year 1865, caused levelling surveys to be made across the country in several directions, and amongst others from Flensburg. All these lines, however, had to be rejected, not only on account of the extraordinary engineering difficulties which they presented, but also by reason of the circumstance that our naval harbour had been established at Kiel in preference to the Alsen Sund. The Government then caused a scheme to be elaborated over a route which had already been pointed out by the Danish engineer, Christensen, as being the most suitable and, possibly also, the only one practicable. In a very able memorandum of Herr Lenze, an official of high rank in the Public Works Department, the circumstances of this project were fully set forth, and the cost estimated at 28 million thalers. The course of the line is from St. Margarethen, on the Lower Elbe, to Eckernförde, on the Baltic. If, however, the canal is to have a military value, it is necessary, for obvious reasons, that it should have its outlet in Kiel Bay, somewhere between Rendsburg and Holtenau ; in other words, precisely at a spot where considerable engineering difficulties present themselves. Councillor Lenze has estimated the additional cost over this line at ten million thalers, or altogether at thirty-eight millions, but this calculation was made eight years ago, and we all know what an increase has taken place since then in the price not only of all *matériel*, but still more of labour. In this particular case, where the volume of soil to be displaced will be as much as fourteen millions of *schachtruths*,[1] the rise in wages will constitute a very serious factor in the scheme. You would therefore, at the present time, certainly not be able to construct the canal at a less expense than that of fifty or sixty millions.

[1] Measure of a square rood to a foot thickness.—[Note by Translator.]

Now, Gentlemen, that the canal earnings will not be sufficient to allow of the payment of interest on this sum is, I think, beyond doubt; and we should have to consider the advantages to navigation and commerce and military operations which would be gained at such a great sacrifice. The number of ships annually passing through the Oere Sound is estimated at 40,000, and it is believed that at least the larger part of this number would make use of the canal.

From this category should, naturally, be excluded, in the first place, those ships bound for Norway, and those sailing north of an imaginary line drawn approximately through the middle of the North Sea to Hull, because these ships would have to follow a circuitous course in order to pass through the canal, which would cause them loss of time—and time is money, especially in the case of steamers. Regard must further be had to climatic considerations. In our northern climate, the canal would be frozen for 100 days; besides, it must not be forgotten that navigation in the Baltic is brought to a stand-still in the winter. Navigation is, therefore, carried on only during the longer summer-half of the year; and it must be remarked that in the height of summer a further diminution of canal traffic must be anticipated, for the reason that dangerous storms and delaying fogs are not to be apprehended, and that ships would select the old route through the Cattegat in order to save the canal dues which cannot, in any case, be light.

Traffic would, therefore, be limited to the two equinoctial seasons. At these times a large number, perhaps too large a number, of ships would wish to use the canal. It is intended that the canal shall throughout be 31 feet below the surface-level of both seas. It is known that the water-levels of the two seas often vary considerably. It is well known that a strong westerly wind blowing up the Elbe dams it up, and it is not unusual at such a time to see the river rise twelve feet above the mean water-mark. The same wind drives the water out of Kiel Bay, and the water-levels there vary as much as eight feet. There may therefore happen to be a difference at any given moment of sixteen to twenty feet in the surface-levels of the two seas. A current would thus be created which would not only very much impede navigation, but which would also necessitate the construction of very costly canal works. At least one lock at the western outlet would be indispensable.

I would wish to point out that though several smaller vessels can be passed through a lock at the same time, the operation in the case of one large vessel requires the expenditure of one and a half hour's time. If, therefore, hundreds of vessels should lie waiting at the gate of the lock, the saving of time in passing through the canal would easily be neutralized.

I now ask of you, Gentlemen, for whom are we building this canal? I may be mistaken, but I believe that our Baltic ports carry on their trade with Scandinavia and Russia, and our North Sea towns with England, America, etc. Even in the event of the completion of the canal, it is hardly to be expected that any great amount of traffic would be carried on between Dantzig and Bremen, or Stettin and Hamburg. It is rather for Sweden and Russia, for America, France, and other countries that we construct the canal. Now do you think that, under these circumstances, the countries I have mentioned would consent to share in the cost of the undertaking? Perhaps! Gentlemen; but in that case the canal would be an international one ; it would then have lost all its strategical value, for in the event of war we should not be able to use a neutral canal. The importance of this fact will be apparent when I state that in the last war a considerable quantity of supplies, and even small war vessels, were forwarded to Jade Bay through the Eider Canal, which was even then available for transit. Whether the existing canal might not be improved at an incomparably smaller expense—that is a question which I leave undecided.

To come to the question of military utility, it is maintained that the canal would furnish us with the means of moving our fleets from one sea to the other, thus enabling us to put forward a double force in either. Gentlemen, this assumption is not altogether a correct one, if only for the reason that our navy may be engaged in both seas. In a war in which Denmark should be allied with France against us the presence of our fleet in the Baltic would be indispensable. Of course we could, under certain circumstances, turn the Baltic fleet to account in the North Sea, though I think that ships such as the *Prinz Friedrich Karl*, or the *König Wilhelm*, could not be employed at all in the North Sea.

I sum up my conclusions in one sentence. If we feel moved to expend a sum of from forty to fifty million thalers, for the purpose of improving our naval strategical position, then I would propose that, instead of a canal, we should build a second fleet.

RHINE—EMS CANAL.

PRELIMINARY DEBATE ON THE BILL RELATING TO THE CONSTRUCTION OF A SHIP-CANAL FROM DORT-MUND, *via* HENRICHENBURG, MÜNSTER, BEVERGERN, AND NEUDÖRPEN, TO THE LOWER EMS.

Sitting of the House of Lords, 30th June, 1882.

Gentlemen,—The subject now engaging our attention has already been exhaustively dealt with in the other House, as well as by your Committee. It is in the highest degree difficult for me, as perhaps for others amongst you, to correctly gauge the relative values of the arguments in favour of, and against, the project, for on one side are actual figures, on the other only expectations.

That the canal will ever be able to pay interest on

the invested capital is certainly very doubtful. On the other hand must be considered the great advantages which it would afford for the transport of goods and material of large volume, only a part of which could be carried by the railway. I would further ask of you carefully to weigh the opinion, which I myself hold, that the Government, which submits the project to your decision, and which has doubtless most thoroughly considered the far-reaching consequences of its proposal, is in a better position than anyone else can be to form a correct estimate of the nature and degree of the general advantages of the scheme as opposed to its financial disadvantages. From a military point of view I must decidedly advocate the development of our railway system, in preference to that of our canals.

It is not to be expected that canals will ever be utilized for the transportation of troops, but I recognize that a well-organized canal system will be of great advantage, even from a military point of view, more especially for the provisioning of our frontier fortresses, and for the formation of the colossal store magazines required for an army in the field.

It appears to me, however, that the project ought to receive a hearty welcome, especially on the part of those interested in mining and agriculture. As a matter of fact, railways confer but very little benefit on agriculture, and they are of actual advantage only to certain restricted districts which lie in the neighbourhood of halting-points or stations. To a very great extent our products must be transported in bulk over great distances, and however much you may lower the railway rates, the advantage gained by rail transport must always be neutralized by its cost. As a matter of fact, railways are rather a hindrance than a help in the transportation of goods, for it is certainly a drawback that our road wagons have to wait whilst each train that passes through our fields goes by. I consider, Gentlemen, that railways and canals are the

complements of each other. Railways cannot supply
the place of canals, nor canals of railways; nor do I
apprehend that they will enter into mutually destruc-
tive competition with each other. That this does not
take place is apparent, not only on the Rhine, but also
here in Berlin, where an immense traffic is carried on
by means of the river navigation, in spite of the fact
that eight or nine main lines of railway, leading from
all quarters, converge here, and that the water routes
are of an inferior description. I hope that by the
construction of the canals—and in this matter I rely
with confidence on the energy of our Minister of Public
Works and Railways—an impetus may be given to
the further development of our railway system, and,
without making pointed reference to the political
circumstances of neighbouring countries, I must remark
that our railway system urgently requires extension;
but I hope that side by side with such extension there
may also be a development of our canal system. For
my part, I shall vote for the proposition.

THE POSTAL AND RAILWAY SERVICES.

PRELIMINARY DEBATE ON THE BILL RELATING TO THE
DISPOSAL, IN FAVOUR OF THE OFFICIALS CON-
CERNED, OF THE SURPLUS REALIZED IN THE ADMIN-
ISTRATION OF THE FRENCH POSTAL SERVICE BY THE
GERMAN POST OFFICE, DURING THE WAR OF 1870-71.

Sitting of the Reichstag, 3rd June, 1872.

Deputy Reichensperger has made mention of the
fact that other officials, besides those of the postal
department, had rendered most useful service during
the campaign. I fully endorse the statement.
Gentlemen, I would wish to seize this opportunity of

calling attention to the manner in which the railway officials also distinguish themselves by their exceeding devotion and loyalty to duty. If the railways in the field were not able entirely to meet the very great demands made upon them by the military headquarters authorities, it was not the fault of the railway officials. I believe that in the organization of traffic in war certain improvements may perhaps be made ; but the devotion to duty of the officials, and their zeal, left nothing to be desired. The merit of the railway officials cannot, however, lessen the merit of the postal officials, and it is with great pleasure, and without misgiving, that I shall cast my vote in favour of the proposed measure.

SECOND DEBATE ON THE SUPPLEMENTARY BUDGET FOR 1871, RELATING TO THE SUPPLEMENTARY VOTE FOR THE POSTAL SERVICE.

A Resolution had been laid before the House advocating the gradual abolition of the appointments held by retired military officers as postmasters. Moltke opposed the Resolution, which was nevertheless adopted.

Sitting of the Reichstag, 19th May, 1871.

Special stress has been laid by the last speaker on the question of examinations, but I am of opinion that a person may pass a brilliant examination for the postal service and yet make but a sorry postmaster. Certain personal qualities are required for the position, such as great exactness, devotion to duty, and application, and these are virtues which surely are fostered by military service. We see it in the great demand existing for retired military men for the most varied spheres of employment. Every military man who retires on a pension experiences the desire to fill some new office of usefulness, such as is afforded by the postal service, and

I am certain that Postmaster-General Mittel has a wide
enough field of selection to enable him to refuse
appointments in the postal service to any but qualified
applicants.

I beg that the Resolution may be negatived.

SECOND DEBATE ON THE LAW RELATING TO THE EMPLOYMENT OF RAILWAYS IN WAR, WITH SPECIAL REFERENCE TO THEIR APPROPRIATION FOR THE MILITARY SERVICE.

Sitting of the Reichstag, 19th May, 1871.

I merely wish to remark that the military authorities
attach the greatest possible importance to the circumstance that the railway lines should be kept in perfect
working order, and that they should on no account be
deprived of that material or rolling-stock which is
essentially necessary for the maintenance of traffic.

SECOND DEBATE ON THE BILL RELATING TO THE EXTRAORDINARY GRANT FOR THE IMPERIAL RAILWAYS IN ALSACE-LORRAINE.

An amendment to the Bill was introduced, proposing an additional
vote of 550,000 thalers for the construction of a railway from St.
Ludwig to the "Rheinhütte," the grant to cover half the cost of
a permanent bridge over the Rhine, together with the necessary
defensive works.

Sitting of the Reichstag, 6th June, 1872.

I merely desire in a few words to throw light on the
military aspect of the question. We have given up the
idea of raising difficulties with regard to the principal
passages of rivers by demands for the establishment of
works of fortification in connection with them. It is

sufficient that we should be able to destroy the means
of passage, as is always the case when bridges are so
prepared that they may be blown up. We protest,
however, against the construction of bridges of boats.
Bridges of boats afford an enemy great facilities for the
establishment of pontoon bridges—the ramps which
lead down to the river's bank are available and assist
the operation considerably. From the point of view
of the defence of the country both the bridges are
welcome to us, but not in the same degree. That at
St. Ludwig lies on the line which, leading from Ulm to
Augsburg, passes for a short distance through Swiss
territory and, by so doing, ceases to be of use to us in
the event of war. If, therefore, financial means, as
well as private enterprise, should be insufficient to
carry through the construction of both the bridges,
then we should very much prefer the line by Alt-
Breisach. I gladly associate myself, however, with
the resolution brought forward by the last speaker, as
in my opinion the only question at issue is which line
should be constructed first.

SECOND DEBATE ON THE BILL RELATING TO THE EX-
TRAORDINARY GRANT FOR THE IMPERIAL RAILWAYS
IN ALSACE-LORRAINE.

The Proposition of Deputy Schmidt, advocating the re-introduction
of the Lauterburg-Strassburg line into the Bill, had been struck out
in Committee. Moltke having energetically spoken in favour of the
Proposition, the Bill was eventually passed in its original form.

Sitting of the Reichstag, 6th June, 1873.
Gentlemen,—I wish to recommend Deputy Schmidt's
proposition to your favourable consideration.
A glance at the railway map will show that there
are three lines of railway running in a westerly and
a south-westerly direction *from* Strassburg, a circum-

stance of great importance for the defence especially
of South Germany. We cannot, however, utilize this
advantage to its fullest extent so long as we have only
two lines leading to Strassburg.

The preference evinced by the military administration for travelling over three lines, rather than over
two, has been described by one of the previous
speakers as a form of luxury. Gentlemen, one more
through-line means a difference of two days in the
concentration of the army, and makes the beginning
of operations possible at a correspondingly earlier
date, and what that means I need not, recalling
past experiences, waste another word in demonstrating. Such a third line of railway would be
the Lauterburg line, for its extension backwards to
Germersheim is assured. The majority of your Committee were of opinion that this line should not be constructed out of Imperial funds, on the ground that it
promises to be a lucrative investment and will, therefore,
presumably be built as a matter of private enterprise.
If, however, you abandon the line to private persons
you renounce the profits for the Empire and surrender
them to a private company. Finally, in case of loss,
the deficit will, after all, have to be paid either out of
the general revenues of the Empire, or else by the
individual States, which are severally responsible for
their respective contributions to the common expenses
of the Empire.

Moreover, you not only surrender an advantage for
the Empire, but you also incur a loss, for, clearly, the
shorter line *viâ* Lauterburg will compete very seriously
with the longer western line. It has been said that it
is not the task of the Empire to construct only divi-
dend-paying railways. Certainly not, Gentlemen, but
if the State is required to build railways which no one
else will undertake to build, as unremunerative, that is
surely no reason for preventing the State from building
such railways as do promise a return.

Further, it has been proposed that, in order to avoid the disadvantage of competition, the concession should be withheld from private enterprise for a certain period of time; but, Gentlemen, a measure which would thus for an indefinite period stand in the way of a useful undertaking would certainly not recommend itself. But even if I suppose that the Lauterburg line should be constructed by a private company, and that it should be quickly taken in hand and completed, even then the military requirements would not be entirely fulfilled. Gentlemen, should we ever be called upon to concentrate the army in a westerly direction, Strassburg, as a main junction of railways, must at once acquire the utmost importance. You know that the erection of a great central station at Strassburg is already in progress. In the eventuality I have just mentioned, an exceptionally large number of military transport trains must pass through this station and a great part of these would be detrained in the station itself. The trains would follow closely on each other, from hour to hour; the line must be cleared of one train before the next arrives. For a short time the traffic at such a station is of an overwhelming character, and the strictest order is necessary. It is therefore clear that the entire management should lie centred in one person. Now, supposing that the Lauterburg line were to be constructed by a private company you would then have a dual control in the Strassburg station, and that is certainly not at all desirable. I therefore urgently recommend that the Lauterburg railway should, as the others were, be constructed out of Imperial funds.

SPEECH IN CONNECTION WITH A PETITION FROM THE CITIZENS' ASSOCIATION IN CELLE, RELATING TO THE CONSTRUCTION OF A RAILWAY BETWEEN HANOVER AND HARBURG.

Sitting of the Prussian House of Lords,
26th March, 1876.

From a military point of view every railway is welcome, and two railways please us better than one. But when I consider the matter from the standpoint of agricultural interests, I am obliged to recognize that since the year 1872 a considerable change has taken place with regard to railways, not only because trade and industry are depressed, but also because a great number of railways have been constructed which are many of them merely competition lines. Now I hold the opinion that competition in the matter of railway fares and rates cannot practically be maintained, but I look upon competition in the matter of railway construction as a pure waste of national wealth.

We have seen how private companies have constructed lines, which it was well known beforehand could not be remunerative, for the sole reason that they feared that some other company might construct them and that this might cause them injury. The State itself has appeared as a competitor, and it was obliged to do so in order to safeguard its own interests; as, for instance, in the case of the great Wetzlar railway, which is, in part at least, a competitive line. Although the subject under discussion has been brought forward in connection with a petition from the town of Celle, I submit that we should refer the matter back to the Government for futher consideration, not on account of the town of Celle, but on the ground of expediency, because we believe that the line can be dispensed with. Even if some hundreds of thousands of marks have already been expended, this circumstance does not appear to me to constitute a reason for a further outlay of as many millions.

Finally, as regards the railway communications between Holstein and the remainder of Germany, they are, it must be acknowledged, defective, but they would not be improved by the construction of a line between Harburg and Hanover. No, the weak point is the condition of the section Altona-Hamburg, and it is there that the first improvement should be effected.

ON THE BILL RELATING TO THE ACQUISITION OF SEVERAL PRIVATE RAILWAYS FOR THE STATE.

Sitting of the Prussian House of Lords,
17th December, 1879.

The honourable members of your Commission have referred to the reflex effect which the subject under discussion will have on military relations. The matter is a very simple one, and can be disposed of in few words. It cannot be doubted that the conversion of the most important railways of the country into State lines is, in a military sense, most desirable. Railways have in our time become one of the most important factors in war. The transportation of large masses of troops to given points constitutes a task of the most complicated and comprehensive kind, which must be continuously kept up to date. Each new connecting line necessitates an alteration in the work. Even should we not travel over all the lines, yet we must lay claim to their respective rolling stock, and it is patent that there would be a substantial simplification if, instead of having to deal with forty-nine authorities, we had practically to deal with only one. Gentlemen, I do not by any means wish to ignore the debt which we owe to private railways for the work done by them at critical periods, but I am convinced that a still greater success is achievable.

I am not in a position, Gentlemen, to offer an opinion
as to how the State, in the event of war, is to raise the
money necessary for the purpose. I would wish, however, briefly to suggest another consideration. Fears
have been expressed that the issue of a very large sum
in State bonds may again lead the public to invest
their capital in extravagant and dangerous speculations.
Yet it appears to me, that the present conditions are
quite different to those obtaining in the years 1871 to
1873. At that time the *milliards* poured in from
abroad. There was a surplus of convertible securities
and financial bonds which went to swell the number of
those already existing, and, unfortunately, a portion of
the capital, which it was sought to invest, was absorbed
by enterprises which were swindles. It was as when
a person unexpectedly wins a great prize in some lot-
tery, which is generally not particularly well spent.
In the present instance it appears to me that
we have to do rather with an exchange than with an
increase of securities, as the railway shares called in
will be replaced by a proportionate number of State
bonds. I am prepared to believe that a large proportion of the public will gladly secure a safe, if moderate,
interest, guaranteed by the State, in exchange for
railway dividends representing a variable and, of late
years, a constantly diminishing return. There are
many persons, especially among the well-to-do and
industrious middle classes, who are in perplexity as
regards the proper investment of their savings, and I
consider that the best course open to them is the
acquisition of fully guaranteed State securities. The
man who has become the possessor of a few State bonds,
and puts them by, will be no social democrat.

As regards the second sentence in section 4. I am personally convinced that the Government will make use
of the far-reaching plenary power with which it may
be invested, only for the benefit of the State finances—
a benefit which will in its extent be proportionate to

the measure of free action allowed to it in taking advantage of each momentary opportunity.

I shall vote for the whole proposition.

THIRD DEBATE ON THE IMPERIAL BUDGET.—IMPERIAL STATE RAILWAYS.—STANDARD TIME.

(Moltke's last speech in the Reichstag.)

Sitting of the Reichstag, 16th March, 1891.

Allow me to say a few words on the subject of a standard time for railways, a matter which has been already discussed in a previous sitting. I will not detain you long, especially as I am quite hoarse, a circumstance which I beg you to excuse.

The fact that a standard time is quite indispensable for the internal working of railways, is universally conceded, and will not be gainsaid. But, Gentlemen, in Germany we have five different standard times. In North Germany, including Saxony, we use Berlin time; in Bavaria, Munich time; in Wurtemburg, Stuttgart time; in Baden, Karlsruhe time; and in the Rhenish Palatinate, Ludwigshafen time. Thus we have in Germany five zones; and all the inconveniences and disadvantages which we dread encountering on the French and Russian frontiers, we experience to-day in our own country. This is, I may say, a ruin which has been left standing, a relic of the time of German disruption—a ruin which, now that we have become an Empire, should be completely erased.

Gentlemen, it is but of trifling consequence that the traveller should at each successive station find a new time, and a time different from that indicated by his watch. But it is of great importance that the existence of all these different railway times, to which must be added all the local times, seriously increases the difficulty of railway management, and that it does so more especially at times when military exigencies cause increased demands to be made on the railways.

Gentlemen, in the event of mobilization, all time-tables issued to the troops must be calculated according to local times and the standard times of South Germany. Naturally the active troops and the men to be called in from the reserves take their time from the clock in their quarters or homes. The case is similar with regard to the tables which are to be despatched to the different railway administrations. But the North German railway administration calculates only according to Berlin time; consequently all time-tables and lists must be arranged to correspond with Berlin time. This continual conversion may easily prove a source of error—error which may involve consequences of great moment. The complicated nature of the process greatly aggravates the difficulty of suddenly adopting the measures necessary in the case of the blocking of traffic, or of accidents on the lines.

Gentlemen, it would be a great advantage if we had a standard time for the whole of Germany, even if it only applied to the railways. For this purpose the fifteenth meridian east of Greenwich is the best adapted.[1] This meridian passes through Norway, Sweden, Germany, Austria, and Italy; it would eventually be well adapted to meet the case of a possible introduction in the future of a standard time for Central Europe. Using this fifteenth meridian, the so-called Stargard meridian, as a basis of calculation, differences in time occur at our extreme frontiers, in the east of 31 minutes, and in the west of 36 minutes. Gentlemen, the public has soon accustomed itself, in America to greater, and in South Germany to less, differences of time.

But, Gentlemen, a standard time for the railways does not remove all the disadvantages to which I have

[1] A standard time, based on this meridian, has very recently been introduced into Germany.—[Note by Translator.]

briefly alluded; this object can be attained only by
the adoption of an universal time-reckoning for the
whole of Germany, that is to say, by the abolition of all
local times.

On the other hand, the public entertains (to my
mind, unreasonably) all sorts of objections to this
course. The weighty opinion of the learned among
our astronomers has certainly been expressed in this ad-
verse sense. Gentlemen, science demands much more
than we do; it is not satisfied with a standard time
for Germany, or even for Central Europe, but it would
establish a standard time for the whole world, and the
desire is perfectly justified, considering its points of
view and its objects.

But this one universal standard time, based on the
meridian of Greenwich, cannot possibly be introduced
into daily life, and then the retention of all the local
times becomes necessary. Further, as regards its
application to railways, all experts have pronounced
against it.

Gentlemen, the learned of the astronomers say: "We
admit that a standard time is necessary for the railways—well, let them have it—but let them keep it for
themselves, they should not wish to introduce it into
public life, for only a small portion of the general
public makes use of the railways." To this I would
reply that a still smaller portion of the public consists
of astronomers, geodetical surveyors, or meteorologists.
If science has to make investigations and observations
at certain points, then it may with safety be left to it
to determine the exact local time at these points.
That is a work which can be done once for all, and in
perfect tranquility in the study. Our railway officials
would, however, have to make the calculation repeatedly
in the midst of the bustle of business, and possibly in time
of emergency—besides, the number of railway travellers
is not so small. It has been calculated that on the
average seven railway journeys are undertaken annu-

ally by each head of the population. The travellers of greatest consequence, Gentlemen, are the troops, which must be moved to the frontiers for the defence of the country, and they are certainly those who deserve the greatest consideration.

But further,—it has been doubted whether the introduction of this standard time into private life would not create difficulties, and special stress has been laid on the inconveniences which factories and manufacture would suffer.

On this point I am obliged to oppose the views previously enunciated by my colleague, Herr von Stumm. If the difference in time between the fifteenth degree and any other place, say Neunkirchen (about 29 minutes) is known, then it cannot be difficult to modify the factory time-tables according to it. If the director of the factory wishes in March to see his workmen assembled by sunrise at 6 a.m., the time-table would give the hour as 6·29 a.m. Should he want them in February at 6·10 a.m., the time-table would show 6·39 a.m., and so on.

As regards the agricultural population—well, Gentlemen, the country labourer does not pay much attention to clocks; in fact few possess any; he watches the break of day, and then he knows that the farm bell will soon summon him to work. When the clock in the yard goes wrong, as it generally does— if it goes a quarter of an hour fast, then he goes to work a quarter of an hour too early, certainly, but on the other hand, he leaves work a quarter of an hour earlier: the working day remains the same.

Gentlemen, it is rarely the case in practical life that punctuality, reckoned to the minute, is required. In many villages it is customary to put back the school clock 10 minutes, in order that the children may be present when the master arrives. Even the clock in the Court of Justice is sometimes put back to let the parties assemble before the proceedings commence. On the other hand, in villages situated near a railway the clock is usually set a few minutes fast, so that the people may not miss their trains. Yes, Gentlemen, and even this august house prescribes an academic quarter of an hour's grace, a quarter of an hour which has at times to be somewhat extended.

But once again, the difference between solar time and mean time has been referred to. Deputy v. Stumm was quite correct in adding this difference to those which already exist. But, Gentlemen, the point must be dealt with both positively and negatively. At certain times the difference must be added, at others it must be subtracted. The maximum of 16 minutes is only reached on four days during the year. Gentlemen, has any one of us, who regulates the order of his life by an accurate timepiece, ever noticed that in one quarter of the year he has been as much as 16 minutes too early in sitting down to dinner, or that he has gone to bed as much as 16 minutes too soon, and that in the next quarter he has been as much too late? I doubt it.

Gentlemen, such a fact as this, that the general public absolutely ignores and will never discover a difference, which is certainly not trifling, between solar and mean time, seems to me to demonstrate that the anxieties which exist with regard to the abolition of local time are quite groundless.

Gentlemen, we cannot here by vote, or resolution of the majority, establish a regulation which can only be brought into operation by the ordinary procedure of the the Federal Council (Bundesrath), or perhaps later by means of international negotiation. But I believe that such negotiations will be facilitated if Parliament declares itself to be sympathetically disposed towards a measure which has already been adopted without serious difficulty in America, England, Sweden, Denmark, Switzerland and South Germany.

THE FORTIFICATION OF COLOGNE AND STRASSBURG.

FIRST READING OF THE BILL PROVIDING FOR THE REMODELLING OF GERMAN FORTRESSES.

The Bill proposes, amongst other things, that the fortresses of Spandau and Cologne should bear the expenses of extending the limits of the towns. Deputy Reichensperger (Krefeld) opposes the proposition, and speaks in favour of the preservation of the mediæval gate-towers at Cologne.

Sitting of the Reichstag, 27th March, 1873.

I only wish to make a few remarks in reply to the exhaustive and able speech of the previous speaker. The case, to my mind, is very simple.

Military requirements demand the strengthening of the fortress of Cologne. We effect this by the pushing out of advanced works, which will be no mean advantage to the city of Cologne, as making a bombardment much more difficult, if not quite impossible. Military interests, as regards the extension of the city's enceinte, are not matters of present debate, extension is demanded in the most imperative interests of the town itself. What residents will profit by it,—that is another question. The extension might have been effected, if some six millions more had been added to the estimate. But, then, whose duty would it have been to bring the matter forward? The whole body of taxpayers; in other words, that very large number of persons who can have no interest whatever in the extension. It appears to me therefore perfectly equitable that the town itself should contribute to the expense.

With regard to the beautiful old gate-towers, they were, in the present condition of Cologne, an obvious military disadvantage. They would indicate to an enemy the points of sortie, the places of busiest traffic, and the points against which he could direct his fire. This disadvantage would cease to exist, once the enceinte of Cologne should have been pushed further afield, and then I think that no objections could be urged against the preservation of these interesting historic monuments.

DEALING WITH A QUESTION PUT BY DEPUTY GUERBER REGARDING THE CONVENTION WITH STRASSBURG FOR THE PURCHASE OF SUCH GROUND PROPERTY AS WOULD BE LEFT UNOCCUPIED THROUGH THE EXTENSION OF THE RAMPARTS.

Sitting of the Reichstag, 7th Febuary, 1876.

The member putting the question has implied that I asked the town of Strassburg whether it desired an extension. At least, so I understand. I never was commissioned to do this, but when I was in Strassburg I certainly made inquiries with a view of ascertaining in which direction an extension would be desirable.

The member putting the question has placed the military interest in the front rank. Gentlemen, we are not behind others in desiring a well-built city with wide streets within the fortress rather than a narrow and crowded one; but there will be no urgent military reason for the enlargement of the city enceinte when once the detached forts, now under construction, are completed. The extension is entirely, or, at any rate chiefly, desirable in the interest of the city.

The speaker gave us to understand that it was intended to extend the city in the least favourable of all directions. Gentlemen, the city cannot be enlarged towards the east, where the citadel lies; towards the south are the inundations and swampy ground, so it cannot be extended in this direction either. To the best of my knowledge the extension will take place northwards and westwards towards Contades, that is, in the best direction for an extension. Have not other great towns in like manner expended large sums in the acquisition of building-land? Stettin, for instance, quite recently. Gentlemen, it may safely be predicted that a city like Strassburg, after all that has been done for it, and all that it is intended still to do, the founding of the University, the improvement of the railway and canal systems—after all this, I say, it may safely be anticipated that this old German city will experience a great rise in prosperity as soon as it has got room to develop.

II.

INDIVIDUAL, POLITICAL, AND MILITARY QUESTIONS.

ON THE BILL RELATING TO THE PUBLIC DEBT OF THE CONFEDERATION.

In connection with the loan of ten million thalers, which was sanctioned by the Reichstag of the North-German Confederation, on the 22nd October, 1867, for the development of the Federal navy and the coast-defence systems, a Bill was introduced relating to the Public Debt of the Confederation. Notwithstanding the strong opposition to it of the Federal Chancellor, an amendment was adopted by the Reichstag, imposing legal responsibility on the officials of the Public Debt Committee, and giving to the Reichstag the power of impeaching them. The Bill was, in the Session of 1867, wrecked through this amendment, but in the following Session it was again introduced, and the debate on it began on the 21st April, 1868, when the amendment, so strongly opposed by the Government, was again proposed by Miquel. In committee it was thrown out on an equality of votes, but in the House itself it was accepted by 131 votes to 114, in spite of a very incisive speech by Count Bismarck.

The Bill was at once withdrawn, and simultaneously orders were issued directing that all work for the navy, which was not absolutely necessary, should be either stopped, or considerably reduced. This was the first serious conflict between the Reichstag and the Government of the Confederation. How much Moltke was interested in the question is shown by the draft of a speech, in which he gives an impressive warning not to sacrifice the practical necessities of the country for the sake of a theory. He addressed to the House the urgent appeal, "to consider some means of remedying the consequences of the Motion." Such means were found in an agreement to entrust the management of the loan, for naval purposes, to the Administration of the Prussian State Debt, under the supervision of the Federal Chancellor, and of a Federal Debt Committee, composed of members of the Federal Council and the Reichstag. On 15th June, the compromise was accepted by 151 votes against 41. When the Opposition on this occasion took exception to the great expenditure for war purposes, Moltke seized the opportunity to justify a defensive policy, which was demanded by circumstances, and which it was possible to carry out only by means of a strong army and navy—the defensive policy of a Germany which had still to be united.

DRAFT OF A SPEECH.

In connection with § 7 of the Law for the Management of the State Debts, we have once more been witnesses of the efforts exerted so to regulate the State machine, that each portion should only work within defined limits, that arbitrary movement should be nowhere possible, and that nothing in the movement should rattle.

Gentlemen, let us be careful not to screw it up too tightly, or we shall increase the amount of friction and the engine will either come to a stand-still or burst.

We were engaged in promoting the best interests of the country in a practical manner by means of good laws, when suddenly we were confronted with a theory, which indeed recognizes ministerial responsibility, but only in piecemeal fashion.

The history of all countries has shown this theory to be impracticable.

When Charles I. of England refused to uphold the responsibility of his ministers, he followed them eight years afterwards to the scaffold, and if to-day the President of the United States of America has been impeached,[1] the result must be either an acquittal, or the discontinuance of that form of Government which exacts this responsibility.

The commander of an army who may be about to execute some operation, the results of which can never be certain, or the statesman who may be charged with the direction of some momentous policy, will never

---

[1] President Johnson, the successor of Lincoln, was arraigned before Congress, for his favourable disposition towards the Secessionists.

allow himself to be influenced by the apprehension that he may be summoned before a court-martial, or that he may be called upon to appear before the Civic magistrates of Berlin. He has a very different responsibility, that towards God and his own conscience in respect of the lives of thousands of his fellow-men and the good of the State. He has more to lose than merely his freedom and his fortune.

Political crimes are only punished because they fail. It is vain to attempt to confine the life of a State within the lines of one paragraph of the law.

Had we lost the campaign in 1866, it is possible that a bloodthirsty Assembly—not Herr Lasker and Herr Twesten alone—might have demanded the head of the Prime-Minister Count v. Bismarck-Schönhausen, which now, fortunately, sits comfortably on his shoulders.

Whether they would have got it is another question, but in theory they would undoubtedly have been justified in demanding it, because State money, and that to a very considerable amount, was expended before the House of Deputies had (with a majority perhaps of only one vote) sanctioned the outlay.

As things turned out well, we have an indemnity instead. As matters now stand, thanks to a number of votes which are usually recorded against the Government, we have a feeble majority which cripples the efforts of the Government in favour of § 7. On all sides it is conceded that we must have a fleet; but how can the Admiralty enter into contracts for a number of years, when at any time chance fluctuations in the intentions of the House may prevent them from acting up to their engagements?

We need coast defences, and it may be in the near future, in order to protect the riches of our commercial towns, but this practical requirement must remain unsatisfied until we can agree upon a theoretical system. Gentlemen, I think that those of you who have brought

forward this motion must be personally dismayed by its
very success, and that the House could not have done
you a better service than by rejecting your amendment;
it could not show more consideration for your patriotic
feelings than by devising means by which the evil
consequences resulting from your motion may be
averted.

Sitting of the Reichstag, 15th June, 1868.

What sensible man would not wish that it were
possible to apply to peaceful objects the enormous
expenditure incurred by Europe for military purposes?
But such a result can certainly never be attained by
international agreement as suggested by one of the
previous speakers. War is, in reality, but the carrying
on of diplomacy by different means. I see only one
chance of such a desirable consummation; it is, that a
Power should arise in the heart of Europe which,
without desiring conquest, would be strong enough to
impose peace upon its neighbours.

It is for this very reason I believe that if this blessed
work is ever to be accomplished, Germany will be the
doer of it—but, Gentlemen, not before Germany is
strong enough—that is to say, when she is united.

In military matters also, Gentlemen, we follow the
progress made elsewhere in science and in inventions;
but an invention is far from being of value merely by
its creative possibilities; the question is to perfect the
invention. Our excellent needle-gun (Zündnadel-
gewehr) was invented many years ago; but it has taken
us more than 20 years to transform it into a really
trustworthy weapon and to reproduce it a million
times. It would be far from enough, therefore, to
watch what is being accomplished elsewhere, we must
take the lead ourselves. It has been said that the
humane Russian Government wishes to see all hollow
projectiles done away with. Gentlemen, the truth is
simply this, that in Russia they do not wish to adopt

explosive bullets, but I very much doubt whether the Russian Government will abolish shells and shrapnel as long as other nations retain them.

We have been further informed, that guns will eventually pierce all armour-plates; if the deputy who made the statement can assure us of this, we should be able to dispense with very costly experiments; but I fear that we may have to wage two wars before this question can be settled, wars in which we shall require armour-clad ships as well as fortifications. How the argument can possibly be turned to prove the worthlessness of the scheme for fortifying the harbour of Kiel, I fail to understand; it appears to me rather to prove the contrary. Gentlemen, our neighbours know well enough—even those who pretend not to know—that we do not wish to attack them; but let them know too that we shall not allow ourselves to be attacked. For this we require an army and a fleet, and I trust the patriotism of this distinguished House to accept the law proposed by the Government.

In the same sitting Moltke makes a brief correction of a mistaken impression produced by his speech.

Gentlemen, I hope that I shall not make a further digression from Article I. than the previous speakers, in briefly stating that I did not say we needed the unity of Germany in order to possess a great army and a great fleet, but conversely, that we require army and fleet in order to attain that unity, which it is to be hoped may at some time lead to a reduction of this great expenditure.

FRANCHISE RIGHTS OF THE ARMY AND NAVY.

SECOND DEBATE ON THE IMPERIAL ELECTION LAWS.

On the discussion of § 2—which deals with the franchise rights of the army and navy, so long as the persons concerned are on the active list—the regulations concerning the Reserves had given rise to objections, as there appeared to be some doubt as to when these might be said to be on the active list. The article was however accepted in the form desired by Moltke.

Sitting of the Reichstag, 19th March, 1869.

Under ordinary conditions of peace, the men of the Reserve and of the Landwehr are in their homes and have a perfect and unrestricted right to vote. An exception is made only when they are called to the colours. But when are the Reserve and Landwehr said to be with the colours? It is on the eve of war. Can you wish to impair the discipline of the army at such a time by subjecting a portion of it to political influences?

Gentlemen, let us be thankful that we in Germany have an army which simply *obeys*. Look at other countries, where the army is no protection against revolution, but where, on the contrary, the army is the hot-bed of revolution.

I urgently recommend you never to take any steps which may alter our position in this respect.

I need hardly refer to the reproach addressed to the Government that it might perhaps call out the Reserve, in order to exert an influence on the elections through the consequent withdrawal of some votes from your side. You need only observe that the Government here, of its own initiative, renounces a large number of conservatives votes, for conservative votes may always be obtained in the army without any departure from legal mode of procedure.

In passing, I may further remark that the whole question does not involve any issue of great consequence, seeing that perhaps nine-tenths of the whole army serving with the colours are under 25 years of age. The amendment which proposes to substitute "with the colours" for "on the active list" is the only one with which I can declare myself to be in agreement. I beg therefore, for my part, that all other amendments may be rejected, and that you will accept the proposition of the Government with this modification.

EXEMPTION OF MILITARY PERSONS FROM COMMUNAL TAXATION.

A motion was introduced by Hagen, after the abolition of the Presidential Decree of 22nd December, 1868, relating to the application of the Prussian regulations to military persons, so as to include them in the liability to communal taxation within the territories of the Confederation. Thirteen petitions were presented from Saxony, Gera and Brunswick to the same effect. The motion was rejected, but the majority agreed in declaring that the question should be legally settled on the basis of the unity of the Federal army.

Sitting of the Reichstag, 28th May, 1869.

I do not intend to speak about the validity of the Presidential Decree, but on subjects affecting us more closely. There has been much contention as to whether this subject falls within the province of communal or within that of military legislation. I must draw attention to the fact that in the communal and military legislation of Prussia it is laid down as a leading principle that military persons on the active list are exempted from all taxation. This exemption is based on and is justified by the consideration, that the income of military men is fixed by the necessities of the case. When Prussia raised a national army there was furnished to it what was considered, under the conditions then existing, to be necessary and sufficient, neither more nor

less. It could not ever have been the intention therefore of the law-makers that any deductions should afterwards be made from the amount which was considered
necessary to achieve a specific and important object.
It certainly was not possible, on other grounds, to
exempt the military from indirect taxation, as it even
then existed. The exemption from direct taxation has
however remained unassailed through a long series of
years; only when after the lapse of decades all the
necessaries of life came to be almost doubled, without
any appreciable increase of former pay—the lieutenant
received 4 thalers—only then (it was during the time
which followed closely on the disorders of the year '48)
were military men first made liable to direct class and
income taxation. It only remains to say, Gentlemen,
that this immunity, which is based on the natural order
of things, was not a specially Prussian institution; the
same principle holds good in most other armies, though
not in all; it does not hold good, for instance, in that
of the United States, which is taxed, and heavily taxed,
by the State and by the communes; but all that I have
to say on that point is that the American subaltern
draws 120 thalers, the Prussian subaltern 26.

I will not exhaust your patience with a description
of the conditions existing in the great armies of our
neighbours; I will confine myself to the mention of an
army, with which you will be more in sympathy, and
which is still held up by many as the ideal to be aimed
at, I mean the Swiss army.

Gentlemen, in the latest bill for the military organization of the Swiss Confederation (§ 187), you will find
the following passage: "All persons in the military
service of the Confederation, all personal effects pertain-
ing to the military service, all military vehicles, provisions and liquors, are to be exempt from all assess-
ments, taxes or excise duties in the cantons and
communes."

"The same disposition holds good for the military

institutions and workshops of the Confederation, and their working funds are not to be subjected to any cantonal or communal taxation."

You will see, then, that in a republic and in the enlightened year 1868 this idea of a total immunity of the military from taxation is accepted as a matter of course.

I have already stated that we deviated from this principle in 1851: we were subjected to direct taxation. Our circumstances are matter of public knowledge, for every one is acquainted with the amount of the pay we draw, and the allowances we receive, and we are taxed for the whole amount. There is nothing whatever to be urged against this, if it is admitted that we should be taxed at all; it would, however, certainly be desirable that an equally clear light should be thrown on the circumstances of other professions, in which case the income tax would doubtless yield a considerably greater revenue than it does at present.

Gentlemen, I will not again refer to the common law of the land, which emphatically enunciates the exemption of the military from all personal burdens; I will only remind you of the regulations for towns, which were joyously welcomed in 1808, and which, in classifying the towns according to the number of their inhabitants, declare emphatically that: "the military are not to be included." The military are not wards of the State (Schutzbefohlenen) nor are they citizens, they have a separate existence, and such is their organization that they can exist by themselves. The army has its artisans and artists, its cooks and musicians, its doctors and its clergy; it is perfectly self-contained. You know, Gentlemen, that we cannot make choice of our place of abode, we have less latitude in this respect than civil officials even, for amongst the latter transfers in the lower appointments are seldom made, and a civil official has the option of refusing an appointment which would take him to a place where he thinks he could

not live. We cannot do that. Incidentally I may
remark, that I consider the taxation of civil officials
quite as illogical as the taxation of the military. The
case of the civil officials is quoted and it is said : How
unjust that the military should not be liable to taxation
in the same manner as are the civil officials. Yes,
Gentlemen, I am of the same opinion, but the injustice
does not lie in the exemption of the military, but in the
liability of the civil officials.

Without option we are then transferred to some
given town and there we come under the commune, but
are granted no communal rights. How, then, can you
lay upon us obligations towards the commune ? We do
not elect the civic authorities, we have no claim to the
town revenues, and no knowledge of how they are
administered ; neither have we any voice in the
expenditure. We are in no way affected if the town
builds a townhall or a market, or if it founds a bathing-
establishment or a hospital.

When a soldier is ill he is taken, not to the town
hospital, but to the military hospital ; if he is invalided,
the town is not burdened with him, but it is the
military exchequer which must provide for him.

Should he become incapable of earning a livelihood,
or be indigent, he goes back to his own village, into
his own particular commune, but the town does nothing
for him. The towns do not present us with parade-
grounds or rifle ranges, we have to purchase both, and
must ourselves prepare them for use ; the town gives us
no free quarters, we have to pay the lodging allowances
(Servis'), and if the allowance is inadequate, then, as
you know, the military authorities are very willing to
increase it, if only you will grant the necessary means.
Gentlemen, the military are thus, as a matter of fact,
guests in the town which they garrison ; guests, not in

---

¹ I.e., The allowance (according to a scale, and varying with the
position of each town, in a specified schedule) which is paid to the
citizens furnishing the lodging.—[Note by the Translator.]

the sense of persons whom you receive, whom you
entertain, and on whom, may be, you bestow a parting
present; no, Gentlemen, not that, but guests who pay
their bills.

A benevolent pity has been extended to the military
man: Why? because through exemption from communal
taxation he is robbed of every home, and the army is
distinct from the people. Gentlemen, when has there
ever been amongst us any question of a distinction
between army and people? The same man who last
year was of the people, is this year of the army, and
two years after he is again of the people. The army is
a part of the people, and not the worst part, and it is
really not necessary to impose a tax on them in order
to impress that fact upon them. And now as regards
the question of a home—Yes, it is true that a battalion
with an average strength of 568 men possesses as many
homes, but in its constitution as one body the battalion
is not rooted to its place of garrison, its place of garrison
does not hold its destiny, and it will never become its
home. Were it even to remain there 50 years, yet its
component parts would go on changing continually.
The home of the army is the Fatherland, is the territory
of the whole North-German Confederation, wherever
the King may send it.

It is further said to us: Yes, but the military profit
by the many and beautiful institutions which they find
in the towns. Yes, Gentlemen, we profit by them in a
measure, an infinitesimally small measure, we profit by
them, as no one can be hindered from doing, just as we
profit by air and light. The town certainly allows us
to walk on its footpaths, but it is not for us that it
paves the streets; it does not burn one extra jet of
gas for our benefit; it need not appoint a single night-
watchman because of the military, for we guard ourselves by day and by night. If you still insist that the
military share certain advantages in the towns, then I
ask: Do not the military perchance, on their part,

also confer certain advantages? And do these advantages not absolutely preponderate? Gentlemen, on what do the towns depend for their flourishing condition, their growth, and their prosperity! Surely on the welfare, on the development of power, and on the political position of the State generally.

I have been told, that here, in Berlin, after the decimating wars of the beginning of this century, landed properties were worth perhaps 20,000 thalers, which would fetch 120,000 thalers and more to-day. Well, Gentlemen, two unsuccessful campaigns might reduce the value of land, in Berlin and other towns, to its former level, and I need not expatiate on the significance of such a possibility for a city in which two-thirds or three-quarters of all the ground property is heavily mortgaged. But in the present case, when it is a question of saddling the military with a new and, I am convinced, a perfectly unjustifiable burden, I may be permitted, if only incidentally, to remind you that the army has won, not lost, two campaigns. If Prussia, if Germany to-day occupies a position in the world different from that which it formerly held, it is to the army that this is, at least indirectly, due, and the towns might show themselves grateful for the service rendered.

Should this, however, also be forgotten, Gentlemen, let me have the honour of demonstrating to you, with the aid of figures, the strictly positive advantages which the towns derive from the presence of the military. Look at Luxemburg for instance. As is well known the fortifications there are being razed; the progress of the work has been slow and consequently very little profit has, so far, been realized from the land recovered; and yet, notwithstanding, the Luxemburg Government has deemed it only just to hand over 140,000 francs to the town of Luxemburg in order in some degree to conpensate it for the losses it suffered through the removal of the former Federal garrison. Gentlemen,

the towns do thus derive advantages, especially as
regards their less wealthy inhabitants; the poorer
citizens profit in a garrison town by trade in the
necessaries of life to the extent of the difference between
the cost of production and the market price. This
difference is so considerable that if it be multiplied an
hundred-fold, or a thousand-fold, according to the
strength of the garrison, the result will represent a very
handsome sum of money. If this is not so, how does it
happen that the towns, which are so ready to complain
of the burden imposed on them in the form of a garrison,
raise an even louder complaint when this burden is
removed? how does it happen that each year petitions
are forwarded to the War Ministry from various towns,
praying that they may be given a garrison?—a garrison,
mind you, which is not subject to communal burdens.

Gentlemen, bestow a brief glance on the budgets of
the towns. Take Berlin as a case in point. During
the year 1865 it received 750,000 thalers, in the form
of communal contributions to the malt and grinding
and slaughtering taxes; as its share in the gross
receipts from the grinding and slaughtering tax,
237,900 thalers; from the game tax 20,000 thalers;
altogether a total of 1,008,000 thalers, or a third part
of the total revenue of this great city. Well, Gentlemen, it may honestly be said that the military contribute a share of this third part and of the items named.
Now look at the expenditure. We will pass over the
interest on the town debt, which we, the military, did
not contract; over the public works expenses, with
which we are in no way concerned; over the handsome
round sum of 360,000 thalers for administrative
purposes; and then we come to the public schools, set
down at 535,000 thalers. Now, Gentlemen, soldiers of
twenty years of age do not as a rule send children
to school, and the sons of officers are educated almost exclusively in the Royal Grammar-schools
(" Gymnasien ") and cadet-schools. Where the

children of military men do, however, attend the city
schools, it is always feasible to exact higher fees from
the parents, a course already adopted by the town of
Oldenburg. The next item to this is for the serious
sum of 710,000 thalers for the city's poor-law system,
that cancerous growth of great towns which is assuming
such vast proportions.

Gentlemen, the soldier is himself poor. Only be good
enough not to deduct anything further from that which
he now has, and he, on his part, will claim no help—
help which, by the way, he knows it is useless to ask
for. Incidentally let me remark that any individual,
subject to a compulsory poor-rate, may, if he feel the
occasion demand it, very easily and very fully indemnify
himself by withholding his voluntary contributions for
poor relief, soup-kitchens, crèches, refuges, in short for
the whole list of generally fruitless experiments to help
the suffering, down even to the charity concert;
voluntary subscriptions which do not, however, protect
him against daily verbal and written solicitations.

In the last place, Gentlemen, comes the principal item
of 746,000 thalers for police administration. Well,
Gentlemen, the military maintain its own strict police
organization. And I ask of you: Who stands behind
the police? We have seen the Civic Guard behind the
police, but you will remember that the thing did not
work well, and that it was necessary to requisition the
military after all. Gentlemen, if you had not garrisons,
you might have to spend double or treble as much as
you now do for police purposes.

It comes to this, then, Gentlemen, that on the revenue
side of the city's balance sheet you find the military
paying, but that on the other side, the side of expenditure, you nowhere find them as receiving anything. No, Gentlemen, if we are to make up accounts,
you may rest assured that the balance would be much
in favour of the military, and that it would be more
reasonable to expect the towns to do something for

their garrisons, than inversely for the garrisons to be taxed by the towns.

People have even gone so far as to demand the imposition of a tax on the pay of non-commissioned officers and privates. I shall not dwell long on this point, Gentlemen. Our young soldiers, the development of whose physical powers is still progressing and from whom we are obliged to exact a great deal of work, have excellent appetites and would gladly eat a pound of meat daily, could we but give it to them. Should you, however, impose a consumption-tax on the military victualling establishment, then the present few ounces of meat will soon disappear from their broth. In towns where there is no grinding and slaughtering tax, you are actually driven to make deductions from pay in a manner which is contrary to regulation, as otherwise you could not count upon getting the 1 sgr. 3 pf. at the end of the month, and the collection of the money would have its own peculiar difficulties; for you cannot distrain the soldier, the only goods in his possession belong to the crown, and you cannot arrest him, for you would soon have the whole company in the prison instead of on the rifle-range.

Gentlemen, this whole subject has been introduced in somewhat high-flown language. It has been said that the Presidential Decree has created deep and widespread dissatisfaction, that the national sentiment of justice has been violated; the expression "a howl of indignation" even has been dragged out from the arsenal of somewhat rusty figures of speech.

Gentlemen, the indignation may have been felt in the treasuries of towns, but not, I believe, in widespread circles. Where conscription is universal there is hardly a family without son, or brother, or some relation in the army and, in these most wide-spread circles of thousands of families, people will already have begun to congratulate themselves on the fact that those belonging to them are not to be taxed for purposes foreign to their interests. Look at the petitions; there are a dozen Royal Saxon and Ducal Brunswick towns, Gera, Weimar, Oldenburg and, as we now learn, Darmstadt, almost all joining in chorus with the civic authorities of Dresden. On the other side we have no representations.

It is not only desirable but necessary that, within the same army, not only pay but taxation should be of an uniform character. Now can you conceive anything more unequal or more unsuitable than communal taxation? Transfer an officer of a regiment from one battalion to the other, from Minden to Bielefeld for instance, and it makes a difference to him of 23 per cent. if he pays communal taxes. He may have been stationed in Boppard, Greifswald, or Görlitz, in one of the good old towns which have known how to maintain their revenues, and where he paid only 3, 4, or 5 per cent.; but send him to Berlin and he will have to pay 50 to 100 per cent. Should he have the misfortune to go to Elberfeld, he will have to pay, I am told, 320 per cent. There is no attempt at adjustment in this matter, Gentlemen, it will be said. There ought to be adjustment; the State must step in, the State must pay extra local allowances. It is astonishing how much is expected of the State, how much it is relied upon to provide for everything, and all the while every care is taken to cut off each fresh means of rendering assistance.

No, Gentlemen, the question now before us is simply one of increase in the general burden of taxation. The inhabitants of the country must be taxed in the interests of the towns.

Gentlemen, I can understand a man getting up and saying: The military have still too much pay; we can boldly deduct something—say five per cent.—this will allow of our abolishing the duty on salt, or remitting the amount direct to the taxpayers. Such a statement I could combat, though not the consequence of the motion.

But if anyone says: We must admit that it is impossible to deduct anything more from the military, but let us raise the taxes, let us put the surplus into the pockets of the military, but only in order that it may be handed over the next moment to the treasuries of the towns, then I cannot say that I should apprehend your approving of this motion, and I content myself with pointing out, besides the injustice inflicted, the impracticability of carrying out such a proposal if even regard be had only to the clerical labour and business involved. The intendance officials would not only have to seek out each body of troops, but each military person, in order to know when the smaller payments in A cease, when the larger in B and C commence. I congratulate the Chief Audit Office which would investigate and confirm such a chaos of references, with the thoroughness characterizing that department.

Gentlemen, the question at issue is simply this: Are five-sixths of the army to surrender their ancient rights, in order to accommodate themselves to the recently joined sixth part, or are a certain number of towns in the countries, lately admitted to the Confederation, to renounce for the future an income which has hitherto been levied—certainly not in an illegal manner, but I believe with a very small measure of justice—from those persons in the army who are connected with them?

I must further draw attention to the fact that the method of levying the communal taxes vary, in form and substance, in each of the different countries which have lately joined the Confederation. There is another something which calls for reform. The final and necessary result would be that you would have to say: Here, Coburg or Brunswick, is the standard to which the kingdom of Prussia, the kingdom of Saxony and all the others must conform.

Gentlemen, your Committee has proposed to you

to re-establish the condition of things existing before
the issue of the Presidential Decree, that is, to legalize
the want of uniformity until the matter can be otherwise dealt with. The Committee has made no suggestion as to an arrangement, because none of the proposals
put forward in Committee secured a majority. A
proposal has now been made, on this side of the House,
simply demanding the extension, to the whole of the
territory of the Confederation, of that order which
undoubtedly obtained in Prussia on the day of the
proclamation of the Constitution of the North-German
Confederation. Gentlemen, I can only most earnestly
urge upon you to accept this Proposition. I believe
that in doing so you will lend your support to a
measure which is just, useful and practicable.

Gentlemen, the army does not, as a matter of fact,
claim a favour to the prejudice of other classes, but it
claims to live, and what is indispensable for its existence,
that you ought not to curtail.

THE GERMAN ARMY OF OCCUPATION
IN FRANCE.

The report of the Committee on Petitions gave rise to a discussion
on the alleged defective provisioning of the army of occupation.

Sitting of the Reichstag, 2nd May, 1871.

I find that there is no representative of the War
Office present. As the General Staff is not responsible
for the food supply of the army, I may, as one
who is not directly concerned, speak with perfect frank-
ness on the subject.

If I understand the previous speaker aright, the first
point raised was that damaged commodities had been
issued to the troops. Gentlemen, when on the proclamation of the armistice a new method of rationing the

army was adopted, we were in possession of an immense quantity of stores, which we calculated would, as hitherto, provision the army for a long time to come. It is natural that endeavours should have been made, from motives of economy, to use up these stores, especially bacon, of which there was a large supply.

The various army headquarters having been called upon to furnish reports as to any complaints that may have been made, the following reply has just been received from the Headquarters of the Third Army, "There are no complaints." Naturally, Gentlemen, a certain amount of discontent exists, owing to the present enforced inactivity of the men after the inspiriting and encouraging progress of the war itself. They are wearied and vexed because the disorder in France prevents their returning home.

The rations, as a matter of fact, are ample, as has indeed already been pointed out; $\frac{3}{4}$ lb. of meat constitutes a perfectly sufficient diet, not to speak of the supplementary articles of food, the amount of which I cannot just now remember, besides an allowance of $2\frac{1}{2}$ sgr. (3d.); Gentlemen, in the aggregate this represents a very considerable expenditure.

If I have further correctly understood the speaker, he laid stress, I believe, on the fact that a French army would live quite differently in Germany. Yes, Gentlemen, that is exactly the difference. We have been moderate everywhere and have only taken what was necessary and sufficient, and no more. I believe I can assert, that no war was ever waged, especially with such enormous masses of men engaged, in which the army was so well provided for as our army was in this campaign. It has been made clear that in war (as has been very correctly asserted) no method of supply for the army is too expensive, unless it be a bad one. For instance, we took with us costly preserved foods which, distributed at the proper time, were of great service. I am convinced, Gentlemen, that the army will not refuse the expression of its gratitude to the chief of the Intendance Department and his capable subordinates.

First discussion of the Bill dealing with the application of the savings effected in connection with the money paid by France for the food supply of the German army of occupation.

The savings effected in connection with the money paid by France for the food supply of the German army of occupation were to be employed exclusively for the benefit of the army, for the support of non-commissioned officers, for free appointments to the Corps of Cadets, for the institution of a life-insurance organization, for the construction of the Staff College buildings (Kriegs-Akademie) and for the fixtures and furniture of official residences. In the Reichstag the question was raised whether the House possessed the right of making grants from this money for other, more general, purposes.

Sitting of the Reichstag, 11th March, 1878.

Gentlemen,—I believe that the preamble of the Bill will have made it sufficiently clear to you in what manner the savings in question were effected. I have only a few words to say regarding the nature and origin of this money.

When General v. Manteuffel assumed the command of the army of occupation in France, he privately made an arrangement with representatives of the French Government by which, in lieu of the previous supplies in kind, a fixed money contribution was thenceforward to be paid for each man and horse in the army. That this contribution was fixed at a reasonably high rate appears to me to be a fact for which much credit is due to General v. Manteuffel. Thanks to his prudent care, and to the excellent management of his Military Intendant, Herr Engelhardt. it was possible to assure to those troops which were not then able to follow their comrades home, a comfortable existence on foreign soil in the midst of an absolutely hostile population. The men received ample rations and, in addition, a sum of money which permitted them to drink wine, which is allowed in France to the poorest workman, and which contributed so very much to the preservation of a good state of health among the troops. For the special purpose of providing wholesome food a manufactory of preserves was at that time established in Mainz which, later on, was very much extended. This factory will certainly in the future render most valuable service to the army generally on the occasion of any great concentration of troops and more especially in the event of war.

I would not enter into this subject now, had not "the enthusiasm for pea-sausage (erbswurst)" been alluded to. Gentlemen, preserved foods have the great advantage that they contain just those elements, albumen and hydrate of carbon, in almost exactly the proper proportions, which are necessary to the nourishment of a working man. Every self-chosen meal contains too much of one constituent, too little of the other; the first goes uselessly to waste in part, while the other does not nourish sufficiently. Preserves have the further great advantage of being portable, so that a man can carry enough food for several days on his own person, and they have this additional advantage, that they can be very quickly cooked. How often does it happen that troops after having been engaged for hours in cooking are suddenly alarmed and have to throw out the contents of the camp-kettles, continuing their march without having satisfied their hunger.

Preserved provisions have one disadvantage, they are too expensive. But, Gentlemen, when the highest mental and bodily efforts are demanded of a man, he should not be allowed to hunger. In the field no kind of food supply is too expensive, except it be a bad one.

It has been already brought to our notice that the officials, as well as the wives and children of the married soldiers, were provided for, and, I think, this is

only fair. The officers, who had to pay heavily for all
the necessaries of life, received, in addition to their
field-allowances, a further allowance according to their
rank. That this allowance was not claimed by the
Commander-in-Chief has been already mentioned, and I
thank the previous speaker for his reference to the fact.
This very considerable amount, as reckoned by the
scale of payment proper for such an office as that of
Commander-in-Chief, and by the time ($2\frac{1}{2}$ years) during
which it accrued, is included in the savings. General
v. Manteuffel, like all our generals, returned from
France no richer than he went.

Gentlemen, when a body of troops saves money out
of its messing-funds, they are entitled to the disposal of
it. Here we are concerned with a great saving, which
a portion of the army has effected out of its messing-
funds, a matter which the military administration have
a right to deal with by prerogative. There can be no
question that General v. Manteuffel was perfectly
entitled to distribute to the troops the whole of the sums
received according to the agreement made. He might
at once have divided the savings among the four divisions, or he might have added five silver groschens to
the allowance of each man, and in that case there would
have been no question of savings to-day. He did not
deem it advisable to adopt either course, as the
difficulty of maintaining strict discipline in the army
would have been thereby increased, a fact which has
been acknowledged even by our adversaries—at least
by the candid ones. He did not wish that France
should become a Capua for the troops remaining in the
country. He considered that the more fitting course
would be to use the savings of a portion of the army for
the benefit of the army at large. It was with this
intention that, even during the occupation itself,
considerable sums were remitted to the Prussian and
Saxon War Offices.

But, Gentlemen, after the occupation came to an end,

the military authorities would, in my opinion, have been perfectly justified if, without reference to anyone, they had distributed all these moneys at their discretion, for the benefit of the army, so long at any rate as the Pauschquantum[1] system obtained. To-day Parliament undeniably has the right of controlling the employment of these moneys.

Gentlemen, it was the army that won the *milliards* and the army it is that has saved these millions here—saved them, mark it well, not out of State or Imperial funds, but out of its own means. Gentlemen, I believe I may appeal to your sense of justice, or at any rate to your sense of fairness, when I beg that you will leave these moneys in their entirety and without deduction to the army for purposes which you will recognize as necessary and very desirable, and for which new grants will otherwise have to be demanded from Parliament.

PUNISHMENT BY ARREST.

SECOND DEBATE ON THE REGULATIONS WITH REGARD TO ARREST AS CONTAINED IN THE CODE OF MILITARY LAW.

Sitting of the Reichstag, 7th June, 1872.

Gentlemen,—I fully recognize the humane purport of the amendment introduced by Deputy Eysoldt and his supporters. I must however express myself as altogether opposed to it. I believe that too great a relaxation in the severity of punishments will only make

---

[1] Pauschquantum—an annual allowance, fixed at 225 thalers (£33 15s. 0d.), paid to Prussia by the States composing the North German Confederation for the maintenance of each man furnished by them to the army of the Confederation. The system was abolished in 1875, when the first regular Imperial war-budget was submitted to Parliament.—[Note by the Translator.]

their infliction of more frequent necessity. If we wish
to make a law for the army, Gentlemen, we must not
consider it exclusively from the point of view of civilian,
or lawyer or doctor, but rather from the point of view
of a military man. Authority from above and
obedience from below—in one word discipline is the
whole soul of an army. Discipline alone makes the
army what it should be, and an army devoid of discipline
is, under all circumstances, a costly institution,
insufficient for the requirements of war, and a source of
danger in peace time.

Gentlemen, it is by no means by punishments alone
that we maintain discipline. The whole education of a
man has to be taken into account, and, in reply to the
mover of the amendment, I would wish to point out
that if our punishments are more lenient than in other
armies, it is precisely this fact which assists in the
further education of the soldier. More important for
the soldier than what he learnt at school is his subsequent education in the ranks, his training in habits of
order, exactness, cleanliness, obedience and loyalty; to
put it briefly, in discipline, and this discipline it is that
has enabled our army to issue victorious from three
campaigns. Nevertheless, Gentlemen, we cannot altogether dispense with punishments; you will admit that
an exceptional degree of authority is required in order
to induce thousands of men, under the most trying conditions, under suffering and privations, to stake health
and life on the execution of an order. Such authority,
Gentlemen, can only exist and thrive if duly protected.
The under-officer must have a position of privilege as
compared with the private, and the officer must be
specially privileged as compared with both the one and
the other. In this respect there certainly exists an
inequality in the law, as pointed out by the previous
speaker. It is not however so much a question of the
privilege of an officer, as of the privilege of seniority,
and in this connection I would point out that through-

out the army each one may be a senior one day and a
subordinate the next. The General in command of an
Army Corps, so soon as he has relations with a more
senior officer, becomes a subordinate. In the same
manner a simple private becomes a senior so soon as
duty calls him to that position. Every sentry, every
lance-corporal in charge of a patrol, has to exact obedience.

Gentlemen, there is no occasion to resort to the more
severe punishments in the case of the vast majority of
our men, who can easily be controlled by instruction,
admonition, censure, at most by mild disciplinary
punishments ; but we have sometimes to deal with really
bad characters. When all pass through the ranks, the
bad characters, which are to be found in every nation,
must, of course, do so with the rest. You see, we are
compelled to accept every man who has entered upon
the year in which he becomes liable to military service,
and who is healthy, and who measures a certain
number of inches. The Levying Committee cannot
inquire into the moral characters of the recruits.
Consequently we have to take men who would perhaps
be candidates for the house of correction, if not saved
from that misfortune by a severe military education. It
is just this military education also, Gentlemen, which
prevents us from agreeing to a very short term of service ; for discipline cannot be drilled into a man ; habit
must make it second nature.

To return to the punishments. Considerable reduc-
tions have been made in the severity of the punishments, such, for instance, as the lessening of the period
of close arrest, by at least one-third. In this matter we
have expressed our concurrence. Short but severe
punishments answer perfectly the interests of the
military service, but we should never be able to get on
with short and light punishments.

The hard bed of the soldier has been represented as
a form of cruelty. Gentlemen, we doom each one of

our men to this hard bed whenever he is on guard, only with the aggravation, which he has not when in arrest, of being called out, every four hours, to mount sentry for two hours in the wind and rain. Gentlemen, a hard, but dry bed, protected from both wind and weather, is an unspeakable boon when compared with a bivouac on the snow or on a wet ploughed field such as our soldiers have often had to endure. How gladly would a soldier, or even an officer, have slipped off from a bivouac like this to a similar berth.

If you allow the refractory and idle soldier, when under arrest, to have his mattress, and if you only stint him of his usual food every third day, he idles away his period of arrest in sleep, and rejoices in the fact that his comrades have to do his turn of guard, and that he has not to do his drill. Gentlemen, such punishments do not suffice us. Bear in mind that the more severe punishments are directed, not against the orderly and well-conducted soldier such as you meet on the street or on the drill-ground, but against the few bad characters.

THE COMMISSARIAT IN PEACE AND WAR.

SECOND DEBATE ON THE LAW DEALING WITH SUPPLIES IN WAR.

The Committee proposed an addition to para. 8 (Lodging and Stable Allowances), whereby these allowances should also be granted to troops who, while on the line of march or in billets, would be entitled to quarters for a longer period than one day, the amount being restricted to one half of that allowed in ordinary times of peace. Moltke opposed this proposition, which was, nevertheless, carried.

Sitting of the Reichstag, 12th May, 1873.

With regard to marches and billets the question

hinges not so much upon what the military authorities demand, as upon what the locality in question can supply. In many cases the person furnishing the billet will provide complete board and lodging ; it may however also often happen that all the accommodation he can offer will be an empty shed. In the first case the half allowance would be too much, in the second too little, and it is impossible justly to estimate and requite the service which has been actually rendered. I fear that by an alteration in the wording you will in the future open the door to a great number of groundless claims. My view is that, when one tract of country has suffered more than others through marches and billeting, a given sum of money should (at any rate after a successful war) be handed over to this particular district, its equitable distribution being left to the authorities. It must certainly be the universal wish that this Bill should be passed, and I would most urgently impress upon all the need of supporting the proposals of the Government in this matter.

SECOND READING OF THE BILL DEALING WITH COMMISSARIAT SUPPLIES FOR THE ARMY.

Herr Schorlemer brought forward an amendment to para. 11 in accordance with which no cultivated land should be made use of during manœuvres : Moltke spoke against the amendment, which was lost.

Sitting of the Reichstag, 8th January, 1875.
Gentlemen, I would only wish to point out that, whereas vineyards, nursery-gardens, etc., are comparatively small plots of ground, round which troops can pass, a meadow may often extend for miles, and, if passage across it is absolutely forbidden, the obstacle presented is as great as if the manœuvre-ground were intersected by a large river. The high rate of

compensation for damage will of itself act as a wholesome deterrent in preventing too large a use being made of such meadows. I would, however, wish to retain the legal right of passage, subject to proper compensation.

RELATIONS WITH AUSTRIA.

Moltke in his speech of 16th February, 1874,[1] had emphatically repudiated any covetous intention on the part of Germany as regards any portion of German Austria : he was nevertheless, on the occasion of the debate on the " Bill for the Prevention of Ecclesiastical Misdemeanours," reproached by the Clerical Party, represented by Deputy Lender, with having declared that complications with Russia and with other States would be prejudicial to the interests of the German Empire. It was also laid to his charge that he had remained silent on the subject of Austria, although matters had since come to light which revealed the entire truth. The following is Moltke's reply.

Sitting of the Reichstag, 24th April, 1884.

Deputy Lender, as well as several other speakers in former debates, have, in the most astounding manner, endeavoured to discover, in words uttered by me in a previous speech, an *arrière-pensée* affecting Austria. As a matter of fact, I do not know what use we could make of territory wrested even from France or Russia. It is not necessary for me, Gentlemen, to refer to all the States of Europe, and possibly also of America. Enough if I say, that in our German countrymen in Austria, who live happily under the rule of their illustrious Imperial Family, we have good friends and, in case of need, perhaps allies. My impression is that we desire no conquests,—but that we intend to keep what we already possess, under all circumstances.

[1] See p. 104.

THE SOCIALIST BILL.

On the occasion of the introduction of the Socialist Bill, which followed immediately upon Hödel's regicidal attempt, Moltke spoke only in the first debate. The Bill was thrown out at the end of May, 1878, by 251 votes to 57. In the debates on a later Bill and its amendments, Moltke took no part. He was, however, deeply interested in the matter, as his letters show. After the dissolution of the Reichstag in June, 1888, Moltke was induced to stand for a constituency chiefly by the anticipation of measures directed against the Socialists which it was proposed to introduce in the course of the next Session. On the 20th June, 1878, he wrote to his nephew, William von Moltke : " In the present state of affairs, where it is a question of carrying through the important laws with regard to social democracy and the reform of taxation, I cannot very well refuse to stand as a candidate for parliament, having been proposed in two particularly unfavourable districts, namely Heydekrug and Teltow-Storkow. My one hope is that, in each case, I may fail."

Moltke did not approve of the annulling of the Socialist Law in January, 1890. He expounded his views on the subject of social reform in a letter,[1] written some months before his death on the 10th December, 1890. He holds the execution of such reform (which, however, he looks upon as an urgent necessity) to be only feasible if undertaken by a strong monarchy, possessed both of the will and the power to carry it through ; he considers these laws for the safeguarding of the State as the necessary and hopeful inauguration of this reform. "The further progress of this safeguarding of the State can only be checked or delayed by a want of understanding between those in whose favour it is to operate, and at this point it is that the iron necessity for the display of force comes in. The law against social democracy was the more humane measure as it worked deterrently. With its repeal nothing remains but a course of merciless repression." He had already, in his speech of the 24th June, 1878, spoken in favour of the adoption of reasonable measures of prevention, and this speech had made a very considerable impression, even amongst those opposed to the motion. There was general agreement that he had uttered golden words which, throughout the country, would fall upon fruitful soil ; nevertheless his deduction, that the measure proposed should be passed, in order to avoid the necessity of adopting one containing severer provisions, was not concurred in. On the 2nd June followed Nobiling's attempt, and on the 21st October, 1878, the new Socialist Law, considerably more stringent in its tenour than the former one, came into force.

---

[1] Compare " Moltke as a Correspondent."

Sitting of the Reichstag, 24th May, 1878.

I sincerely hope that the Honourable Members, who yesterday and to-day have opposed the Government measures, may not, all too soon, be placed in the position of having to demand of the Government the introduction either of this very law, or of one similar to it, but imposing, possibly, even greater restrictions. It is quite possible that the measure requires improvement in several points, and that many paragraphs will have to be altered; it appears to me, however, that the conviction has everywhere gained ground that we are in need of some better protection against the dangers which, by the progressive organization of social democracy, threaten the State in its innermost constitution. I fear that the leaders of this organization are already now pressed back to within measurable distance of that line beyond which they will be required to make their promises and pledges good.

These gentlemen will be the first to understand what difficulties this will involve. They cannot gainsay the fact that the first distribution of property must be followed by a hundred more; that where all are equally rich, all are equally poor; that want, misery and privation are inseparable conditions of human existence; that no form of Government, no legislation and, generally, no human disposition, will ever banish misery and want from the world. What would become of the development of the human race if these cogent elements had no place in God's creation! No, the future will not be without its cares and its toil; but a man who is hungry and cold considers little what the future may have in store; he snatches eagerly at the means which the present offers him. Passions long restrained, blighted hopes, will incite him to deeds of violence which his leaders are utterly unable to prevent: for Revolution has hitherto devoured its leaders first of all.

What, then, is the position of the Government? Gentlemen, we should cease to look upon the

Government as, in a certain sense, a hostile power which is to be held in check, and hampered as much as possible. Let us invest the Government with that fulness of power which is indispensable to the safeguarding of all interests! The history of the Commune in Paris attests the consequences that follow when a Government allows the reins of authority to slip out of its hands, and when the direction of affairs is controlled by the masses. The opportunity was then offered to democracy to carry out its ideas, under circumstances when, at least for a time, it could set up its own ideal form of Government. Nothing, however, was gained, Gentlemen; much, on the contrary, was destroyed. The official French reports of this sad episode in the history of France allow us to peer into an abyss of depravity; they depict circumstances and events of the 19th century which one would have deemed impossible if they had not occurred under our very eyes—before the astonished gaze of our armies of occupation, which would have made short work of the whole thing had they not been obliged to look impassively on, with " ordered arms."

Gentlemen, our labouring classes, even the most misguided amongst them, do not contemplate such consequences as these, but, on the downward road, it is always the better elements which are carried along by the worse. Behind the Moderate Liberal comes the man who is prepared to go much further than he. That is the mistake which so many make; they believe that they can, without danger, bring things down to their own level, and there stop, just as if they could abruptly arrest the rush of a train going at full speed—without peril to the necks of the passengers. Gentlemen, from behind the honest revolutionist those dark shapes may be descried emerging, the so-called Bassermann apparitions of 1848, the *professeurs des barricades* and the *pétroleuses* of the Commune of 1871.

Gentlemen, you may to-day throw out this Bill in the

well-grounded expectation that the Government will be
strong enough to deal with any violent excesses and, if
necessary, to put them down by armed force; but,
Gentlemen, that is but a sorry shift—it averts the danger
of the moment, but it does not remedy the evil from
which the danger springs. If now we have here a way
pointed out to us, by which it may be possible to avoid
the employment of such pitiable means by adopting
preventive measures, by a sensible temporary restriction
of misused liberty, then, I say, we should lend a helping
hand in the interest of all social and national order, in
the interest especially of the suffering classes among
our fellow-citizens, who can never be benefited by any
sudden overturning, but only by the slower processes
of legislation, moral education, and individual labour.
For my part I intend to vote in favour of the motion.

INSTITUTE FOR THE EDUCATION OF SONS OF SOLDIERS, AND PREPARATORY SCHOOL FOR UNDER-OFFICERS AT NEU-BREISACH.

SECOND DEBATE ON THE IMPERIAL BUDGET FOR 1882-83.

Between 1882 and 1887 the grant for the above Institution was
four times thrown out, and it was not until March, 1887, that it was
voted.

Sitting of the Reichstag, 16th December, 1881.

One of the previous speakers has laid stress upon the
fact that it was far more difficult formerly to maintain
the supply of under-officers than it is at present. Yet that
is no valid reason why we should not improve matters
for the future. He takes the view that if the Alsatians
would only reconcile themselves to Germany, there
would be no difficulty in finding under-officers. Yes,

it just comes to that, we must accustom them to regard themselves as Germans, and to this end universal service is the best propaganda. Some years ago, when his Majesty the Emperor was in Alsace, all the young men who had served in the army flocked from their villages in red military caps, which they wore with pride. It is the young generation that we must work upon, for we can never make Germans of the old men. The matter has also a political significance and I appeal to you to support the Government in the question of these establishments.

Moltke spoke on the same subject in the debate on the budget for 1885-86.

Sitting of the Reichstag, 19th January, 1885.

There is hardly anything more to say on this subject; I shall only make a few further remarks.

The previous speaker has urged against this proposition that, whenever it has been submitted to the House, it has been rejected. Yes, Gentlemen, but, on the other hand, as often as it has been rejected, it has been brought up again by the Government. Apart from all political considerations, it has to do with an institution for providing some 2000 or more under-officers, who are wanted to complete the establishment of the army. It is, in every sense, desirable to win such excellent material, as the population of Alsace, for the rank of under-officers,—that body which, next to the corps of officers, is the most important element in the efficiency of the army. From Breisach, which formerly possessed a far stronger garrison than now, come urgent complaints. The inhabitants resent the loss of the troops. Breisach, like so many small towns, is accustomed to live by its garrison. Now there are sites in Breisach which might be used for the school, and I believe that the proposition can be recommended on financial as well as on military grounds. I ask you to accept the proposition.

BARRACKS AT GROSSENHAIN.

SECOND DEBATE ON THE IMPERIAL BUDGET FOR 1883-84.

Sitting of the Reichstag, 9th December, 1883.

Particular aversion has been expressed in this place to the installation of officers' quarters in barracks, and still more to that of officers' messes. These views cannot, surely, be based on financial considerations, for the lodging allowance of those officers who are to be quartered in barracks will be saved, and this amount will more than cover the interest on the initial cost of the plan.

An argument has, however, been advanced on a point of principle to the effect that the introduction of these innovations would tend to keep officers aloof from other classes of society, and that their *spirit of caste* would thereby be fostered. True, Gentlemen, but then for *caste-spirit* we soldiers have another name ; we call it *comradeship*. *Comradeship* is that strong link which binds the officers of a regiment together in all their interests for mutual support, in joy and sorrow, in peace and in war. It was *comradeship* which, in our last campaign, moved other troops to hasten up from all sides to render assistance and support to small detachments which were hard pressed ; and it was to this spirit that the successes achieved were really due.

In listening to the debate in this House one might be led to believe that a distinction existed in the army between officers of noble birth, and those drawn from the middle classes. Gentlemen, such is not the case ; when an aspirant-officer has been approved of by his brother-officers, and has joined their ranks, the spirit of *comradeship* admits of no further distinctions being drawn. No one could succeed in introducing such a rift into the army; such an attempt would be like a useless waste of powder.

Moreover, Gentlemen, there can be no question that, where hundreds of young soldiers are living together, they require superintendence both by night and day. Gentlemen, there is a great difference between the order given generally to a body of men with whom the officer is not familiar and the order which makes a soldier say to himself, "This order concerns *me*. My commanding officer knows *me* individually." The company officer knows every man in his own company, but it is not to be expected that he should also know every man of the other companies, every man in the whole battalion, and that, Gentlemen, is the simple reason why it has been decided that, in every company, one officer shall be quartered in barracks.

With regard to the officers' messes, these may perhaps be denounced also as the outcome of class prejudice; but we are of opinion that it is not becoming that an officer should dine in any casual "eating-house." If he goes to a high-class restaurant it will cost him from 1 to 2 thalers, and this is more than his pay will permit of. In barracks, however, in his mess, he will get a good dinner at far less cost; and even the officer of slender means will sometimes be able to indulge in a glass of wine, obtained directly from the producers at cost price, and free from the middleman's commission.

I believe, Gentlemen, that I am right in saying that the officers of every regiment have now got their library, map-room, war-game and other facilities for professional study. Where would these prove of most use? Where could they be to better purpose than in some place in the barracks, which all the officers must visit every day, where such a common room would foster the advancement of their professional studies as well as their social intercourse?

Gentlemen, if we deprecate the building of barracks for economical reasons, we are quite within our rights;

but when it is once admitted that they are necessary,
then we should leave it to the military authorities to
construct them in the manner considered most desirable
from the military point of view.

LAW RELATING TO MILITARY PENSIONS AND GOVERNMENT OFFICIALS.

Moltke only interposed with a very short remark during the debate
on the first Pension Law, in the later amendment of which he took a
very considerable part.   At the sitting of the 13th May, 1871, when
Herr Miquel raised the question as to whether soldiers born in
Alsace-Lorraine, who had served under the French flag in the late
war, should be treated with as much consideration as the German
soldiers, the War Minister, Von Roon, replied that he believed that so
generous a proposal would not, on principle, be refused, and that the
interests of their now German fellow-countrymen residing in Alsace
and Lorraine would have to be considered in the " Invalids " Bill.
Moltke considered it his duty to make a qualifying remark, as
follows :—

" With reference to the Alsatians, I would only desire to call
attention to the following point—that a great number of them took
part in the war as *franc-tireurs*, firing on our soldiers one day and,
the next, putting away their rifles and appearing as civilians. I
consider that some distinction should be drawn here."

In 1884 a Bill to make certain changes in the Law relating to
Military Pensions and Government Officials was brought forward for
debate ; the Bill was, however, only finally disposed of in March,
1886.   The question turned on the provision to be made for the
widows and orphans of persons having served in the army or navy.
The Bill was wrecked on the provision, approved by the Reichstag
but declared unacceptable by the Minister for War, that all unmarried
officers were to pay 3 per cent. of their pay as a contribution
towards the widow's fund.   The Opposition also made it a condition of
their support of the Bill that the immunity of officers, as regards
communal taxation, should be done away with.   Moltke felt it
incumbent upon him to make several speeches in connection with
these questions during the course of the debates.

FIRST DEBATE ON THE BILL FOR THE ALTERATION IN THE LAW RELATING TO MILITARY PENSIONS AND GOVERNMENT OFFICIALS.

Sitting of the Reichstag 24th April, 1884.

If I animadvert on one of the points raised by the

previous speaker, I mean his second point; and if I deprecate the communal taxation of officers, I must premise that I do not speak in the name of any party, but express merely my own personal conviction. Gentlemen, I should like, with all brevity, to narrow the scope of the subject under discussion. I believe that from a financial point of view its importance is greatly over-estimated. Gentlemen, our officers' corps is drawn from all the educated classes of the nation, but this by no means implies that they are chosen out of the more wealthy classes. Parents, whose means allow of their sons studying, do not as a rule destine them for the profession of arms. The largest contingent of our officers is supplied by the class of the unmonied Prussian nobility. This nobility, formerly possessed of large estates and considerable wealth, has ruined itself in the service of the State; it has become poor by having, from time immemorial, embraced as its vocation in life the glorious, but far from lucrative, profession of arms. The number of officers who inherit property from their parents is exceedingly small. The vast number of young officers who marry upon the minimum income, fixed by regulation, of 600 thalers, and who have no more than this to enable them to live in a manner becoming their position in life, find themselves in such straitened circumstances, that you really cannot take anything from them. There are also, incontestably, officers who are well-to-do, and even rich: candidly, I do not think the number of these can be very large.

Gentlemen, bearing in mind the fact that a large proportion of the towns have, by alienation and sub-division, parted with their former fair possessions in woods and pasture-land, I heartily wish them, too, better revenues; but I fear that it is not from the officers that they must expect to get them. As I said before, there are a number of officers who could, incontestably, bear increased taxation. But first and foremost comes the question, by what just title should officers be mulcted for

G 2

the benefit of the towns? And here, Gentlemen, I must emphatically asseverate that the towns do absolutely nothing for their garrisons. Gentlemen, all the fine institutions of a town, the lighting of the streets, the pavements, the canals, the laying-on of water to the houses—all this, Gentlemen, is charged to the tenant by his landlord, and the officer has to supplement his lodging allowance in order to pay it. We have no claim on the fine charitable institutions of the towns, we nurse our own sick and provide for our own invalids. All exhibitions, places of amusement, everything else, in fact, that the towns have to offer, are available only for ready-money. What thanks, then, do we owe them?

In spite of all this it is sought to impose a fresh tax. How will the proceeds of this tax be disposed of? Who will maintain that they will be applied solely for the benefit of the garrison, even if we leave the officers out of the question? What will become of them we are not told; we are not represented on the municipal boards, and indeed we have no right to ask what will become of them; but, Gentlemen, where there is no privilege there can be no obligation.

Gentlemen, it is well known that officers are subject, as every one else is, to all State taxes, direct as well as indirect; they are indeed liable to the former to a greater extent than many other persons, whose affairs are not so exposed to scrutiny as is the pay of officers and officials. As regards communal taxation, officers have been for the last generation exempted from it in Prussia. All municipal regulations, even those which have undergone revision, state most emphatically that a military man is not to be classed in the same category with the civil inhabitant, and that he is, when entitled to lodging allowance, exempt from all direct communal tax-ation as well on his official as on his non-official income. The Decree of 1867, and the Federal Law of 1868, both lay down the same rule. What, then, has occurred since 1868 to cause a departure from these principles? Well,

Gentlemen, what has happened is this, that since then we have had a great war, a war won by the army, which has brought milliards of money into the country ; and if, as seems to be the case, these milliards have not proved altogether a blessing, the blame at any rate does not lie with the army.

And this further has happened, that the South German States have joined the Empire. It appears that in some of these—I believe in Bavaria and Würtemburg—other regulations govern communal taxation. Yet that does not strike me as a reason why that portion of the Empire which is immeasurably larger, and older, should abandon its institutions ; on the contrary, it seems far more reasonable to expect that the new-comers should accommodate themselves to us.

Gentlemen, the whole question of taxation, and, in large part, the whole social question, turns upon this, that the rich and well-to-do must pay more—the poor and badly-off less—in the matter of taxation, and upon this point we are agreed ; but as to how this is to be effected we have never yet been in accord. We have carried on debates through entire sessions, in hour-long speeches, on tobacco-tax, stock-exchange tax, spirit-tax, sugar-tax, etc., etc., and on occasion of each proposition it has been demonstrated, with great acumen, that just this proposal is the one which commends itself least.

At this rate we are making no progress. More is expected from the Government every day, but no further provision is made to increase the revenue. Gentlemen, I believe that the well-to-do classes certainly can, and will have to, bear increased taxation, and I do not in any wise leave out the well-to-do officers : all we want to know is, for whom are we to be taxed ? If the taxation is for the benefit of the community at large, for the Empire, for the State, the preserver of social order, for the State, the universal benefactor, especially of those who have something to lose, then we will submit to taxation, I cannot quite say cheerfully, but willingly. But I can see no reason whatever why an officer should be taxed for the benefit of a town which does absolutely nothing for him, which he does not himself choose as a place of residence, and from which he may at any time be transferred to another town which also does nothing for him. Gentlemen, if such a reason could be found, it would justify the town of Berlin, for example, in demanding such a tax from each Honourable Member of this House who is a stranger to the city. Yes, Gentlemen, you are not free agents as regards the choice of your place of residence when serving the State, for Berlin is assigned to you; you enjoy all the advantages and benefits of this residence just as much as we, but, like us, only in return for ready-money. The only difference between us is that you, at least, have still a real home elsewhere than in Berlin, whilst the officer, as long as he serves, has no home anywhere, and therefore should not be taxed for one. You owe the city no more than we do. It is not the city but the Empire which builds our barracks, and builds your palace, for which, by-the-bye, the army furnished the necessary millions.

Gentlemen, the proposal to tax officers is, in my opinion, not to the purpose in this Law. What possible sense can there be in saying, "We admit that the lot of those officers who are past serving must be improved, but it must be at the expense of the officers who are still serving"? I hope that this clause may be thrown out in committee. Whether, then, you accept the Pensions Bill (making it retrospective in operation, too, I hope) will depend upon this, Gentlemen—whether you believe that the Empire owes some little gratitude to the men who risked everything and devoted their lives' best energies in fighting our battles.

At the same sitting.

Only a few words! Dr. Windthorst has paraded the fact, that officers' children are permitted to attend the schools, as a special boon conferred by the town. Well, Gentlemen, it must be unreservedly admitted that the towns make great and laudable sacrifices in the matter of schools, but, so far as that goes, it is quite a simple matter to make the children pay higher fees, as indeed is done. But that is no reason why all officers, whether married or single, should be taxed.

Then it has been further pointed out that account must be taken of the fact that towns have built military buildings, barracks, riding-schools, etc., for the military. True, but this brings me to the other side of the question—not what the town does for the garrison, but what the garrison does for the town! I shall not linger on this argument; it is not everywhere welcome that the garrison is, in the last resort, the guardian of public order, especially in large towns and in those cases where the available police force is inadequate. I shall, however, bring out another point. The pay both of officers and privates is, taking them individually, extremely modest, but, when taken collectively, it represents enormous sums, which are entirely expended in the towns to the great advantage of the classes connected with manufactories, industry, and the retail trade. How great this advantage is we see by the numerous applications received from time to time at the War Office, petitioning for the establishment of garrisons in towns, or protesting against their withdrawal.

FIRST DEBATE ON HERR V. KÖLLER'S MOTION FOR AN ALTERATION IN THE LAW RELATING TO GOVERNMENT OFFICIALS. (INCREASE OF THE PENSION RATE FROM $\frac{1}{80}$ to $\frac{1}{60}$.)

The motion was accepted on the 9th December, 1885.

Sitting of the Reichstag, 2nd December, 1885.
I have but little to add to the pleas urged by Deputy

v. Köller in favour of his motion, and I am glad that, apparently, the claims of the government officials have throughout been recognized as justifiable; but, Gentlemen, the claims of officers who are about to retire from active service are not less well grounded. I consider it of imperative moment that this question, which has already been in abeyance three years, should now be brought to a satisfactory issue, and I have therefore felt it to be my duty, to bring forward a Military Pensions Bill, which, when printed, shall at once be distributed to the members of the House.

FIRST DEBATE ON MOLTKE'S MOTION WITH REGARD TO THE ALTERATION IN THE MILITARY PENSIONS LAW.

As the increase of military pensions had already been refused, except on the condition that officers should no longer be exempt from communal taxation, Moltke now brought forward the earlier Government proposal in its original form. In order to silence the scruples of the Reichstag in this direction, it was proposed by the Government that the exemption of officers from communal taxes should be ruled out of court, in so far as their private incomes or the pensions of half-pay officers were concerned. The acceptance of the motion followed on the 8th and 10th April, 1886.

Sitting of the Reichstag, 10th March, 1886.

The Military Pensions Law has already been discussed in several sessions, and has been considered by three committees. It will be difficult to say anything new on this subject, and I shall not waste your time and your patience on matters which have already occupied your attention.

First of all I must refute the accusation which has been levelled against me from the opposite side of the House (the Left). It has been said that the introduction of my motion was distinctly a party move, hostile to the success of the Government-Officials Bill. Gentlemen,

I may whisper to you in confidence that my proposition was never contemplated by the Conservative party, nor even once broached to them. The Government-Officials Law no more originated with the authorities than did my motion originate with my party; and if nevertheless I have in this matter received the support of my political friends, I am very grateful for it. It was, however, of my own accord that I decided to bring this motion forward, because I said to myself that without a stir in the matter the Bill would, in all probability, be again shelved for a considerable time, and that the officers, who have for many years been vainly awaiting a final settlement of the question, would once more be doomed to bitter disappointment.

Gentlemen, the Government-Officials and the Military Pensions Bills have been simultaneously laid before you, but as distinct proposals, each standing or falling by itself. The reproach, therefore, which has been brought against the Government, that two years ago it introduced the two Bills amalgamated into one, is undeserved. I am of opinion that the Government was entirely justified in doing so. For, Gentlemen, the two Bills are framed on exactly parallel lines. In tenor, subject, and form they are intimately related—I should rather say inseparably. I can conceive the rejection of both Bills, say on financial grounds, or the acceptance of both, but I hold that it would be unjust to approve of one (whichever it be) and to disapprove of the other.

But now what have these gentlemen done, these very gentlemen who have reproached the Government for having—as they express it—coupled together two kindred matters? They have not themselves hesitated to introduce into the Bill a matter entirely foreign to it.

Gentlemen, even the most skilful dialectic hardly convinced any one in the previous discussion that this subject is germane to the matter in hand. From the very beginning your Committee entertained doubts as to whether it was justifiable in any way to enter into

further discussion on the subject of these taxes, which
are altogether beyond the scope of the Bill proposed by
the Government, and whether undue pressure was not
being exercised on the Government in making the
acceptance of the Bill conditional on the acceptance of
the amendment. Gentlemen, the Pension Law gives,
the taxation clause takes away: the relation surely is
one of contrariety and not of affinity. The two measures
are not in any one particular addressed to the same
persons; the one affects retired officers, the other those
on the active list. Even the title of the Bill would
require alteration. Recourse was had to the wording:
"alteration and *amplification* of the Pensions Bill."
Well, Gentlemen, you cannot take it amiss that the
Government did not view this "amplified" Bill with
favour. To have done so would have meant the
creation of a hazardous precedent; hazardous especially
for us if the Bundesrath, turning the tables, should only
consent to consider the propositions and wishes of this
House in return for compliance or concession on other
matters foreign to the point at issue. All parties should
stand aloof from such bargaining.

As regards the taxation of officers, the Bill which has
been laid before us to-day opens up a new phase of the
subject, inasmuch as the Federal Government cancels
the hitherto existing exemption of officers from taxation,
and leaves the matter to be dealt with by the legislature
of the country. Then the taxation of officers will
undoubtedly form an integral part of the whole question
of communal taxation. Now I do not know, Gentlemen,
I cannot possibly foresee, what attitude you will adopt
with regard to this Bill in its altered form. Should
you approve it, I believe that you will thereby remove
the stumbling-block which till now has stood in the
way of a satisfactory settlement as regards both these
Bills. As soon as the Bill is relieved of that which does
not properly belong to it, an understanding will easily
be arrived at; for, Gentlemen, the questions of increasing

officers' pensions in the future from $\frac{1}{80}$ to $\frac{1}{60}$, and of reckoning service from the age of eighteen, have already been fully discussed in this place, and against these, I believe, no serious objections have been raised. Should you insist in singling out, from amongst the voluminous and weighty matters connected with communal taxation, the one point of the taxation of officers for earlier treatment, then, Gentlemen, I should reserve to myself the right to discuss here the feasibility or otherwise of the whole project. I think, however, that I may venture to reserve the consideration of this somewhat comprehensive question until such time as this Honourable House thinks fit to come to such a resolution.

Gentlemen, my motion is, word for word, a repetition of the former Government proposal. It contains nothing which is retrospective in its action. I have refrained from burdening my motion with any conditions which might make it difficult either for this House or for the Government to give their assent to it. And yet I must say that a certain amount of retrospective action is so extremely desirable, and is so much in accordance with the claims of justice, that I feel bound to plead energetically for it. I am convinced that this course will meet with the approval of the Opposition. A motion dealing with the matter has already been introduced in your Committee, in favour of which the representatives of the Government have delivered a carefully-considered verdict. I hope that they will be able to find the limit to which retrospective action may be extended without involving any unreasonable financial sacrifices. I hope that the necessary means may be obtained for the Imperial Pensions Fund. First and foremost, however, it is my wish that my motion should at once be accepted in the simple form in which it has been drawn up.

I ask you, Gentlemen, also to view the Pensions question from another, more general, standpoint. It

is obviously desirable that those officers, who under the
burden of advancing years feel that their physical in-
firmities interfere with the proper execution of their
duties, should not be forced to continue a service which
is beyond their strength, out of anxiety for the future
both as regards themselves and those belonging to them.
But, Gentlemen, we have to do in the present instance
not only with this particular class of persons, however
numerous, but we have to consider also a question of
grave political import to the State.

The remark was made here on a previous occasion,
"Who would have thought that, after a war which
had produced such changes in Europe, peace would
have been preserved for fifteen years?" Gentlemen,
we owe this blessing to the wisdom of our Emperor
and to the policy of our Chancellor—a policy (so far
as we can judge) such as the world has never seen
before, which has enabled a powerful State at once to
solve internal social problems, and to make use of its
might, its prestige, and its ascendency, not for the
oppression of its neighbours, but for the maintenance
of peace with them—and not only that, but for the
promotion of peace amongst the neighbours themselves.
But, Gentlemen, such a policy can only be carried
through when supported by a powerful army ready
for war. The machine of State, deprived of this mighty
driving-wheel, must come to a standstill, and the diplomatic notes of our Foreign Office would no longer
carry weight. The army, Gentlemen, has been the
foundation upon which it has been possible to establish
this policy of peace ; the army it is which assures weight
and support to diplomatic action, but only so long as it
is really efficient, and capable of intervening when a
peaceful solution is no longer attainable. And, Gentlemen, the army ages with its officers, not only with
those of senior rank, but (and this is a reflection of
much more serious consequence) with those who occupy
the very important posts of captains of infantry and

their fellow-officers of similar rank in other branches of the army.

Gentlemen, if the army is to fulfil the objects required of it, if you wish to see it powerful and vigorous, then you must grant to it its Pensions Law.

III.

CONSTITUTION OF THE GERMAN ARMY.

THE great questions of army organization, especially as regards the peace establishment, of the duration of its maintenance, and also of the duration of active service, have always, since 1867, been the subject of constantly renewed and exhaustive debates, at times of passionate altercation, in the Reichstag. These were the questions on which Moltke spoke most impressively and most emphatically. Even in an earlier discussion on those clauses in the "North German Confederation Bill" which dealt with the military constitution of the Confederation, Moltke had made an attempt to keep the peace establishment of the army as long as possible independent of all Parlimentary decrees, whilst he came forward, at the same time, as a steadfast champion of the three years' active service scheme.—The peace establishment was first brought into question in Article 56 of the "North German Confederation Bill," when it was fixed at 1 per cent. of the population in 1867. On increase of population a fresh percentage, varying in proportion to increase, was to be fixed every ten years. To this Moltke proposed an amendment whereby the peace establishment, and the attendant annual expenditure, were to be maintained until the publication of a new Law of Federal Union. This amendment was lost by 138 votes to 125 ; instead of it an amendment by Herr Forckenback was accepted by 137 votes to 127, whereby the existing percentage was to hold good until the end of 1871, after which time the peace establishment was to be fixed by law. By the acceptance of an amendment proposed by Herr Ujest-Bennigsen it was further resolved that the sums voted, as well as the peace establishment, should remain unaltered until a change should be made in the Federal Law. With the discussion of the Imperial Military Bill of February, 1874, an attempt was made to effect such an arrangement by law, and once again the most lively controversies arose in connection with the question of the peace establishment. On this occasion also a satisfactory solution was not arrived at, but the compromise, which was accepted by the Government, of granting a fixed peace establishment for a period of seven years, was carried by 216 votes to 146. In the spring of 1880 the subject again came up for discussion in the debate on the Bill for Amplifying and Amending the Imperial Law of 2nd May, 1874. This Bill demanded an increase in the peace establishment of some 26,000 men, on the basis of the actual population ; it demanded further that the men of the first category of the "Ersatz" Reserve should be compelled to undergo trainings during peace time; and it demanded, finally, that the laws regulating transfer from the Reserve to the Landwehr, and from the Landwehr to the Landsturm, should undergo revision. It was agreed by 186 votes to 96 to fix the peace establishment for a further septennial period (viz. up to March, 1888). In November, 1886, however, the Imperial Government introduced a new Bill, which laid down the peace establishment for the period from the 1st April, 1887, to the 31st March, 1891, a measure which increased the number of infantry battalions from 483 to 534, and of field artillery batteries from 340 to 364. In the sitting of the 14th January, 1887, however, the majority of the House declared itself in favour of accepting it only for a triennial period. The result was an immediate dissolution of the Reichstag. The newly elected Chamber, in its sitting of the 7th to 11th March, 1887, accepted the measure in the sense of the Government proposals.—In the short and unobstructed debate on the great Defence Bill which was brought forward in December, 1887, to reorganize the system in connection with the Ersatz Reserve, the Landwehr, and the Landsturm, Moltke took no part. It passed its second reading (without amendment,) on the 6th February, 1888, and its third reading on February 8th.—Moltke spoke on military matters for the last time on the occasion of the debate on the latest Military Bill, by which the peace establishment was increased by 18,500 men, the artillery arm alone being raised from 364 to 434 batteries. On the 28th June, 1890, this Bill, which fixed the peace establishment from the 1st October, 1890, to the 31st March, 1894, was read for the third time and passed.

PRELIMINARY DEBATE ON SECTION XI. OF THE NORTH-GERMAN CONFEDERATION BILL (THE CONFEDERATE ARMIES).

Sitting of the Reichstag, 3rd April, 1867.

The first gentleman who spoke has revived the question of a two years' period of service. It is a question which has often been the subject of discussion ; allow me once again to briefly throw some light upon the matter.

A two years' military service has been demanded on

the score of national financial expediency. Whether two hundred thousand able-bodied men serving for three years, or three hundred thousand serving only for two years, are temporarily withdrawn from productive labour, comes exactly to the same thing.

Military service does certainly not represent productive labour, but it has for its object, and actually compasses, the security of the State, without which every form of productive labour is impossible ; it forms the school which trains the young generation to order, exactness, obedience, and loyalty—virtues which are not thrown away in their later relation to productive labour.

The same argument is always used that the young men must remain a third year with the colours, and the fact is passed over in silence that seven whole annual contingents, the oldest and the fathers of families, will henceforth never be called up for military service, and consequently withdrawn from their business. This advantage is certainly, from a national financial standpoint, of great importance. I only make an allusion, from a financial point of view, to the sums raised by local taxation for the " sustenance of families."

It is perhaps much more possible to advocate the two years' service system on financial grounds. The peace establishment stands in the way, and it cannot be denied that, from a financial point of view, a reduction of the peace establishment is most important and desirable. There only remains, therefore, the consideration as to the extent to which such a reduction is permissible from a political and military point of view.

If we cast our eyes around us, we see all our neighbours arming. Why ? We do not know. We threaten no one, we wish to bring order into our own internal affairs. About the fact, however, there is no doubt.

I will not enter the arena of politics ; I will confine myself to the military aspect of the question. It is urged with justice that the three years' service does not allow of all the men capable of bearing arms passing through the military school. Quite true, there is a remainder.

Not in every case, however, for in several districts all the men capable of bearing arms are absorbed, even to the last man. It is moreover true that with a two years' service there would remain just so many able-bodied men as would be sufficient to raise the battalions to a strength of 500 men. This reasoning applies, of course, only to the infantry, for a reduction in the establishment of the special arms cannot be contemplated. Now I will not maintain that such battalions would altogether lose their efficiency if, as with the three years' service, one-third of the men, at most, were recruits; with the two years' service, however, half of such a battalion would be engaged in elementary military training. Now consider the deduction of some sixty under-officers, consider the deduction entailed by the duties that fall upon the other half of the men, such as detachments as guards of military prisons and for transport duties; the daily service of guards (in fortresses, for instance), however limited it may be; the supply of ammunition, which has, at times (at Magdeburg, for instance), daily requisitioned several thousand men; deduct, further, regimental tradesmen, the sick, prisoners, etc., etc., and there is so small a remainder that such a battalion can no longer carry out its tactical training for war, and thus fulfil the very object for which it exists.

It is also true that the two years' service would furnish a larger quota of men for purposes of augmentation in the event of war. But, Gentlemen, there is no lack of men; our War Minister, after having mobilized and placed nine army corps in the field, improvised two more, and would even have been able to create others had they been required. After the battle of Königgrätz we were stronger than we were before it, and on the conclusion of peace we had no less than 664,000 men under arms. Such formations find their limit much sooner in another direction. Picture to yourselves what it means, financially, to maintain an army of 700,000 men, or the 900,000 now asked for, under arms!

Besides this, the possibility of creating such formations is restricted by the limited number of officers. To show you the value of officers in war in leading troops, let me cite just one figure of statistics. We lost one officer for every twenty men. Form a body of troops with an insufficient proportion of really experienced officers, and you will have a mob of brave men, but not troops!

In the course of last year we made nearly 50,000 prisoners, and had 3000 men missing. Of the latter probably only a very small proportion were made prisoners, although the fact cannot be authenticated. Why this enormous difference? I can only ascribe it to the length of service. Financial straits had forced Austria to adopt a system by which the infantry soldier served on the average only one and a quarter to one and a half years. These men fought with the greatest bravery, and in this connection I must bear witness to the glorious example set by the officers in leading them on, for the Austrians themselves also lost a large number of officers. As soon, however, as difficulties arose, order vanished; in village fighting and in wood fighting the men were made prisoners in flocks. With us the call was heard on all sides, "Where is the captain?" "Where did the captain say we were to go?" Gentlemen, this feeling of mutual reliance under all circumstances cannot be acquired by drill, but can only become a second nature with time. To obtain this result two years are not sufficient.

SPECIAL DEBATE ON THE ARTICLE IN THE NORTH-GERMAN
CONFEDERATION BILL RELATING TO THE CON-
FEDERATE ARMIES, NAMELY, ARTICLE 56, WHICH
FIXED THE PEACE ESTABLISHMENT AT 1 PER CENT. OF
THE POPULATION, ON THE UNDERSTANDING THAT THE
PERCENTAGE SHOULD BE REGULATED DECENNIALLY,
TO MEET THE ALTERED CONDITIONS OF THE POPULA-
TION.

A compromise, on a septennial basis, was effected.

Sitting of the Reichstag, 5th April, 1867.

I need speak but a few words in justification of an
amendment which I wish to propose. The question
arises as to what is to happen if, after the expiration of
a term of years yet to be fixed, the stipulations of the
Constitution Bill should lose their effect before a new
Military Law shall have come into force. We have
been told that the Laws and Regulations which were
valid in Old Prussia will apply in like manner to the
whole of North Germany. Were this to be the case,
were everything to remain as of old, then my amendment would be superfluous, though, in any case, harmless. I do not, however, believe that this conception of
the circumstances is, as a matter of course, to be
expected in a new Parliament; I look for some more
positive security.

My amendment has for its object to provide, for so
permanent an institution as the army, the solid foundation of a fixed revenue.

Consider, Gentlemen, that the after-effects of lowering
the peace establishment will continue operative during
periods of twelve years,—aye, and in the immediate
future during a period of nineteen years. You may
perhaps decide upon a reduction in times of peace, but
the effect of such reduction may possibly be realized
only in time of war.

My amendment ought to extend not only to Article

56, but also to Article 58 ; for it is of no assistance to me that the multiplier is constant if the multiplicand is variable. It is quite true that a portion of the military revenue and expenditure remain beyond the reach of Parliamentary control. But, Gentlemen, you have heard from the detailed explanations of the Government Commissioner how closely the expenditure is estimated, and you know that, for every demand for an increase, the Government is dependent on the favourable disposition and patriotism of the national representatives. Vouchsafe to the Military Department the right, within defined limits, to act with a free hand according to its discretion ; the army will be grateful, the liberty of the people will remain uncurtailed, and the representatives of the nation will be relieved of the uncongenial task of having to flounder through discussions on technical subjects about which they know nothing. Suppose, for instance, 100,000 thalers are demanded of you for alterations to knapsacks ; well, Gentlemen, those of you who have never carried a knapsack in a blazing sun cannot know where it rubs. There are many matters which the Military Administration undoubtedly understands far better than a whole assembly of excellent and patriotic men.

Gentlemen, I beg of you voluntarily to limit the sphere of your uncontested privileges ; necessity bursts through bonds that are too tightly drawn. I commend to you the acceptance of my amendment.

Special Debate on the Bill dealing with Obligation to Military Service, Section 6 (Seven years' service in the Standing Army, three of which to be uninterrupted colour-service).

The most important portion of the paragraph lies in Section 6 : " During the remainder of the seven years' service the men will be sent on furlough to the Reserve, unless the annual trainings, necessary augmentation, or mobilization of the army, or, in the case of the navy, the arming of the fleet, should require their recall to the colours." The expression "necessary augmentation" had created distrust ; several amendments aimed at clearer definitions, without, however, exhausting the various possibilities of the case. Moltke expressed himself in favour of the original phrase, which was carried by 165 votes against 81.

Sitting of the Reichstag, 18th October, 1867.

Gentlemen, for me also the main difficulty of this whole paragraph of the Bill lies in the words " necessary augmentation."

With the greatest interest I followed the lucid report of the Chairman of your Committee yesterday : I quite concur in the principle, to which he then gave expression, that the liberty of each individual subject of the State does not depend upon a lenient exercise of Government authority, or, as he put it, on its favour, but on his own right. This is the spirit of legislation in a Constitutional State. But you will also allow that a certain latitude ought to be reserved in the Bill itself for the authorities who administer its provisions, because the conditions under which it will come into operation cannot be determined beforehand. Although Section 60 of the charter of the Constitution fixes the establishment of the army at 1 per cent. of the population, and Section 62 names the maximum expenditure for the maintenance of the army, yet Section 63 reads : " The Confederate Commander-in-Chief fixes the peace establishment." And with reason, for the circumstances cannot actually be foreseen which will justify a reduction of this peace establishment, or necessitate an increase. These cases of necessity are dealt with in Section 6. You will find in several paragraphs that measures which have always been permitted hitherto, and which, though not illegal, were not dealt with by the Bill, are now submitted to discussion, and I understand that it is the intention of the Government in each instance to secure legal sanction for their execution. This is what the Government in the present instance openly say: "In case of necessity we must have the power of calling up the Reserves." These words have given rise to many-sided objections, which I regret to find are entertained by the Chairman of your Committee. A more rigid or a more elastic form of phraseology has been sought for; on the other side, also, an attempt has been made, in most radical fashion, to supply an ultra-rigid phraseology. It has been felt, however, on all sides, that the latter course would make it impossible for the executive power to discharge its highest functions. It has been proposed, on grounds of expediency affecting politics and the country police, to word the matter thus: "Preparations for war having been decided upon;" or else, "On the outbreak of war." I look upon this last phrase as the more suitable, although I am convinced it does not embrace all the contingencies which might render an increase necessary. If we had been compelled last spring—and it very nearly came to that—to increase our armed force in the Rhine Province, and that we had carried this measure out under orders headed "Preparation for war," we should have had war. Considering the excitable character of our neighbours, I have no doubt of it. But we do not wish for war. We wish to perfect our internal relations in peace, we wish to regulate German affairs here in Germany, and only in the event of any one interfering with our doing so, shall we wish for war.

I will only observe incidentally how much I hope that in such an event we shall not put into practice the theory of a militia army. Surely none of us would wish to see the horrors of such a war as we have recently witnessed in America transplanted to European soil. I hope, moreover, that we shall not act upon the theory of the weak offensive army, and the strong defensive one. We should have fared badly so in the last war; we should have to look for the battle-fields, not on the maps of Bohemia and Moravia, but on those of Silesia and Lusatia, and perhaps even further back.

Besides, the army does not divide itself into an offensive army and a defensive army: the same army, which, by attacking the enemy, better than in any other way protects the Fatherland, will also engage in the defence of the interior of the country, should its field of operation unfortunately be thus limited. It would then find in the Landwehr a strong, necessary, and excellent support, as no one can doubt.

The other suggested improvement in the wording, "On the outbreak of war," does not any more than the last meet all the necessities of the case. Gentlemen, let me remind you that already on several occasions it has been necessary to effect frontier reinforcements entailing the dislocation of the troops from whole army corps districts. It has been urged that the inconvenience of employing two weak companies, instead of one of increased strength, would be slight as compared with the alternative of precise legislation.

It is not a question, however, of the employment of companies, but of far larger bodies of troops: the transfer to the frontier of troops quartered in interior districts is a measure which must be carefully weighed. I will not press the point of expense, as other members assign but little importance to it, although indeed considerable sums of money are at issue, for the troops have to be transported, they must have their field-allowances, and so on. There are, however, other considerations in connection with this matter. Our infantry is, for the most part, quartered in fortresses; we cannot simply withdraw them, without more ado; we cannot denude the fortresses, the large towns, and whole districts, of troops: garrisons must be left in them, recruits must be left, etc. The difficulty, then, is no insignificant one. The consideration further arises that, if a mobilization should take place at such a time, great difficulties would be experienced; our troops can only be

effectively mobilized in their own permanent garrisons.
You have first to send back the troops, which involves
loss of time, and time is an important element of
success, or else you have to bring all their effects up to
them. Gentlemen, our mobilization is such a complicated affair—even the minutest detail being the subject
of regulation—that I fear such a course would cause
embarrassments which might be very disastrous.

As regards the elimination of certain clauses, I must
say that I consider it irrational to strike out anything
merely with the view of preventing the adoption of
necessary measures in a given eventuality.

It is not now a question of the calling up of individuals, Gentlemen, but of whole categories. I do not
believe, therefore, that there is any necessity for you to
safeguard individuals against arbitrary acts on the part
of the military authorities. Whether on any given
occasion the calling up of the Reserves was justified
or not, is a matter the decision of which will rest with
you, Gentlemen, when you come to vote the supplies
for such a measure. It will be impossible to defray
this expense with the 225 thalers.

Gentlemen, I believe that we all honestly wish the
laws to be upheld ; the best way to do this is so to
make the laws that they can be observed.

I most earnestly beg of you to allow the words
" necessary augmentation" to remain unaltered.

FIRST READING OF THE IMPERIAL MILITARY BILL.

Sitting of the Reichstag, 16th February, 1874.

Of the numerous objections brought forward by the
last speaker, I will in the first instance only touch upon
one. I hold it to be nothing less than impossible to
determine the war formations of an army beforehand,
for we cannot foresee whether we shall have to make

front towards one or towards two flanks. We do not know whether we shall have to make war with only a portion of our army, as in 1864, or whether we shall be placed as we were in 1870, when, calling forth all our strength, we had to employ entire Landwehr Divisions for the duties of the lines of communication and in the sieges,—when we had to group together, in totally new formations, the oldest classes of the men liable to military service,—when we had, in order to guard hundreds of thousands of prisoners, to arm the veteran " Gardes du Corps " with infantry weapons,—and when we had, during the course of the war, to alter the number of armies and their composition. I have no doubt that these and many other considerations would be elucidated in a discussion in Committee. I would above all direct your attention to the fact that, with the very first paragraph of the Bill now before you, it will be necessary to weigh the question as to whether or not Germany will in future have to support the heavy burden which will be imposed upon her by the maintenance of a peace establishment of 401,000 men. Gentlemen, the matter depends upon the internal and external circumstances of the country. Every Government must employ its revenues in meeting the imperative requirements of all departments of the State before it can entertain the idea of effecting savings or redeeming debts or, least of all, remitting taxes. But now the first necessity of a State is—to exist,—to safeguard its existence from without. Within a country the law protects the right and liberty of individuals ; without, as between State and State, might is the only right. Even an international arbitration tribunal, if it existed, would lack the power of executing its decrees, and its judgments would, in the last resort, be subject to the arbitrament of the sword. Minor States can trust to neutrality and to international guarantees ; a great State must rely on itself alone and stand in its own strength ; it fulfils the conditions of its being, only

if it is determined and prepared to maintain its existence, its liberty, and its rights in arms, and to leave a
country defenceless would be the greatest crime its
Government could commit.

The desire to save the large sums which are annually
expended upon the army, for the relief of the taxpayer,
or for the objects of peace, is certainly most eminently
justifiable. Who would not associate himself with such
a desire? Who does not like to picture to himself how
much of good and useful and beautiful might thus be
effected? But we must not withal forget that the
savings of a whole series of years on the Military Budget
may be dissipated in one year of war.

I will recall to your minds the cost to the country of
the period of time between 1808 and 1812, after an
unfortunate campaign. Those were years of peace,
years when the strength of the army was small, and the
period of military service as short as could be desired in
any country—and yet the Emperor Napoleon could
boast of having wrung a *milliard* from the small and
impoverished State of Prussia. We saved, because we
had to save, on our own army, and spent tenfold for a
foreign one. In any case we should not overlook the
fact that of recent years the Government has praise-
worthily devoted large sums not only to the furtherance
of military interests, but also to the objects of peace.
These sums are, however, totally inadequate; on all
sides more is demanded, and more will be demanded,
and it is for this reason that I am of opinion that we
have certainly not yet reached the point where it is
possible to recommend a reduction of taxation. I think
that each subject of the State, however humble he may
be, should bear some share in its taxation, even if it were
only to remind him that a State really exists which
cares for and protects him, and which he, in his turn,
is called upon to protect; for experience shows that
human nature is incapable of rightly appreciating the
value of even the greatest blessings if they cost nothing.

How also is it possible for the State to forego a portion
of its revenues when, in all departments, so much remains to be done? I only specify Public Education,
because I believe that the school is the point where the
lever must be applied if we wish to protect ourselves
against the internal dangers which are as much to be
dreaded as external attack. I refer to socialistic and
communistic tendencies, which constitute dangers only
to be averted, I believe, by means of social improvements—by a better and more universal education.

Our schools, Gentlemen, do not take in the whole of
our youth, and they conduct the great majority of our
young men only a short way on their path through life.
Fortunately when instruction, in its strict sense, ceases,
education soon steps in, and no nation has, hitherto,
enjoyed an education so universal in its character as
that which we now secure through common liability
to military service.

It has been said that the schoolmaster won our
battles. Gentlemen, bare knowledge does not yet raise
men to the standpoint at which they are prepared to
stake their lives for an idea, for the fulfilment of their
duty, for honour and for Fatherland; nothing less than
education in its fullest sense will bring a man to this
level. Not the schoolmaster has won our battles, but the
military profession, as popular educator—the military
profession, which has now, for nearly sixty years, trained
the nation to bodily activity and to moral health, to
order and exactness, to loyalty and obedience, to love of
Fatherland and to manliness. Gentlemen, from the
point of view even of domestic policy, the army, and
the army in its full strength, is indispensable for the
education of the nation. And how about external conditions? Possibly, a later and more fortunate generation, a part of whose burdens we already bear, may hope
to escape from the condition of armed peace which has
already so long weighed Europe down. For us, no such
smiling prospect is, I fear, in store. An event so great,

so historically important, as the re-erection of the German Empire, is scarcely to be compassed in a short space of time. That which we have wrested by force of arms in half a year we may have to protect by arms for half a century, so that it shall not again be torn from us.

This is a matter, Gentlemen, about which we should cherish no illusions; since the termination of our successful war we have gained respect everywhere, but affection nowhere.

On all sides we are confronted by the distrust lest Germany, having become powerful, should, in the future, prove to be an unpleasant neighbour. Now Gentlemen, it is not wise to conjure up bogies, and out of distrust and anxiety, unfounded though they may be, real dangers can arise.

In Belgium, even to this very day, you will find sympathies with France, but very few with Germany; it has not yet been recognized in that country that there is only one neighbour who can be dangerous to Belgian neutrality, and that it has only one real protector.

In Holland they have already begun to restore the line of inundations and to fortify it anew. Against whom? I do not know. I believe that in Germany the idea of annexing Holland has never even occurred to any one.

It is true that as late as the beginning of this century we captured these very lines; not for ourselves, however, but for the House of Orange. In a small, yet widely-read pamphlet, written with a view of drawing the attention of the English to the defects in their militia system, the consequences are depicted of a landing in England—not from France, not from the opposite coast, but from Germany. In Denmark, from fear of a German landing, it is considered necessary to increase the coast-defence fleet, and to fortify the points of landing on the island of Zealand. At one time we are about to conquer the Russian Baltic Provinces, at another we wish to lure away the German population of Austria.

And now, Gentlemen, let me turn for a moment to the neighbour in whom we are most interested.

France has been compelled to reform her entire military organization. Whilst our armies occupied France, almost its entire army was in Germany; we sheltered, lodged, fed, and partly clothed them, and then, on the conclusion of peace, we restored this army uninjured to France, where it now forms the solid nucleus of all new formations. All our military organizations have now been faithfully copied in France, of course without citing their origin, under French names, as "originally French ideas, offspring of the great Revolution, only the Germans adopted them somewhat earlier." First and foremost universal liability to military service has been introduced, and has had as its basis a twenty years' liability, while ours is only for twelve years; a retrospective action has further been given to the law, so that many Frenchmen, who have long since worked out their term of service, have suddenly become liable once more. The French Government is already authorized to call out 1,200,000 men for the Active Army, and another million also for the Territorial Army. In order to be able to place these men in the ranks by instalments—for, Gentlemen, it is not merely a question of the number of men liable to service, but also of the cadres which they are to complete—I say, that in order to place these large numbers in the ranks, it became necessary to increase the cadres. After Germany had once more reconquered her Imperial Province (Reichsland), we merely transferred the already existing burden to a greater number of shoulders, except in the case of a few of the special arms. Since that time France has made considerable additions to her armed forces, and this in spite of the fact that her population has decreased by some $1\frac{1}{2}$ millions. The number of infantry regiments in existence in France up till the time of the war was 116, it is now 152; consequently there has been an addition of 36 infantry regiments, without counting 9 fresh rifle battalions. Since the peace 14 new cavalry regiments have been formed. Up till the time of the war the number of batteries was 164, there are now 323, i.e. an addition of 159 batteries. This does not complete the list of increases: the peace establishment in France has never yet been so large as it is at present; it has been increased, since 1871, by 40,000 men. The average strength, according to the budget for 1874, is 471,170 men and 99,310 horses. Instead of the eight army corps with which the French opposed us at the commencement of the war, France will in future put eighteen into the field, without counting a nineteenth for Algiers. The Military Budget—I give the figures in thalers for greater facility of comparison with our figures—has increased since 1871 by over 25 millions: it amounts, for the army, in the Ordinary Budget to 125 million thalers, in the Extraordinary to 46 millions; that is to say, 171 million thalers in all. Gentlemen, the French National Assembly, uninfluenced by considerations of State finance, and without respect of parties, has freely made the sacrifice which was demanded for the re-establishment and development of French military power. It even went further: more warlike than the War Minister himself, it has, in the course of this year, forced upon the Military Commission, for a special purpose, namely, the calling out of the *seconde portion*, a sum of 17 million francs. The French communes have not allowed themselves to be outdone in patriotism; they provide exercising-grounds, buildings for officers' clubs, they erect barracks, etc., etc.

All this, Gentlemen, furnishes to us a picture of the prevailing state of feeling in France. I believe, indeed, that the great majority of the French, who undoubtedly bear their misfortune with more self-possession and dignity than one would be led to believe were one only to listen to the French demagogues or only to read the French papers,—I believe that this majority is thoroughly imbued with a sense of the absolute necessity of, above all, preserving peace.   I see a confirmation of this view in the circumstance that a prudent soldier stands at this moment at the head of the French Government.   But, Gentlemen, we have all witnessed how French factions, whose field of action lies in Paris, can hurry the Government and the people on to the most extraordinary decisions.   What is borne to us from across the Vosges is a rabid cry for revenge for the reverses which France herself had courted.

Well, Gentlemen, we have not followed our neighbour's lead in increasing the army ; we hope that the provisions of this Bill will suffice for our needs.   But, Gentlemen, we must not allow the intrinsic value of our army to be lessened, either by shortening the term of service, or by a reduction of the peace establishment.   The first measure, if it is to have any financial value at all, leads to a militia.   Wars carried on by a militia have this peculiarity, that they last much longer, and even on this ground and for this very reason involve far greater sacrifice, both of money and of human life, than all other wars.   I need only remind you of the late American War of Secession, which had to be waged, on both sides, principally by militia forces.   I must not miss this opportunity of communicating to you the opinion of the man who had to conduct the first American campaign, the War of Independence—the opinion of Washington—regarding a militia.   You will find it given in Bancroft's excellent " History of the United States of America."   Never and nowhere could a demand have been more unpopular than that which Washington again and again submitted to Congress, the demand for the raising of a standing army.   This may be matter of surprise to you, but Washington expresses himself in the following terms : " Experience, which is trade's best guide, so completely and so decisively rejects all reliance upon a militia force, that no one who values order, regularity, and economy, and who cares for

his own honour, his character, and his peace of mind,
will stake these on the outcome of an undertaking
which relies for its success upon militia forces."

And a little further on he writes: "Short service
and an unfounded reliance on the militia are the causes
of all our misfortunes and of the growth of our debt."

The war was, as you know, brought to a close by
the appearance on the scene of a small corps of only
6000 men, who were, however, real soldiers.

Gentlemen, France has twice tried a militia system.
The first time that the hated army was disbanded was,
of course, after the Revolution ; the nation itself was
to guard the new-born liberty, patriotism was to take
the place of discipline, whilst the national *élan* and
the masses themselves were to supersede military training. A certain halo even now hovers round the
volunteers of 1791 ; but, Gentlemen, there is also an
impartial account of all this, compiled, by a Frenchman, from the official records of the French War Office.
I will resist the temptation of citing some very piquant
passages ; to do so I should, indeed, have to quote the
whole book, for every page would show how useless
and how costly these formations were, and what a
scourge they proved to their own country. Only after
thirteen years of bitter experience did the French arrive
at the conviction that the army should no longer be put
in the ranks of the volunteers, but the volunteers in
the ranks of the army. When, therefore, such men as
the First Consul and other illustrious generals placed
themselves at their head, then indeed these same
volunteers victoriously overran the whole of Europe ;
but, Gentlemen, they had then become soldiers.

The small volume to which I refer, and from which
such instructive lessons may be derived, appeared in
March, 1870, and six months later we see France
resorting to these same measures, though, it is true,
only in her direst hour of distress. Gentlemen, we
have all by experience gained the conviction that, how-

ever great may be the number of staunch, patriotic, and brave men who may be banded together, they can never withstand a real army.   The French *Garde-Mobile* and their *Garde-Nationale* prolonged the war by several months, thereby entailing bloody sacrifices, wide-spread devastation, and great misery.   They could not, however, change the course of the war, nor could they, on the conclusion of peace, secure more favourable conditions for France.   Again, the mischief wrought by the *franc-tireurs* did not retard our operations by one single day; on the contrary, it gave our mode of warfare, towards the close, a character for severity, a circumstance which we deplored, but could not alter.

The law-suits which to this day, after a lapse of three years, arise in France, present to you a picture of the degeneration, and of the horrors, which infallibly result from the adoption of such a measure.   Gentlemen, if you arm the nation, you arm the bad as well as the good elements.   Of the former every nation has its share, though the latter vastly predominate.   But has not our own experience of armed citizens demonstrated how quickly the trustworthy portion itself becomes dissatisfied, and disappears noiselessly, leaving a clear field to those who are untrustworthy?   Gentlemen! rifles may be distributed quickly, but it takes time to get them back again.

And do you not believe that we also harbour elements such as those which, after the war, got the upper hand in Paris?   Even if we have not got them yet, it is certain that outside influences will very soon see that we do get them.   Even now many of those heroes may have been imported who, in Paris, destroyed the monuments of French glory!   God forbid that we should ever place weapons in such hands as these.

As regards the peace establishment, therefore, Gentlemen, I would earnestly warn you against making it a Budgetary question.   I know well that Honourable

Members of this House believe it to be their duty not to yield on this very point, in order to safeguard to Parliament its undoubted right in the matter of the granting of funds. But, Gentlemen, consider whether, in exercising this right, you will not infringe upon that other right which the nation possesses of being able to count upon your co-operation in a question dealing with the stability of the Empire. It appears to me to be desirable to enter into a fresh provisional arrangement. Let us rather settle, once and for all, what Germany must do for a German army. If you are convinced that, having in view the internal and external state of affairs, we should maintain not less than 401,000 men in time of peace, and if, after mature consideration and trial, it has been ascertained what expense is necessary for this purpose, then you should altogether give up discussing, granting or refusing this same sum each and every year. Moreover, Gentlemen, by so doing your right of financial control is in no wise impaired; it comes into full play on the occasion of each further demand and with each fresh legal adjustment of this subject. The normal peace establishment must necessarily remain constant over a long term of years. By making it a variable quantity you introduce a factor of uncertainty into all the numerous and comprehensive preparations which, if you wish to be assured of your ability to resist foreign aggression, have to be determined long beforehand in minutest detail. Just consider that each reduction has an action lasting for twelve years, and that there is not one of us who can foresee whether in twelve years' time we shall be at peace or war.

Well, Gentlemen, the best-disposed mortal cannot live in a state of peace if it does not suit his evil-disposed neighbour.

I think, however, that we shall show the world that we have become a powerful nation and remained peace-loving; a nation which does not require war in order to acquire fame, and that does not desire it in order to make conquests. I really do not know what we should do with a conquered portion of either Russia or France.

I hope that we not only shall enjoy peace for a period of years, but that we shall also be in a position to impose peace; then perhaps the world at large will become convinced that a powerful Germany in the centre of the Continent constitutes the best guarantee for the peace of Europe.

But, Gentlemen, in order to be in a position to impose peace we must be armed for war, and I am of opinion that we stand face to face with the alternative —either to assume that the political aspect of Europe does not make a strong and efficient German army indispensable, or else to grant the means for the maintenance of such an army.

SECOND READING OF THE IMPERIAL MILITARY BILL, SECTION 1 (THE PEACE ESTABLISHMENT).

Sitting of the Reichstag, 14th April, 1874.

Gentlemen, I consider it a token of respect to address the Assembly from this place. I offer this as my excuse for thus addressing you. As the Assembly is already somewhat fatigued, my remarks shall be of the briefest.

My speeches, though neither numerous nor lengthy, have been quoted by several speakers, and in particular by Deputy Reichensperger. In reply, I may state that I am still as thoroughly convinced as I was before, and that I still at this moment believe that a strong Germany in the centre of Europe is the surest guarantee of peace. But, mark me, Gentlemen, I say a *strong* Germany! So long as one of our neighbours threatens us daily, from the platform and in the press, with a war

of *revanche*, so long must we not forget that it is only
the sword which keeps the sword within its sheath, and
that under such circumstances disarmament for us
would mean war; that war which we would so willingly avoid, and which, I trust, may yet be averted by
the wisdom of the French Government.

Gentlemen, if in earlier days we had known in
Germany how to unite peacefully, the struggle with
France would probably never have arisen.

But, Gentlemen, in 1870 there was as yet no united
and powerful Germany in the heart of Europe, and the
war, with which France took us by surprise, was waged
principally with a view to preventing its establishment.

It was not we who courted this war, neither did we,
during its course, at all misuse our power. It rested
with us, had it pleased us to do so, to drive two and a
half millions of people in Paris into inevitable death by
starvation. No one could have prevented us from
prolonging the blockade for another week or fortnight :
whatever demands we might have made of the Government, it would have been compelled to comply with
them. Due consideration, however, had to be given to
the fact that the Government was not in a position to
comply with extravagant demands. We contented
ourselves, therefore, with exacting the restitution of
those lands which our restless neighbour had wrested
from Germany in the days of her weakness. No reproach can be attached to us on the further score of
war indemnities, for no amount of *milliards* can heal
the wounds which a war, " undertaken with a light
heart," has inflicted upon both public and private
life.

Yes, Gentlemen, Germany, with her dissensions of
the past, has only herself to blame if, in the reconquered country, a German race has been able, in
the long period of 200 years, so to lose its nationality
that even now, in spite of the beneficent treatment
which has been bestowed upon it, it resists the idea of

becoming once more German. Well, we will give our
fellow-countrymen on this side of the Vosges time
during the next two hundred years to become recon-
ciled to us.

It, however, behoves an united and strong Germany
to demonstrate to the world that we possess both the
determination and the power to keep the Reichsland
ever with the Empire.

All round us, Gentlemen, the Great Powers have
materially increased their military strength. We alone
have remained content with the proportion of the
population, 1 per cent., calculated according to an
earlier census. We cannot count upon numerical
superiority, but must rely rather upon the intrinsic
qualities of our army, which depend to a great extent
upon the length of service of each individual man.
The French infantry soldier serves actually with the
colours from three to three and a half years ; we hope,
by reason of the excellent natural disposition of our
men, by educating them, by the introduction of gym-
nastic training, and by reliance on the unceasing toil
of our officers and under-officers—who exert themselves from morn till night—to be able in a yet
shorter period to possess an excellent infantry. How
far, Gentlemen, we can venture to make things easier,
constitutes a technical and purely military question,
and the military authorities believe that last year they
reached the lowest permissible limits of concession.

Gentlemen, the amendment which has been introduced by Deputy v. Bennigsen admits that the
demands made by the military authorities are justified, but it provides that they shall have effect only
for a limited interval. I cannot bring myself to believe
that the leading institution of the Empire should in
any way possess a provisional character. I believe
that it must be fixed legally and definitely. Laws are,
of course, not made for all eternity. If the political
relations of the world were to change in the course of

years, it would be possible also, with the consent of all three factors in the legislature, to give legal sanction to a modification of the figures of the peace establishment. What I altogether fail to perceive is that the composition of the army should be dependent on the sanction of one only of these law-giving bodies. I shall, nevertheless, vote for this amendment, because I believe that a patriotic Assembly of Representatives of the Empire will, at the end of seven years, be unable to refuse that which we recognize to-day to be necessary for the stability of the Empire. I therefore hope that, if only on the basis of this amendment, there may be secured, on the division, a majority which shall be worthy of the importance of the subject, of the prestige of the country abroad, and of the dignity of this House.

DEBATE ON THE IMPERIAL BUDGET FOR 1877–78. EXPENDITURE IN CONNECTION WITH THE CREATION OF 122 NEW CAPTAINS.

The motion in question, brought forward by the committee, was passed.

Sitting of the Reichstag, 24th April, 1877.

Gentlemen, the question now before us will, to a certain extent, meet with opposition ; not because the measure does not in itself appear to be expedient and good, but because, to tell the truth, it includes a fresh increase in the Military Budget.

It was remarked on the occasion of the first debate, and it has now again been repeated, that it is, in principle, inadmissible to sanction, in time of peace, the creation of appointments for officers who will only be required in time of war. The simple answer to this, Gentlemen, is that all officers' posts exist in peace because the officers are required in war. Attention has been directed by that side of the House (the Left) to the far weaker peace establishment of the French battalions; any reference to the far greater number of these weak battalions was, however, omitted. Gentlemen, the grand total of these battalions, with the due proportion of auxiliary arms, amounts in peace time to 487,000 men; whilst Germany, with a population greater by several millions, maintains only a little over 400,000 men. Weak battalions are, from a military point of view, most undesirable. I believe that nowhere more than in France itself do the more experienced military men doubt whether, with companies of fifty, or perhaps only of forty men, it is possible to carry out even the elementary training of the troops in all the various branches, in addition to the unavoidable garrison duties. But, to speak plainly, if it is wished to take the field with 1092 battalions, and if only 641 of these are maintained in time of peace, it will be impossible to make these units very strong, without launching forth into enormous expenditure.

Gentlemen, the French Military Budget, with its weak battalions, exceeds the German, with its strong ones, by more than 150 millions of marks annually in the Ordinary Budget, without counting a large number of supplementary estimates and an exorbitant Extraordinary Budget.

The question of whether a nation, though it be as rich as the French, will burden itself to this extent for all futurity, or whether it is only for a definite and pre-arranged purpose, and with a perhaps not too-distant object, is one which cannot now be solved.

We were also further informed, during the first debate, that an absolute Government would probably, under existing political circumstances, rather reduce the army than increase it. Gentlemen, I associate myself with the Honourable Member both in his hope and in his desire for a lasting peace; I cannot, however, share his confidence as to the probability of attaining it. Happy will be the days when States will no longer be in a position compelling them to devote the greater part of their revenues solely to the protection of their very existence; when not only the Governments, but also peoples and factions, shall have arrived at the conviction that even a successful campaign involves a greater cost than the profit; for there can be no profit in buying material benefits with the lives of men.

But, Gentlemen, what militates against this advance of the whole of humanity is mutual distrust, a distrust in which there lurks a great and ever-present danger.

I consider that the strength of Germany lies essentially in the homogeneity of its population. True that we have, near the confines of the Empire, subjects who are not of German nationality, but that is the historical result of centuries of battles, of campaigns and treaties of peace, of victories and defeats. The limits of a great State cannot be defined by scientific principles.

Well, Gentlemen, these non-German subjects of the Empire fought side by side with the Germans with equal loyalty and with equal bravery; but the statement that all their interests are not coincident with ours is one which surely we have heard more often in this House than any of us can possibly desire. Why, then, should we commit the folly of weakening, instead of strengthening, ourselves by an extension of territory?

I believe that the peaceful tendency of Germany is so self-evident, is so firmly based upon the necessities of the case, that by this time the whole world must have become convinced of it. But nevertheless, Gentlemen, we cannot fail to acknowledge that our western neighbour nourishes a strong distrust of us. If you read the French papers, even the leading ones, you will find in them, to put it mildly, a great antipathy to us. I will say nothing about the scorn, derision, and contumely which they display, for they are devoid both of sense and sincerity.

What the French press, however, does not set forth, but what is nevertheless true, is the apprehension lest the numerous and repeated attacks made by France against a weak Germany, should induce a strong Germany, without ground and without cause, to fall upon France.

This, Gentlemen, accounts for many facts. It explains the gigantic task which France has accomplished in carrying out, in a short period of time, the re-organization of her army, with great knowledge and with rare energy; it explains the circumstance that, ever since the conclusion of the last peace, a disproportionately large portion of the French army, including specially large contingents of cavalry and artillery, has been stationed in Paris, and between it and our very frontier—a force which is in the most complete state of preparation for any eventuality. This state of affairs must in my opinion, sooner or later, necessarily constrain us to adopt counterbalancing measures.

It is, moreover, worthy of attention that in France, where the factions, which of course exist in all countries, although in other respects more abruptly opposed to each other than here with us—these factions, I say, are all at any rate agreed on one point, which is, to grant anything and everything demanded for the army, whilst we, here, wrangle painfully over small items of expenditure. Gentlemen, in France the army is the spoiled child of the nation, its pride and its hope; in France the army has long since been pardoned for its defeats. I will not say that with us the conquests of our army have been forgotten but, if on the next occasion the same services are to be demanded of it, it is necessary that there should not be a too sparing allotment of those means which are indispensable for its further development.

It appears that our neighbours base their hopes of success in the next war on overwhelming numbers, and that, certainly, is a factor which weighs heavily in the scales. We rely rather upon the careful training of our troops, and upon their thorough efficiency. The French are undoubtedly superior to us in this respect that they possess, even in peace time, the cadres necessary for all their numerous formations. You have now proposed to you a measure which, though only in a small degree, remedies this deficiency with us. We have been told that by the creation of thirteenth [1] captains the number of officers will in no wise be increased. That is quite true; but, Gentlemen, it places the number of officers earlier in that position which they will have to fill in war. It is surely quite natural that anyone, who, under the most trying circumstances, is suddenly placed at the head of troops, possibly after being snatched away from some quite different line of life, should in the first moment experience a certain amount of embarrassment —a contagion which, Gentlemen, inevitably spreads through the ranks from the highest to the lowest. Want of decision in giving an order begets untrustworthiness in the execution of it.

The creation of thirteenth captains will permit of the earlier introduction of senior officers into those posts the duties of which should, by force of habit, be performed as a second nature. Gentlemen, you really need not be afraid that the thirteenth captains will be gadding about. There is plenty for them to do.

I feel satisfied that those gentlemen who have taken part in the deliberations of the Committee, will have convinced themselves that we have, indeed, an economical military administration which really only asks for what is urgently required.

I recommend the measure to your acceptance.

The above speech was delivered on the same day as that on which

---

[1] In a regiment of three battalions.—[Note by the Translator.]

the Russian Government issued its declaration of war. It produced the most intense uneasiness throughout Europe, which was already excited by the imminence of the Russo-Turkish war. This uneasiness was especially felt in France. At the next sitting of the Reichstag Moltke, therefore, willingly endorsed and emphatically confirmed the words of Deputy Lasker, in which the latter interpreted his speech in a peaceful sense.

Sitting of the Reichstag, 26th April, 1877.

Gentlemen, as I have been personally referred to in the course of this Debate, permit me to say two words. I thank Deputy Lasker for having understood me rightly, and for having more clearly explained the meaning of my words than I had been able to do myself. When I said that a considerable portion of the French army is posted very close to our borders, I ought to have added that our regiments are contrariwise evenly distributed over the whole Empire.

My object was to anticipate any corresponding measures which we might deem it necessary sooner or later to adopt, and prospectively to divest such measures of an aggressive character. At the very beginning of my speech I described our policy as one which is necessarily peaceful, but does not, on that account, renounce its right to full freedom of action.

First Debate on the Bill dealing with the Additions to, and Changes in, the Imperial Military Law of 2nd May, 1874.

Sitting of the Reichstag, 1st March, 1880.

Who can deny that Europe groans under the weight of an armed peace? It is mutual distrust which keeps the nations in arms against each other. If this distrust can in any way be removed, it will be rather through an understanding between Government and Government than through other means, such for instance as the Babylonian confusion of international fraternity, international parliaments, and other suggested means of like nature.

Gentlemen, all nations are equally in need of peace, and I am convinced that all nations will maintain peace as long as they are strong enough to command it. Many people look upon the Government as a species of hostile power whom one cannot sufficiently curb and trammel. I consider, however, that it should be strengthened and supported in every possible way; a weak Government is a misfortune for any country and a source of danger to its neighbours.

We have all of us witnessed the outbreak of wars which were wished for neither by the head of the State nor by the nation itself, but only by the leaders of parties, who had set themselves up as their spokesmen, and who had drawn after them the impressionable crowd and, at last, also the Government. Cravings after annexation and longings for revenge, dissatisfaction with the state of internal affairs, the striving to draw towards one's self kindred nations which, in the course of time, have been incorporated into other State formations—all this, and much more, may also, in the future, occasion, at any time, fresh developments, and therefore it is that I am afraid that we shall still, for some time to come, have to wear the heavy armour which our historical development, and our position in the world, have forced upon us.

Historically speaking, we are of course, as an empire, only the youngest member in the family formed by the States of Europe, and an intruder is always looked upon with distrust, at any rate until he comes to be better known. As regards our geographical situation—well, Gentlemen, all our neighbours are more or less, I may say, protected from rear attack; they have behind them either Pyrenees or Alps, or else semi-barbarous races whom they have no cause to fear. We are placed right in the midst of all the Great Powers. Our Eastern and Western neighbours have only to form front in one direction, we in all directions; they can transfer, and have already in peace time transferred, a large proportion of their military forces to the neighbourhood of our frontiers, whilst our regiments remain evenly distributed over the whole Empire. We have no occasion to suspect any hostile intention in this. If our neighbours are really apprehensive of danger from Germany then, from their point of view, they are quite right; we must, nevertheless, take this situation into our calculations.

We have also to consider the constant growth of the armies around us. Russia had good grounds, even before the Turkish war, for adding considerably to her already strong military forces, and after the conclusion of peace she carried out and preserved this organization. Russia has created 24 new reserve-infantry-divisions and 24 new reserve-artillery-brigades, and has, in addition, formed 4th battalions for 152 regiments. The Russian press, which is now so agitated, maintained profound silence with regard to this measure, and the whole proceeding obtained hardly any notice in the foreign press.

As regards France, I have not read the article quoted from the Prussian annuals. By the help of the data which are at my disposal, I arrive at quite a different result from that obtained by the former speaker. I will only give a few of the principal figures, and will spare you the details.

In the 1870 campaign France opposed us with 8 army corps; at present she possesses 19. At that time she had 26 infantry-divisions, there are now 38; then there were 26 cavalry-brigades, now there are 37. The strength of the French army on its first formation amounted to 336,000 men; at present, France can oppose us with 670,000 men, according to the budgetary figures. This does not include the territorial army.

I arrive at the result that France has, since 1874—that is to say, in six years—more than doubled her army, and,

Gentlemen, in this same period, or rather since the last peace, we have remained stationary with a percentage based on an antiquated census.

We come, then, to the consideration of the high peace-establishment of our neighbours. France has, according to my calculations—that is to say, as the previous speaker quite justly remarks, inclusive of the gen-darmerie, which, however, in France, is included in the army—497,000 men under arms. Whilst Germany, with a population some millions larger, has only 401,000 men with the colours. This constitutes a difference of close on 100,000 men. The Russian peace establish-ment is double ours, or say 800,000 men.

To arrive at the war strength one must naturally take into consideration the number of annual contin-gents that are available, in other words the length of the period of liability to service, and then you find the result to be as follows,—in France, 20 years; in Russia, 15 ; and with us, 12. Well, Gentlemen, on which side is there a menace, an imperilment of peace ? And with all this we are expected generously to set the first example of disarmament! Has the German Michel ever drawn sword except to defend his own skin ?

If, then, under the circumstances, the Government considers that it is necessary to propose a moderate increase of our peace cadres, can we, unless we wish to remain far behind our neighbours, offer any opposi-tion to such a measure ?

What, then, does the expedient of two years' service offer in its place? We are promised national-econo-mical and financial advantages. I fail to understand how such an opinion can be entertained. If, with the two years' service, the present strength of the battalions is to be maintained, all financial savings as a matter of course disappear ; on the contrary, considerable in-creases would be required for the clothing, arming and equipping of the Reserves and Landwehr-men who would, in such a case, be far more numerous than before.

Nor can we anticipate any gain from the point of view of political economy since, clearly, it can make no difference whether two able-bodied men are withdrawn for three years from productive labour, or three such men for two years. It cannot certainly be meant, although such would appear to be the case, that it is desired to simply strike out a whole annual contingent and to reduce all the battalions by one-third of their strength.

Well, that would certainly effect a financial saving in the peace-establishment, and afford a certain amount of relief for those liable to military service ; but, Gentlemen, as a make-weight to this you must set the military value of the measure, and reflect that, while quantitatively the army remains the same, qualitatively its intrinsic value is considerably depreciated.

Gentlemen, our army stands behind those of our neighbours in point of numbers. It can only make the deficiency good, and it does make it good, by thorough efficiency. This efficiency must not be meddled with.

A two years' service system is the cherished dream more especially of those who are not themselves required to convert, in shortest possible time, a recruit into a soldier, that is to say into a man who can not only march on parade and mount guard, but who can, after having acquired an intimate knowledge of his complicated weapon, and after having acquired perfect confidence in it, act independently under the most trying circumstances. By this I mean a man who has learnt to obey and to command, for even the most junior private becomes a commander as soon as he is placed on sentry duty or leads a patrol. Gentlemen, this task is not so easy as perhaps it appears here at the desk. It is not merely a question of the technical, I might say mechanical, training of the man—we could manage that in the twenty weeks which are here proposed for the training of the Ersatz Reserve ; with this we can produce a material which can with advantage be placed in the ranks of the solid framework formed by the army, but which can never constitute its core. No, Gentlemen, we have to deal with something far different; we have to deal with the development and consolidation of moral qualities—with the military education which transforms the youth into the man. That cannot be drilled into him; it must become a matter of habit and of second nature.

I will not take up your time with a demonstration of the great disadvantages which accrue from weak cadres in the training of the troops and more especially of their leaders. I will not detail the difficulties which weak battalions give rise to on their sudden threefold expansion in the event of mobilization. I will only remark, in passing, that our western neighbours, who are also gifted with military judgment, have not, in spite of repeated demands, seen their way to reduce the period of service in the French army; they hold that three years, which we do not even attain to, do not suffice to complete the training of a soldier.

But, whatever we may think about it, you will admit this much, that there could scarcely be a more unfavourable time than the present for the introduction of so far-reaching a measure.

Gentlemen, it is certainly a subject for sincere regret that an iron necessity compels the German nation to impose on itself fresh sacrifices. It is, indeed, only by sacrifice and hard work that we have at last become a Nation again. But what far greater sacrifices than those now demanded would follow on a hostile invasion? The eldest amongst us can bear personal witness to this. The very credit of the State depends in the first instance upon its security. What a panic would occur on our Stock Exchange, how all our securities would be shaken, were the continuance of the existence of the Empire to be in question for a moment.

Gentlemen, let us not forget that, since the decline of the German imperial power, Germany has been the battle-field of other nations and their objective; that

Swedes, Frenchmen, and Germans laid Germany waste for more than a century. Let us pass to later times. Are not the great ruins on the Neckar, the Rhine, and far into the heart of the country, lasting monuments of our whilom weakness and of the wantonness of our neighbours?

Who would further wish to recall the days when, at the dictation of a foreign ruler, German contingents were forced to march against Germany?

No, Gentlemen, let us, before all things, protect the honour and safety of the Empire; let us defend the long-wished-for, the finally-attained unity of the nation; let us continue to maintain peace so long as we are not attacked, and to enforce peace even abroad, according to the measure of our strength! Possibly we shall not stand alone in this endeavour, but may find allies. There lies in this no threat to anyone, but rather a pledge for a continuance of peace in our part of the world, provided, of course, that we are strong and ready armed. With weak forces, with armies that have to be called up, we cannot achieve our object; the fate of every nation rests with itself.

I look upon the Government proposal as justified, appropriate, and necessary.

First Debate on the Bill dealing with the Peace Establishment of the German Army.

Sitting of the Reichstag, 4th December, 1886.

Gentlemen, I beg most urgently to recommend to your acceptance the proposal of the Government. It is certainly matter of regret that we are compelled to employ a large portion of the revenues of the Empire as a security against danger from without instead of devoting it to internal improvement; it is, however, necessitated by general circumstances which it is quite

out of our power to alter. Gentlemen, the whole of
Europe is bristling with arms. We have only to cast
our eyes right and left and we find our neighbours
armed from head to foot; armed in a manner which, in
the long run, cannot but tax to the utmost the strength
even of a rich country. This state of affairs naturally
presses for an early solution, and that is the reason why
the Government demands an increase of the army even
before the expiration of the septennial period.

From the Introduction to the Bill, which accompanies
the Government proposal, you will perceive how far
we have remained behind the other Great Powers in
the matter of armament. You will observe from it
that, of all the great armies, ours is, relatively, the least
expensive—that it presses less severely than any other
upon the public at large; and that France, for instance,
expends upon her army nearly twice as much as we do.
It is only within the last few days that the very considerable demands made by the French Minister for War
were granted in the Chambers without demur.

The accuracy of these figures has been called in question. Well, Gentlemen, we cannot possibly work out
the calculation here in full Session; that will be done
in Committee. I believe in the accuracy of the statements, for they are founded upon the very best information that we can procure.

We have also been advised to come to an understanding with France. Well, that would certainly be very
judicious; it would be a blessing for both nations and
a guarantee of peace in Europe. If, however, it should
not come to pass—*à qui la faute?* As long as public
opinion in France vehemently demands the restoration
of two essentially German provinces, and as long as we
are firmly resolved never to give them up, so long will
it be almost impossible to arrive at an understanding
with France.

Reference has also been made to our relations with
Austria. This alliance is a most valuable one, even in

ordinary every-day life; however, it is not wise to place sole reliance upon the assistance of others. A great State exists only by reason of its own inherent strength.

If I understand aright, it was argued that the Government proposals referred only to the peace establishment, and not to the war establishment, or, in other words, the war strength. Gentlemen, the proposals ask, in any case, for an increase in the establishment of certain bodies of troops who, being close to the frontier, may probably be called upon to take the field at the very moment of the outbreak of hostilities. By carrying out this proposal the war strength will in no wise be increased; it will merely lessen the number of reserves who will have to follow on later. The measure, however, demands expressly and principally the creation of new cadres, and these will certainly increase the war strength. The cadres of 31 new battalions will increase the war strength by 31,000 men.

Then the question of the two-years' period of service was touched upon. Well, Gentlemen, I will go no further into this matter; the subject has already been exhaustively treated. In the existing political situation, it would be a very serious experiment to upset our whole previous military system and to introduce a new one.

A two-years' service, as a matter of fact, we already have; but to introduce a still further reduction would mean an increase in numbers but a deterioration in quality, and we should thus gain nothing. On the contrary, our best security lies in the excellence of our army.

The financial side of the question has also very rightly been taken into consideration. Well, Gentlemen, I by no means fail to recognize the great importance of a good financial position—but this does not apply during actual warfare, when the question is one of battles and of decisive action, when, in the words of the German *landsknecht*, cartridge-cases are the best

form of negotiable security; in this case, Gentlemen,
all regard for the financial position is set aside; it is,
however, in the very highest degree important for the
preparation for war, for the proper equipping of the
troops, for the erection of fortifications, and for the
efficient administration of the railways. A disastrous
war throws even the best managed treasury into
disorder. Why, it is the army which must safeguard
the treasury.

Gentlemen, I think we have been able, in the course
of a series of years, to convince ourselves that we possess
a circumspect, honest, and economical military administration. Even the measure now under debate has been
principally dictated by motives of economy. We have
abstained from the course, adopted by our neighbours,
of having all our guns horsed even in peace-time, however desirable such a practice may be. The increase
applies principally to the infantry, as being the least
costly arm. One half of the proposed new battalions
will, in order to avoid the necessity of creating fresh
regimental staffs, be attached to regiments already
existing. In short, Gentlemen, we do not aim at reach-
ing to that which, from a military point of view, is
absolutely the most desirable, but at that which
financial considerations render possible of attainment.

And then, Gentlemen, this demand which has been
made upon the country, has been suggested by the
desire to prolong, if possible, that peace in Europe
which has up till now been maintained with so much
difficulty. I am of opinion that, if we throw out this
measure, a very grave responsibility will attach to us;
we shall be answerable perhaps for the misery caused
by a hostile invasion; a responsibility which, though
borne by a hundred shoulders, will yet rest heavily
enough on each. We have, by great sacrifice, attained
to that for which all Germans have longed for so many
years—we have the Empire, we have an united Germany. Would that we also had an unity of Germans

on a question such as is now before us ! The whole world knows that we are not bent on conquest. Let it also know, however, that, that which we have, we intend to keep, and that, to do this, we lack neither determination nor weapons.

SECOND DEBATE ON THE BILL DEALING WITH THE PEACE ESTABLISHMENT OF THE GERMAN ARMY.

Sitting of the Reichstag, 11th January, 1887.

Not one amongst us deceives himself as to the grave character of the times we live in. All the greater European Governments are, as rapidly as possible, taking measures to anticipate an uncertain future. The whole world asks itself: are we to have war ?

Well, Gentlemen, I believe that there is no ruler of a State who would willingly take upon himself the enormous responsibility of casting a burning torch into the inflammable material which is heaped up, to a greater or less extent, in all countries.

Strong Governments are a pledge of peace. But the passions of the populace, the ambition of Party leaders, and public opinion led astray both in speeches and by the press—all these, Gentlemen, are elements which may prove stronger than the will of those who rule. Have we not seen how even stock-exchange interests have kindled wars ?

If, then, in the existing state of political tension, there is any one State which is in a position to work for the continuance of peace, it is Germany, which is not directly concerned in the questions which are agitating the other Powers; Germany, which, since the existence of the Empire, has shown that it has no desire to attack one of its neighbours, unless that neighbour himself drives her to the act.

But, Gentlemen, in order to carry out this difficult,

perhaps thankless, task, Germany must be strong and ready armed for war. If, in such a case, we become involved in war against our own wish, we have then the means of carrying it on. Reject the demands of the Government, and then, Gentlemen, it is my conviction that war must ensue.

It is a matter for congratulation, and one which cannot fail to make its effect felt abroad, that of the great parties in this House there is not one, which, in spite of many different views on internal affairs, would, after conscientious consideration, refuse the Government the means which it asks of us, for providing protection from without; it is only with regard to the duration of the grant that our views differ so widely. I would once more desire to remind you that the army can never be looked upon as provisional in its nature. The army is the leading institution of every country, for on it depends the existence of all the others—all political and civil liberty, all the products of civilization, the finances, the State itself, stand or fall with the army.

Gentlemen, grants for a short period, whether for one or for three years, will not help us. The basis of a sound military organization rests upon permanency and stability; new cadres will be productive of effect only in the course of a series of years.

Gentlemen, I believe I may say that the eyes of Europe are to-day fixed upon this Assembly and on the resolutions which you will form in this highly important matter. I appeal to your sense of patriotism, when I ask you to accept the Government measure uncurtailed and unaltered. Prove to the world that the nation and the Government are of one mind, and that you, Gentlemen, are ready to make any sacrifice, even that of a conflicting opinion, when the security of the Fatherland is at stake.

In the resumed Debate on the Military Bill in the Sitting of the Reichstag, 13th January, 1887, Moltke referred to his previous speech.

Gentlemen, it seems that the few words which I uttered, in the Sitting of the 11th January, have met with various interpretations. I expressed my satisfaction that none of the great Parties in this House would refuse the Government what they demanded as being necessary for the defence of the country, and that the only question which arose was as to the length of time during which the Bill is to operate. This statement was based upon the declaration of the Leader of the strongest Party in the House, who stated that his Party was ready to grant the very last man and the very last farthing. I then, however, also added, according to the stenographic report, that a grant for a short period, say for one or for three years, was of no use to us, that any new formations will only become effective after the lapse of many years, and that stability and absence of change form the basis of all military organizations. It cannot, therefore, be open to doubt, that my opinion is that a period of at least seven years is necessary.

FIRST DEBATE ON THE BILL DEALING WITH THE PEACE ESTABLISHMENT OF THE GERMAN ARMY.

Sitting of the Reichstag, 14th May, 1890.

It may have created surprise that new and considerable sacrifices for military purposes should have been asked for just at this particular time, when apparently the political horizon is more free from threatening clouds than it was even a short time ago, and when we have received from all foreign Powers the definite assurance of their friendly intentions. You will, however, permit me to indicate in a few words, to what degree of security we can look forward under these circumstances.

Not long since, Gentlemen, the assertion was repeatedly made from the other side of the House, at least from the extreme Left, that all our military precautions are only taken in the interests of the wealthy classes, and that it is princes who bring about wars, and that, were it not for them, the nations would live together in peace and amity. First of all as regards the wealthy class, which is, of course, a very large one, which, in a certain sense, embraces nearly the whole nation,—for who is there that has not something to lose?—the wealthy class has, in any case, an interest in all institutions which guarantee to each one his possessions.

But, Gentlemen, it is not princes, and more especially Governments, who, in our days, bring about war. The days of Cabinet wars are past,—now we have only the People's war, and to conjure up such a war as this, with all its incalculable consequences, cannot be resolved upon by any prudent Government, except with the greatest reluctance.

No, Gentlemen, the elements which menace peace are to be found among the People. These elements include, at home, all the inordinate desires of the classes least favoured by Fortune, as well as the occasional attempts of these classes to effect, by violent measures, an improvement in their condition—an improvement which can only be brought about by organic laws, and by the decidedly slow and tedious path of labour. Abroad, these elements take the form of national and racial aspirations, and, above all, dissatisfaction with the existing state of affairs. This may at any time, without the wish of the Government, and even against its wish, bring about the outbreak of a war, for, Gentlemen, a Government which is not strong enough to oppose the passions of the People and Party machinations, constitutes a lasting danger to peace. I believe that one cannot set too high a price on the worth and blessing of a strong Government. It is only a strong Government which can carry through salutary reforms, and it is only a strong Government which furnishes a pledge of peace.

Gentlemen, if war, which has now for more than ten years been hanging like a sword of Damocles over our heads—if war breaks out, one cannot foresee how long it will last or how it will end. It is the Great Powers of Europe which, armed as they never were before, are now entering the arena against each other. There is not one of these that can be so completely overcome in one, or even in two campaigns that it will be forced to declare itself vanquished or to conclude an onerous peace; not one that will be unable to rise again, even if only after a year, to renew the struggle. Gentlemen, it may be a Seven Years' War, it may be a Thirty Years' War; and woe be to him who sets Europe in flames, who first casts the match into the powder-barrel.

Well, Gentlemen, where the point at issue deals with matters of such vast import, when it concerns what we have achieved with such great sacrifice, the existence of the Empire and, perhaps, even the continuance of social order and of civilization, in any case when it concerns hundreds of thousands of human lives, then, indeed, the question of cost can only be a secondary consideration, and any pecuniary sacrifice is justified beforehand.

It is undeniable, as has been frequently pointed out here, that war requires an almost inexhaustible supply of money, and that we should not wreck our finances before the time. Well, Gentlemen, had we not made that great expenditure for military purposes, for which the patriotism of this House and of the nation provided the means, our finances would certainly have been to-day in a far better condition than they actually are. But, Gentlemen, the most brilliant financial position would not, failing the necessary means of resistance, have saved us from having the enemy in our country to-day; for now, as ever, it is the sword that keeps other swords in the sheath.

The enemy in the country—well, we bore that for six long years at the beginning of the century, and the Emperor Napoleon could boast that he had squeezed a *milliard* out of the country, then so small and poor—the enemy in the country would not stop to ask whether a bank were national or private.

We know what happened in 1813 in Hamburg (it was then a French city)—how a French General, then in full retreat, marked his departure by putting the Hamburg Bank into his pocket. The enemy in the country would very soon make away with our finances. A Germany strong in arms has alone made it possible, for her and her allies, to avert for so many long years a breach of the peace.

Gentlemen, the better our forces are organized on land and water, the more perfectly they are armed, the more ready they are for war, the sooner may we hope it may be to preserve peace a while longer, or it may be, on the other hand, to carry on an inevitable war with honour and success.

Gentlemen, every Government, each in its own country, is confronted with the tasks of the very highest social moment—vital questions which war can postpone but which it cannot solve. I believe that all Governments are honestly anxious to maintain peace ; the only question is whether they will be strong enough to do so.

I believe that in all countries an overwhelming majority of the population desire peace, but the decision rests not with them, but with the factions who have placed themselves at their head. Gentlemen, the peaceful assurances of our two neighbours, eastern and western—whose warlike preparations are nevertheless uninterruptedly carried on—these peaceful assurances and other information of a similar nature certainly have their value, but for safety we must rely only on ourselves.

MEMOIRS OF THE FIELD-MARSHAL.

I.

WRITTEN BY SOME OF HIS RELATIONS.

*Fraulein Marie Ballhorn, daughter of a cousin of the
Field-Marshal, writes this memoir of him.*

WHAT the world has seen of the Field-Marshal,
what the nation has learnt and gained through
his abilities, belong to the latter portion of his life.
One is accustomed to think of the hero as of an old
man ; it was his lot not to be seen in the full glory and
zenith of his genius, till he was seventy. He then
appeared a man ready for the occasion ; the result
of his extreme diligence and silent studies became
widely known by the fruits of his work. There were
then but few who knew anything about his early life,
for most of his contemporaries had been called away. I
have been fortunate in being very intimate from my
earliest years with this celebrated man ; he was a near
relation and friend of my father.

My first recollections date from the year 1839, when
the Field-Marshal, then Captain von Moltke, returned
from Turkey. His letters from that country had almost
all been first addressed to Berlin, and sent on by my
father to all the other relations. They made a deep
impression upon us when we were children, even by
their looks, for they were pierced through and fumi-
gated to prevent spreading the plague then raging in
Turkey.

The Field-Marshal's father, the Danish General von
Moltke, was a brother of my grandmother, on my father's
side. He was one of those original people hardly ever
found now-a-days.

His figure, stately even in old age, his noble
features, his head covered with thick white hair, his
military moustache, and bright and jovial manner, won
great interest and respect everywhere. Like his son, he
was very fond of travelling, which in those days was
still attended with great difficulties.

His liveliness often amounted almost to restlessness,
and one of his favourite remarks became quite a *bon mot*
with us. He frequently used to say when we rested
during a walk : " But, my dears, are we to remain here
for ever ? "

He travelled in an open carriage, a kind of Victoria,
drawn by a white horse, which he drove himself, though
he was always attended by a servant. Once he drove in
this way from Kiel to Salzbrunn, taking three girls with
him. Another time he even drove in this favourite
vehicle of his to Paris, and to the South of France. It
seems most unlikely to us now, that all these expedi-
tions were taken for pleasure. The old gentleman,
whose good humour was unchangeable, used to tell of
his manifold experiences in a very amusing manner.
On these travels he often visited my grandfather, his
brother-in-law, and he used to have great fun with us
children. Old Uncle Fritz has always remained in our
remembrance, an object of admiration and respect. He
even once contemplated visiting his son Helmuth at
Constantinople, when the latter was in Turkey. But
as he would have gone even there with his old white
horse, he might have met with many a danger.
However, he did go as far as Vienna and Presburg.

On his return from Turkey, Captain von Moltke
stopped first in Berlin, where he stayed at our home.
It was just about Christmas time when he arrived, and
I well remember the tall handsome man, with a Turkish
fez on his head, in undress, entering the room where
our Christmas tree was, laden with all the treasures of
the East, so at least it appeared to us children. For my
mother he had brought, amongst other things, a tube with

attar of roses which is still kept by our family. There were various kinds of silk shawls, stockings knitted in the harems, embroidery, jewelry, and rosaries, and also two wooden spoons, carved by soldiers in the camp of Nisib, they are still treasured by us ; of course to-day they are only of value for the sake of the giver ; but at that time they were something quite out of the common. He also brought the little Arab horse with him that he rode at the battle of Nisib. He was put into our stables, and on him my brother and myself made our first attempts at riding, of course always with the help of his owner, or that of his groom. The former rode Nisib daily, accompanied by my father. They generally wended their way through the Hallische Gate, where one was soon in the open country. Our old mansion stood at the corner of the Zimmerstrasse and Friedrich-strasse, which between our house and the gate was then only crossed by the Kochstrasse. We children were able to watch the horsemen all down the long street, at that time generally very quiet, almost as far as the gate. The sight made a deep impression on me.

Even at that time our cousin had his silent manner, which later on procured him the name of "The great silent one" (der grosse Schweiger). This silence was a mixture of reflection and shyness, as he himself has sometimes confessed. He did not feel that he possessed the talent of expressing himself easily on the idea of the moment, much less of making, as one says, "Fine speeches," and so his silence was often interpreted as pride. When he wrote he appeared to be another man. After a party at his house he once remarked to his wife : "Of course it was very slow again at the Moltkes' to-day." But little as he liked to talk in society, he loved much to be with children. He had great fun with us ; he used to tell us stories of the Turks and Turkish ladies, and I suppose he invented a good deal to increase the pleasure of his little friends. At such times he used to smile to himself, and he was well pleased when the children's eyes were turned attentively to him. He was always fond of little jokes and fun, and had himself a dry humour which at times animated his handsome face with a slight ironical smile.

One evening, I remember well when he drew a Turkish sentinel in a sitting position, while we were at tea. When he told us that the Turkish women were always veiled, I asked him: "Then, I suppose, you cannot draw a lady for us?" The well-known smile came into his face, he took the pencil and drew a feminine face with sharply bent eyebrows and of great beauty, as it seemed to me.

"But, Uncle,[1] how do you know what she was like?" I asked.

"Well, I peeped behind the veil," he said quite seriously.

I did not understand then, why all the grown-up people laughed at this. As his sketches pleased me much, he was often kind enough to draw little pictures for me. Unfortunately they were all lost as time went on. Who could know then, what value they would have had now.

His love for a childlike, unaffected disposition may have been one of the reasons that led to his engagement, for his *fiancée* was hardly more than a child when he became engaged to her. Only a few days after her sixteenth birthday, she was betrothed to him, then a man of forty. I distinctly remember the impression which this engagement made upon the family. We did not think that Helmuth had chosen wisely, firstly on account of the great difference in age, and then also because Marie was known to all of us as an extremely wild and frolicsome child—how could she be the sedate wife of a serious, learned officer? As he was so silent, hiding his feelings so carefully, nobody would have believed his love so deep and sincere. But in this too he has proved indeed that he was right. The happy

[1] She generally gives him the title of "Uncle."

married life which he enjoyed for twenty-seven years has shown how wise a choice he made. Never did he think of marrying again, after he had lost his wife, though everybody expected him to do so, and though the papers were never weary of hinting at it. Once when he passed with my sister through the Brandenburger Gate he said smilingly to her: "To-morrow the world will again say I am engaged."

I also remember the day on which we greeted our childhood's companion as the Major's wife in Berlin. We were astonished to find in the rather tall, pretty and graceful young woman, still the merry child who had had many an amusing romp with us. Much more astonished was I to see the serious husband watching us with his quiet smile; he seemed to be very happy, though he did not express it in words to my father and mother.

From that time a lively intercourse sprang up between us and the young couple in Berlin, and the sincere friendship which had existed between my father and the Field-Marshal when they were boys did not suffer through any change in their later lives. Yes, and Count von Moltke was the last of all the friends and relations to sit by the deathbed of his cousin Eduard and to hear his last conscious words. He had brought a bottle of old wine for the dying cousin, hoping that it might strengthen him. His changed position (it was in the year 1877) and the great difference in rank had made no change in their friendship.

Of the Field-Marshal's later years the world knows more than I myself, I therefore conclude these early recollections here. They may be of some interest as none of his contemporaries are alive now, who know this time of long ago from personal experience.

Major Henry von Burt, the Field-Marshal's nephew, who was for many years his Aide-de-Camp, gives the following little traits of his character and events of his life.

WHEN the Field-Marshal was on his way to visit the King of Sweden in 1882, he stayed a day at Copenhagen, and he pointed out to me the house where his brother Fritz and he, when cadets, had lived as boarders in the family of General Lorenz. Their room was a small chamber over the doorway. There the two boys suffered from hunger and cold, for the very stingy General did not think much of their comfort, but left them to an old quarrelsome housekeeper, who neither fed them properly nor kept their room warm. She had an old goat who once wandered into the rooms of the General, where she broke a looking-glass. The General broke out in a rage and ordered the animal to be killed, the boys were fed upon her flesh.

We then went to the parade-ground. Here the Field-Marshal remembered how he had once stretched his head forward when they were standing in rank. An officer came up to him, knocked him in the face with his elbow so that it made his nose bleed instantly. The boy began to cry, and the officer shouted at him these words: "Hvorfor holder Du Snuden for?" ("Why do you stick your snout out?") When I asked why he had not complained to his parents, the Field-Marshal replied: "The post went but very seldom then, so we did not come home for years running, and also we imagined that it was as it should be." At last the boy fell ill with typhus, and was taken to the military hospital, which appeared to him like a paradise.

2. The Field-Marshal was very averse to tales about

forebodings and the fulfilment of dreams. Several times he has told me that he dreamt one night in the begining of the sixties that he was ascending a ladder, but that he fell down every time he tried to reach the sixty-sixth step. He never spoke about this dream till after the year 1866 ; and then he remarked, in telling it, that if he had died in the year named, and the dream had been known, everybody would have taken it as a prophecy.

3. Between Meudon and Sèvres lies a little place, Bellevue. On my rides in the neighbourhood of Versailles I had discovered a villa which was forsaken by its inhabitants. From the room in its gable-end there was a beautiful view over the batteries of the siege and over Paris itself. I took the Field-Marshal to the villa where the artist, Count Harrach, found us as we were watching the bombardment; later on he painted the well-known picture, " Count Moltke before Paris," as he saw us then. On this picture a splinter of a shell is to be seen, and the following event is connected with it. One day we had gone by carriage to this villa with Major von Brandenstein of the General Staff, we had watched the bombardment for some time, and had then gone out into the avenue, which leads from Meudon to Sèvres and which was commanded by a battery of Mount Valérien. Suddenly we heard a hissing sound over us, and a few moments later one of those gigantic artillery pieces from the fort exploded at about fifteen paces away from us, covering us with earth and dust. Some splinters of a shell were lying on the ground and Moltke felt one of them which was still hot. I took it with me and it is still kept at Creisau.

On another occasion we drove to St. Cloud and were shown over the castle. It was just as Napoleon had left it. On his writing table lay copies of Schneider's Soldier's Friend with representations of Prussian soldiers. In the Empress' boudoir there was a magnificent mirror which receded when a button was pressed, and

showed a beautiful view of Paris. Everything was
intact, only the eagle which ornamented Napoleon's bed
had been shot away by a cannon ball. Soon after our
visit there, the castle was set on fire by French bullets.

4. In the seventies the Field-Marshal in the Emperor's suite had been present at many reviews and
manœuvres in South Germany. He became so fatigued
before the reviews were quite concluded that he asked
the Emperor to allow him to return to Berlin. After
his request had been granted, he said to me in the afternoon: "Now let us go somewhere, where we can have
perfect rest. Take tickets for us and the servant for
X." We had sent our luggage home, the servant
carried nothing but a little portmanteau.

When we arrived at the station, the station-master
came out saying: "I have added a saloon carriage
for your Excellency." We entered it and left with the
pleasant feeling of having obtained quiet at last. But
no sooner had the train stopped at X., than the
Mayor in tail-coat, white tie and white gloves, entered
the carriage with these words: "Your Excellency, all
is prepared for your reception, rooms have been ordered,
and a carriage is waiting at the station as well as a
cart for the luggage."

The Field-Marshal entered the carriage with the
Mayor and myself, not in a very good humour, the
servant with the small portmanteau went in the cart.
The town was decorated with flags, and some of the
inhabitants were still engaged in putting up wreaths on
the houses; school children were running after our
carriage, and all X. was agog. The Mayor told the
Field-Marshal that it was the anniversary of the
veterans and also the vintage festival, and the people
would be very cross with him, if he did not persuade
his Excellency to honour the feast with his presence.
Rather hesitatingly Moltke accepted, and soon after
the carriage stopped before the hotel. The landlord
welcomed his guests respectfully and showed them a

suite of rooms that had been arranged for them. The Mayor was rather pressing about the feast, till the Field-Marshal answered somewhat sharply: "Will you allow me at least, to wash a little first?" But soon after we were sitting in an open carriage again, followed by enthusiastic young people. It began to rain gently, but in the course of an hour we had reached the vineyard which was crowded with people. We left the carriage, and the policeman made room for us to go slowly and single file through the crowd; now and then we stumbled over a little *dachshund* who had lost his master and hoped to find him in the path that had been cleared for us. At last, when we had reached the summit, we sat down by a simple citizen seated with his family on a crowded wooden bench, who offered us a glass of must.

Meanwhile it had begun to rain hard ; an old woman offered the Field-Marshal her umbrella, which, however, he declined, being in uniform. A thundering " hurrah ! " was his reward. Then we were taken to see some fire-works, which, however, did not go off well on account of the rain, and which altogether were not very effective as it was not dark enough. After this we went on till we reached the carriage, which took us back to our hotel. I ordered supper, and after we had taken it, Moltke leant comfortably back in his arm-chair, saying : " Now let us have a game of patience and then go to bed." No sooner had I spread out the cards on the table than a knock at the door was heard ; and on our calling " come in " the Mayor entered in the same official dress. " The singing club of the town wishes to serenade Your Excellency and the fire-brigade to give a torch-light procession. There is a balcony near this room and it would be a great favour if you would show yourself there to the assembled crowd." Suspicious clouds were gathering on the old gentleman's forehead, they were noticed by his companion, but not so by the harmless official. I hurried down and quickly ordered the Field-Marshal's favourite songs, and after this festivity was ended we succeeded in finding quiet and rest in our beds.

But no sooner had daylight broken than another knock at my door, and again the Mayor appeared in his tail-coat, etc., to announce to us that: "The town-band had assembled outside the house to serenade the Field-Marshal." I tried to impress upon him, that "the old gentleman needed rest, that one could not wake him up so early"—it was of no avail, I had to act. Reluctantly I entered the bedroom, and rather nervously I called him. When he heard what was the matter, he broke out: "Have I come here to rest, and am I not let alone for a moment?" I appeased him as well as I could, reminded him of the fact that all was done with the best intentions, and that it would make a bad impression if he did not show himself pleased.

"Very well," he said, "but after this we will leave by the very next train and go straight to Berlin." And so it was. The old gentleman was in a very bad humour at the time, but whenever I reminded him in later years of the incident, he laughed till tears ran down his cheeks adding: "Yes, and up to my room the passage was lined with people, I could not leave it in the morning after I had taken my coffee, without being greeted with thundering hurrahs."

5. At one time when the Field-Marshal was at Ragatz, taking waters there, he went through the wood to the village of Pfäfers. It was very hot, and as he was thirsty he went for some refreshment to an inn. The landlord said to him :—

"I suppose you are taking the waters at Ragatz?"

"Yes."

"Molkte is said to be there?"

"Yes."

"What does he look like?"

"Well, what should he look like? Just like one of us two."

6. Once he went from Ragatz to Lindau, as he thought, incognito; he ordered a room on the ground floor in the "Bayerische Hof." As he was tired he went to bed early but forgot to draw his blinds down. When he was just going to sleep, he heard music drawing near, and soon it was beneath his windows, which were lit up by the shine of the torches of the fire brigade. It was clear that he had been recognized after all, and that he was going to be serenaded again. The difficulty for him now was how to get dressed without being seen. He dared not strike a light. But, as he himself afterwards related, the glare of the torches lit up his room, and the curious crowd stood close to the windows, their noses pressed against the panes. In spite of all that, he felt that he must rise, and at each piece of dress that he put on loud and endless hurrahs were heard.

MEMOIRS OF THE FIELD-MARSHAL.

II.

FROM THE CIRCLE OF HIS EARLY FRIENDS.

*Lieutenant - General von Hegermann - Lindencrone's
Reminiscences of Count Moltke, written in a letter to
Major Helmuth von Moltke, nephew and for years
Aide-de-camp of the Field-Marshal.*

Copenhagen, Oct. 1st, 1891.

AS a sequel to my letter to you of Sept. 7th, 1891,
I begin here to write down my recollections of the
years which I spent with the Field-Marshal Count
Helmuth Moltke, principally of our early years, but
also of our meetings in later times. These communications may give an insight into his noble character and
the straightforward way in which it developed according to his view of right. I first became acquainted with
young Helmuth von Moltke and his brother Fritz at the
house of my parents, where both of them visited regularly during their holidays, and to which they had been
introduced by my brother Fritz, who was a cadet with
them at the Academy. When I joined them at the
Academy in 1816, I came into still closer contact with
the two brothers. In appearance they were rather unlike each other. Fritz von Moltke had a more serious
expression and sharp features, yet occasionally he too
was lively and cheerful. Helmuth von Moltke was
fairer and taller, he had a slim figure, finely-cut features
and an aristocratic bearing. His beautiful blue eyes,
speaking eyes they were that awakened confidence at
once, never lost this lovable expression even in his old
age. My father and mother as well as all the other
members of our family grew very fond of the brothers

and between them and my brother Fritz an intimate
friendship sprang up which lasted till death. I who
was six years younger than Helmuth, looked up to the
older comrade with a natural respect but also with an
ever-increasing devotion. He returned my affection
with brotherly love which bound me to him as much as
his chivalrous manner attracted me. We often met
other cadets at Rolighed, an estate near the sea about
a quarter of a mile from Copenhagen, and at the Castle
where my father was in command of the Riflemen
quartered there. It was natural that our games and
occupations generally had a military character, as we
were all intended for this position in life.

Beside the usual games, such as all kinds of ball games,
athletics, etc., we imitated with much zeal the games of
the old Romans, such as the throwing of the disk. We
often used the round bottom of a barrel which, as it had
sharp sides, frequently made painful cuts when it happened
to run against the stick with which the adversary tried
to turn the barrel bottom from its course. As we were
allowed the use of some boats which lay in the harbour
near a chalk factory in which my father was a partner,
we often rowed about on the Oresund and made ex-
cursions to the Isle of Saltholm, which belonged to the
chalk factory and where the chalk pits were. There we
also practised our horsemanship on some old horses
which were bought every year to take the chalk to the
ships, which again conveyed it to the works. Helmuth
found much pleasure in these amusements, and always
was a skilful and bold rider over the dangerous ground
cut up by many ditches. He used to ride on a pecu-
liarly shaped saddle which was said to have been kept on
the island since the time when Carl Gustav had besieged
Copenhagen. The pommel was in the shape of a large
metal lion's head and the cantel was enclosed by a large
metal basket. Helmuth took great interest in this historical saddle. An accident at a game with the not very
beautiful name of " Pulsog " once threatened to disturb

our sport in a sad way. The purpose of the game was that one party of the players had to push a ball with the aid of sticks into a hole in the ground, while the opposite party tried to prevent this, at the same time knocking their adversaries' sticks in another direction. Once when Helmuth was trying to put his ball into the hole and my brother Fritz was trying to prevent it, the fight grew very violent, all the more so as both of them were very quick and nimble. The players were using some heavy sticks that day, which at one time had been used to defend solitary houses exposed to violence from wandering vagabonds. Just at the moment Helmuth was going to hit his ball into the hole, and stooped down to make better use of his stick, my brother Fritz, who was trying to knock Helmuth's stick aside, hit Helmuth's head with such a powerful blow that the latter fell down unconscious.

Our endeavours to bring him to himself were without success, we therefore carried him up to my room and sent out some one on both the roads that lead from the citadel to Rolighed to stop our doctor who was expected to come home for his dinner about that time. When he arrived, about three quarters of an hour after Helmuth had received the blow, he found him to be in a very dangerous condition, for Helmuth had given no sign of life and looked like a dead person. At last after some treatment he began to breathe, and after an hour's time he was able to speak again. It can easily be imagined what an anxious time this was for all of us and especially for my brother Fritz who had very nearly killed his own friend. The unfortunate blow, however, had no bad consequences.

The brothers, especially Helmuth and my brother Fritz, occupied themselves with various things; they wrote articles on history, especially war history; which were published in "The Current of Time" ("Tidens Ström"); they also worked at a game of mimic warfare, in which their interest was continually increasing till it filled up many of the hours which could not be spent out of doors. I well remember, I think it was during the Christmas season in 1815, that they constructed a place which represented a kind of rock, on the top of which they erected a temple-like building, it was surrounded by a battlemented wall in the shape of a bulwark. A path led up to the fortress, and up it the assailant had to go to take the castle, which was defended by the others. Both parties were equipped like real soldiers. Whether the assailant should go on or be compelled to retreat was decided by throwing dice; the game was called "The road to the Temple of Honour." Even in those days Helmuth had the talent of sketching with a firm hand characteristic pictures of such objects as interested him. How he developed this talent later on is seen by the many illustrations in ink or pencil of the descriptions which his letters contain. With a vivid desire of increasing his knowledge and a clear power of conception of everything he came in contact with during his life-time, he preserved a high degree of modesty which often caused him to be silent on occasions when he would otherwise have asked questions or given his opinion. But whenever he did give his opinion it did not fail to awaken the interest of the listeners. At our home a number of eminent men used to visit, amongst others Bishop Münster, the great thinker M. S. Orsted, a brother of the naturalist, Professor Sibbern, Professor Ohlenschläger, and amongst our comrades was the cadet A. V. Scheel, who became later the well-known jurist, minister of justice and auditor-general. With the greatest interest and attention Helmuth Moltke used to follow the conversation of these distinguished men; he was always anxious to get information from their writings, if they were at all accessible to us. In this way he took a great fancy to the poetry of Ohlenschläger and also to his legends and tragedies like "Ewald" "Rolf Krake," etc.

One day after Moltke had received his commission, and was quartered with the Oldenburg Infantry Regiment at Holstein, he came to Copenhagen and asked my father's advice upon a proposal in a letter that he had received from an old relation in Prussia, who, I think, occupied a high position. He wrote as follows :— " I have been told that you have good capabilities and that you are in earnest with anything you undertake. If this is so, and you will follow my suggestion, I should advise you to enter a larger army, instead of the small Danish one. I think you would find greater satisfaction and have better prospects for the future if you were inclined to make this change."

My father discussed the matter thoroughly with Moltke and advised him decidedly to follow this suggestion, provided that he himself felt inclined for it. It is well known how Moltke entered the Prussian service, how he worked with never-failing zeal till he reached the highest positions in the military career, profiting by all the various posts in which he was placed and improving himself unceasingly. I cannot say for certain if it was principally my father's advice, or the unanimous decision of Moltke's family that led to the change in his path of life.

The following incident is a proof of the deep interest Moltke took in the works of our poets, and how he preserved it up to his latest years. In the year 1844 some gentlemen of the General Staff and I visited him and his charming wife in Berlin, where he then lived near the Brandenburger Gate and the Zoological Garden. He said that he thought the Danish language very pretty, if it were cleverly used by those who understood and liked it ; he asked me to recite some of the lines that we had learnt by heart together, if I remembered any, he would previously explain the meaning to those who did not understand Danish. When I requested him to mention something that he could remember, he chose the poem " Hakon Jarl."

" Es brüten die Nächte so schwarz und bang
Das Siebengestirn blinkt so matt, etc." [1]

and also a funeral dirge over the death of the botanist
Vahl:

" Decken grüne Pflanzen auch dein Grab." [2]

It was very pleasant to notice how that which was
characteristic and beautiful in the poems he had learnt
in his young days still appealed to him.

His interest in æsthetics developed more and more
with his wide experience. In the year 1846 his brother
Adolf and he came to stay with us at Jägersborg.
One evening we went to the theatre where we saw
" Staatsmann und Bürger," and " Quäker und Tän-
zerin." The parts were excellently played by the
actors whom the theatre was fortunate enough at
that time to possess. His delight with these plays was
great, and he broke out into the words : " Except the
' théâtre français' there is no stage in Europe which
could produce such acting. The representation is so
natural and artistic that one has no time to think how
the individual actors play ; one believes one is living
through something, forgetting that one is only looking
on."

During this visit of his we took a drive to the *Thier-
garten* where we had once encamped as cadets near the
old shooting box "l'Érémitage ;" we could still trace
the lines which had marked out the camp.

The old associations, the magnificent forests of oak
and beech and a romantic bubbling brook which flows
into the Oresund as well as the great number of deer,
all this was a real treat to Moltke : he took as great delight in nature as in art. This visit of his was a very
great pleasure to my wife and myself.

Though Moltke had been away from Denmark for

[1] "The night is brooding so black and bleak
The seven stars are shining so pale," etc.
[2] "Though green plants deck thy grave."

years, we had kept up our relations with him through
Fritz Moltke, who remained in this country till he
went, in his old age, to live with General Helmuth
Moltke, after both of them had lost their wives. Helmuth Moltke often wrote to his brother Fritz, who kindly
gave us now and then one of his letters to read, and he
also allowed my brother Fritz to keep some of them.
On my visit to him in Berlin, in 1844, Moltke said to his
friends, " Now you can hear from Hegermann if the
description I have given you of our life at Copenhagen
when we were cadets was right." He then repeated
his words before me. " The cadets received a truly
Spartan education, being treated strictly, much too
strictly. The tone in which we were spoken to was
very harsh, there was no trace of love or sympathy
in it ; in moral training the institution was not a
success, a mistrust was often shown which was
extremely hurtful in its effects, though the motives
which produced it may have been praiseworthy.
Those pupils who came out of this Academy unharmed,
went through a severe but hardening training ; but it
must be admitted that this Spartan education has produced able and in every sense soldierly men.

" The feeling of comradeship and the inviolable fidelity
which was observed from first to last by every cadet,
was a very attractive feature in our life there. No
severity of any kind could induce anybody to break
this fidelity."

The next time I met Moltke was in Paris, in 1856, on
his way home from England after the betrothal of the
Crown Prince of Prussia to the Princess Royal of
England. As soon as he learnt that we were there, he
looked us up, and asked me if I would like to join the
suite of the Prince to see some military practices, in
which case he would give notice to that effect. I was
sorry to have to decline as I had not reported myself
officially in Paris, neither had I my uniform there.
Hereupon he offered to let me know each time

when a practice which might interest me took place, that I might see it as a civilian.

I met Moltke once more, and this was the last time, in November, 1863, as I passed through Berlin on a mission to St. Petersburg. I found him unchanged and as amiable as ever, but it seemed to me that something was oppressing him. During a conversation with him and his charming wife he asked me for my photograph, he had seen one at General Schlichting's after the return of the General Staff from Denmark, where I had presented the troops selected for the Xth allied Army Corps. I gave him the photograph, asking at the same time for one of himself, and he said, showing me some to choose from : "Do you really wish to have mine?" When I left, he accompanied me downstairs, into the entrance hall, where he asked me, if our Sovereigns were to quarrel, would our old friendship come to an end. I answered that our mutual relations would under any circumstances remain unchanged, even though we should appear to the outside world to be separated in such a case as the one he mentioned. He asked me if I should be at home in the evening, as he would like to see me and have a talk with me.

I was able to be at home by ten o'clock, and was looking forward much to seeing him, all the more as perhaps a long time would pass before we could meet again. But Moltke did not come, probably he thought that I was staying, as I usually did, at Hotel Meinhardt which was not the case, and he could not very well go about asking where I lived. When I returned from St. Petersburg, Moltke was not in Berlin.

After I was attached à la suite and was living at Björnemke on Funen I heard repeatedly that Moltke spoke of my family in the friendliest terms. I only mention these facts as a proof of how faithfully Moltke remembered his friends, and for how long a time. We had had so much happiness through Moltke's friendship in our old home, that that alone would have been reason enough to keep up a sincere devotion to him and his brother.

What I have told now belongs to my dearest memories; they are connected with him who is gone home, and with his friendships with me and my family. It has been a drawback that my failing sight has obliged me to dictate these communications. I must not forget to add that after the conclusion of the war I repeatedly had the pleasure of receiving letters from the Field-Marshal, one of them on the war of 1864 is eight pages long. This letter was a reflection of the whole personality of Count Moltke who was so dear to me, I could recognize him as I had known him in our early years, and I could trace his character through all the difficult circumstances which had occurred in his and my life.

Honour to his memory—as to a dear friend, but also for a time, a formidable enemy.[1]

Reminiscences of Count Moltke's stay at Briese by Frau Lony von Schimpff, née Countess Kospoth.

I AM now in my eighty-first year and my last days are passing away quietly. I live much in the remembrance of olden times, without losing my interest in the present. I can hardly express the pleasure I have had in seeing Moltke's letters to his mother published; they also include an episode of my early years. If I look back to the year 1828 and to the home of my childhood, I often wonder at the great changes that have taken place. Everything was simpler

---

[1] General Hegermann-Lindencrone commanded the Danish Cavalry Division during the war of 1864, and from the middle of February the assembled forces in Jutland.

then, the Napoleonic wars were not quite forgotten, nor had they lost their effect. They had been purifying; life in general was influenced by an ideal way of thinking, not by the modern realism. My parents lived carefully, in spite of considerable landed property, but they knew how to make life comfortable with a little.

I was then seventeen years old, and was just being prepared for my confirmation. I had a cousin, Bianca von Forçade, staying with me who was an intimate friend of mine—ours was a genuine girl's friendship. We were not at all pleased at first when Lieutenant von Moltke took up his quarters at Briese as topographer. He was received most cordially by my father and mother, but perhaps we girls were rather stiff at the beginning; however, we soon became great friends. Of course everything in the house centred in my father and mother. My father, Count August Kospoth, was the personification of kindness and cheerfulness, he had artistic tastes, he painted much in a kind of miniature style, occasionally wrote poetry, and was fond of music; my mother, Julia *née* von Poser, a daughter of Major von Poser of Peuke, formerly *aide-de-camp* of Frederick the Great, and of his wife Henriette *née* von Loeben—was a highly gifted, noble, and beautiful woman. Besides us two girls, our family circle at Briese included my brother, who was nine years older than myself and very musical. The scene of our quiet life was Schloss Briese; the approach to the courtyard led through beautiful limes, nine rows deep; behind the house was a beautiful, well-kept garden with a large orange-house. Everything was what we should call now-a-days in good style, a pattern of rococo taste. The garden was laid out in the *Lenôtre* style, and we had many merry hours and pleasant walks in it, and here our guest used to display his physical skill in jumping lightly over the hedges. We read and painted a great deal, wrote poetry, had music, sketched costumes and designs, made up little scenes of plays, in which the figures of the

Greek mythology took a large part, then the fashion. We interested ourselves greatly in Moltke's topographical work, and we gave him a pair of fingerless gloves to protect his hands, which he always kept in a faultless condition, from the sun. Sometimes we went in a big carriage drawn by four Polish horses and driven by a clever Polish coachman, who was not always quite sober—to visit friends or relations in the neighbourhood; there were the Reichenbachs at Zessel, the Schwerins at Borau, the Posers at Domsel, the Randows at Krakowahne and others.

So the weeks passed by quickly, and with great regret we said good-bye to our delightful guest, little thinking what a great future was in store for him many years after. He had told us how lonely his life often was, how, at Christmas, he had walked through the streets of Berlin to see the lit-up Christmas trees through the windows. For Christmas Eve of 1828 we sent him a little dressed-up tree, grown on Silesian soil, and little presents which referred to the time we had spent together, and he mentions them in a letter to his mother.

More than half a century had passed when I sent my congratulations to the friend of my early years, on his 90th birthday, whereupon he wrote me the following answer :—

Berlin, Oct. 31st, 1890.

DEAR FRAU VON SCHIMPFF,—You have given me much pleasure by your kind lines. I am very grateful to you for having remembered me so kindly through half a century; I, for my part, still remember most vividly the kindness I received in the beautiful castle of Briese.

Your son, who for some time was on the General Staff here, has left the remembrance of an excellent officer. You must be proud of him.

Hoping that you, too, are enjoying health and content-

ment in your advanced years, I remain, in highest
esteem and with many thanks,
                        Yours sincerely,
                              COUNT MOLTKE,
                                    Field Marshal.

The handwriting of the man of ninety was firmer
and more beautiful than that of the manuscript poems
of the young man. The drawings of his which I have
are most carefully executed, his writings are done more
carelessly. I have been told that Count Moltke
practised writing still, when he was quite a man, to
improve his hand. In everything he did, he strove
after perfection. And that is why he attained so
much.

*The retired Major von Kameke at Halle put the follow-
ing records, after the death of the Field-Marshal, at
the disposal of his family. He too had recalled
himself to the Field-Marshal's memory, by writing
him a letter of congratulation on his ninetieth
birthday. He received the answer which is published
below.*

THE first time that I came into contact with
Moltke was in 1830, and afterwards in 1832, my
first and his last year of appointment at the topographical office. There we drew nearer together
in confidential intercourse. Moltke had hardly any
other friends amongst his comrades, he lived much
alone. and really was not very accessible. He was
thought proud, otherwise he was taken little notice of
(he was then second lieutenant). We two met almost
daily, and played a game of chess regularly, he played
very well and won almost always. When I went to his

rooms in an afternoon, I used to find him standing at his writing desk, where he translated Gibbon's History of Rome, from English into German, for a publishing firm. He made a little extra money by it, as his allowance was very small, being almost without any fortune. This reason made him at first decline the offer of General von Krauseneck, Chief of the General Staff, to be on the General Staff. He was not able to buy the horses which would have been necessary for the coming manœuvres. But Krauseneck's discerning glance detected Moltke's eminent intellectual capabilities, and he assisted him with advances from the coffers of the General Staff. He also gave him the appointment to Turkey. From Constantinople, Moltke wrote to me about his life there, he had a sloop and six saddle-horses at his disposal. After the battle of Nisib, which had been undertaken contrary to his express advice, he returned home, being most kindly released by the Sultan. When we met again in 1842 we took daily rides together. After that, our ways in life parted.

Berlin, November 2nd, 1890.

DEAR KAMEKE,—Amongst many congratulations on my birthday, your letter has given me special pleasure.

I had quite lost sight of you since we lived so closely together before the Potsdamer Thor in the forties.

I went to Rome and since then had never heard of you again. I think, of our contemporaries, only Randow at Potsdam is still alive. Now I find you at last in your hiding place at Harzburg, that pretty little mountain town, and I thank you with all my heart for having remembered me so kindly after all these years. I often think of our youthful companionship, our games of chess, and many other things. You must be over eighty now, but I hope that you are in good health, in spite of your years, and that you live contentedly. I share in my old age the deafness which ended your military career so prematurely. Thanking you again, I remain, with my best wishes in old friendship,

Your faithful
Count Moltke.

The contemporary of the Field-Marshal, mentioned above, Lieutenant-General von Randow, was born on January 6th, 1801, and died on January 13th, 1891. He was from 1856 to 1881 Director of the great Military Orphanage at Potsdam. He, like Major von Kameke, was the Field-Marshal's friend through life. These letters breathing true friendship are so similar to the one above that they are best given in this place.

Creisau, Oct. 8th, 1881.

DEAR OLD FRIEND RANDOW,

I see from your letter written on the 1st inst. that you have concluded your career of active service, with an honourable recognition of your many years of successful work. I should be thankful to do the same, and to spend my last days here in retirement on my own ground. Though the giving up of one's regular occupation must at first necessarily leave a blank, new interests are soon found, and with your many-sided, cultivated mind such will certainly not be wanting.

When we both worked at the topographical office—I think both equally poor, both on the lowest steps of the military hierarchy, studying tactics and in company partaking of our not very sumptuous dinners—surely neither of us thought then that we should climb up to the highest steps of the ladder. Very few comrades are left from those times of manifold hardships, and old age is felt more keenly at seeing all round one's old acquaintances and old friends pass away. But we cling all the firmer to those who remain and who keep up the true friendship of earlier years. And so I wish with all my heart that the conviction of duty faithfully done may console you for many a sad loss, and that you may enjoy a long and happy old age.

With kindest regards,

Your Excellency's most devoted

Count Moltke,

Field-Marshal.

Berlin, January 6th, 1891.

Much honoured Friend ! Dear old Comrade,— This day gives me occasion to offer your Excellency my heartfelt and well-meant congratulations on your ninety-first birthday.

I know that you have had severe bereavements in your family, lately. At our age it is natural, but sad, to see those dear and near to us pass away from us. There remains only the hope of being reunited with them all the sooner. Life becomes poorer every day, but it makes one cling all the firmer to what is left.

May the New Year at least bring rest and contentment in looking back upon a long life spent in activity and the fulfilment of duty.

Even though I should not receive any reply to these lines I know that you will remember in old friendship

Your heartily devoted

Count Moltke,

Field-Marshal.

Lieutenant-General H. A. von Gliszinski, late Director in the War Office (died 1886), recalls the Field-Marshal in his autobiography left in manuscript, from which his son, Major-General von Chammier-Gliszinski, kindly contributes the following paragraph, as well as a letter of the Field-Marshal to his father.

AS the students at the War School spent daily several hours together, we all had common interests, were also almost all of the same age, and had the same standing in the army and pretty well the same social standing and scientific education ; it was therefore natural that we should keep together like intimate acquaintances, somewhat as the students of the universities. Not one was a stranger to me, although I only formed real friendships with a few.

From this small number stand out the names of Moltke and Roon. The latter had already been a friend of mine at the Academy of Cadets; Moltke's acquaintance I did not make till we met at the War School, in October, 1823. He had only a short time previously joined our army, having been in the Danish service. He was then a young lieutenant in the 8th Infantry Regiment. His appearance was much the same as in later years, and he himself remained almost the same. I have never again met a man who throughout life changed so little as Moltke. As we were in the same *coetus*, I met him daily for three whole years. We worked out many a difficult mathematical problem together, and he often advised me well. To me he did not appear superior, nor did he distinguish himself more than his comrades. But, afterwards, all the greater grew the difference. While he continued his study with diligence and earnestness, I did nothing in that way for years, but, on the contrary, forgot much of what I had learnt before.

After that time we met now and then officially till, twenty-three years later, in July, 1849, I was ordered to Magdeburg as Major and officer of the General Staff of the IVth Army Corps; and, as he was Chief of the General Staff there, I was under his immediate command. It was a troublous time during the Badische Campaign, and we were on very difficult ground, for Magdeburg was in a very disturbed state and the 24-pounders of the armed citadel were directed towards the town. Under such circumstances our old friendship was quickly and most warmly renewed, we agreed well in our official position as well as in social life, and we both were conscious of it.

And this friendship was still further cemented by our respective wives. Moltke had, shortly before, married his charming, amiable, and very kind-hearted wife, who was very young then; she soon became much attached to us, and often asked and accepted good advice from my wife. The ladies, too, were glad to find their views coinciding in this important political crisis, and so, during the nine months which we spent at Magdeburg, we founded a firm friendship which not only lasted till the death of Moltke's wife, but has since even become closer and more intimate. In 1855, when Moltke was appointed first Aide-de-camp of Prince Frederick William, he had to go to Berlin. He was then a colonel, and was comparatively master of his time. Whenever my wife or myself went to Berlin, we always received a hearty welcome at the Moltkes'. My wife used to stay at their house, which I generally declined to do. Very often I have accepted friendly services from him, and have never failed to render him such whenever I found an opportunity.

After I retired from the service, and left off giving parties or going to them, we met the Moltkes only in simple friendly intercourse, which was sadly ended by the death of his wife, about Christmas time, 1868; I, however, frequently went to play at whist with Moltke.

Now and then, but seldom, he would come, with his
brother, to my house to play a rubber, or we met at
Scheller's; but he preferred our playing at his house
from half-past six to half-past eight, when the evening
was ended with tea, and bread and butter, so that I
was usually at home by ten o'clock.

In July, 1870, on the outbreak of the war, I took
leave of Moltke, fearing that we should never meet again.
It was on this day, as he was leaving the Royal Palace
for his carriage, that he heard the following remark,
showing confidence in him, from a street arab, " *Nanu,
Moltke, mach man wieder en juten Plan*," [1]—a remark
which gives proof of his great popularity.

By God's grace, my faithful, old, and tried friend has
found an opportunity of using his excellent gifts during
his career, and of gaining a great reputation, which
has given him a name never to be forgotten in the
Prussian Army.

We publish here a letter written when Gliszinski was Chief of the
General Staff of the Garde du Corps, and Moltke occupied the same
position on the General Staff of the IVth Army Corps.

Magdeburg, February 13th, 1851.

DEAR GLISZINSKI,—I have read some passages from
your amusing and capital letter to His Excellency and
our officers, they were very delighted with it.

It seems quite clear to me that our politics were not
taking the right direction, for every step brought us
into deeper swamps. I think we ought to turn back,
but that cannot be done without loss and mortification.
But even the uninitiated can see that we do not occupy
the place due to us. I cannot get rid of the idea that
the mobilization on the 2nd of November was intended
as a demonstration, but on the 6th it was ordered from
a sudden fear that matters were becoming serious,

[1] " Now then, Moltke, make a good plan again."

which does not seem to have been realized at all before. Then 20,000 Austrians and 15,000 Bavarians might have rendered the mobilization of the IVth and IIIrd Army Corps and of the Garde-du-Corps quite impossible. For the last thirty-five years the organization of our army has only allowed us to have the ordinary number of men under arms; but in the possibility of a conflict, we must not defer the mobilization. However, we were allowed the valuable space of four weeks, and after we had collected 400,000 men, we evacuated Baden and Hesse, gave up Holstein, and accepted all the conditions that were made!

The day before yesterday, Royal and Imperial Austrian soldiers were quartered at Magdeburg, this time only twenty men, next time there will be 200, etc. On the eve of an outbreak of war, high authorities like the Commander-in-Chief and his staff ought to receive some political information. We did not know officially if we were making preparations for a war with Russia, France, Austria or Denmark. We were concentrated quite calmly near Merseburg, expecting to make our winter quarters at Leipzic, when we were very much surprised to hear from the Commander-in-Chief that we were to assemble as quickly as possible between the Mulde and Elbe, to be able, if necessary, to join the 2nd and 3rd Army Corps, and the Garde-du-Corps. We heard later on that a position on the defensive was to be taken behind the Nüthe. No sooner had we marched off, when a new order was received. The combination of the Militia Cavalry Regiments was not yet completed when the Militia Cavalry was disbanded.

The fourth battalions were not yet formed (with the youngest men) when an order was given that they should be formed with the oldest men, and now I should not be astonished if this new system were abandoned altogether. The highest authorities were continually wavering, which entailed numberless changes for us. I even fear that the conquest of Neuenburg—Vallendis will not set us up again. It was hard on Roon to be sent to another place while the Army Corps was still mobilized. If the orders of the War Minister were not all carried out without delay, the fault lay not in the persons to whom they were given, but in the orders themselves. The blow was to have been dealt to the commander, but it struck the Chief of the General Staff. I think it is almost decided now that promotion from the line to commanderships is a mistake, and I do not doubt that your appointment will be ratified.

The last few months have been a real test of the capabilities of the authorities. Almost everywhere the mobilization took place under difficult circumstances. We did not have one single man from the regulars of the whole Army-Corps, neither infantry nor cavalry, in our Corps; we had no Intendant, no Principal Medical Officer, no officer from the General Staff. The instructions for the mobilization were all vague, and numerous special orders had to be given. I hope we shall have learnt some lessons for our 40 millions! We have gained one experience, and that is that the way in which business is at present conducted is utterly useless during the mobilization; this refers especially to the audit system. We have had more than a thousand letters every month at the office of the Commander-in-Chief. As this office has to correspond, when the Army is on a war footing, with 5 divisions, 1 Pontoon Convoy, 1 Reserve Artillery, 1 Intendant, and different civil authorities, these 1000 entries required 15,000 replies. Six clerks were engaged from morning till night, Sundays and week-days. When the Office is for a month at Dessau and another month at Merseburg, it can be done. But if the clerks have to march, the officers to operate, the whole building tumbles down and the important as well as the unimportant entries must cease. But this is very bad at the *Intendantur*. Old Lehmann [1] has left during our two months'

---

[1] Intendantur-Rath of the IVth Army Corps from 1836-1851.

absence 1700 numbers unanswered. The militia battalions have booked half a million advance money, partly
dating from the autumn of 1848. The militia cavalry
is a new creation of the last mobilization, without aide-
de-camp, without accountant, without office, and without regulations. But what can one say of the newly
invented militia guards of the second levy!—but
enough of waste of ink and temper!

His Excellency who thinks a great deal of you,
wishes to be remembered as well as the gentlemen of
the Staff. It is an excellent officer's corps, what a pity
that part of them have been ordered home again!

My wife is much concerned about the Austrian occupation of Holstein. She finds it very hard to defend
our politics as she wears intense black and white colours.
She asks assistance from me! but I don't know how to
give it her.

My best compliments to Frau von Gliszinski. We
miss her very much here. Steinmetz has gone too now,
and Magdeburg is more miserable than ever. Please
to remember kindly

Your
MOLTKE.

*Prince Bismarck writes in answer to the Geheime
Justigrath and Professor Dr. Dahn on the 6th
of April, 1892.*

IT would be presumption on my part to make any
comment on my departed friend Count Moltke; I
can only say that in our personal relations under all
circumstances, even under the most difficult, he has
always been an affectionate friend to me. To say more
would either be an empty phrase, or it would be against
the " ne sutor ultra crepidam."

MEMOIRS OF THE FIELD-MARSHAL.

III.

HIS WORK DURING THE LAST DECADE OF HIS LIFE.

IN the year 1869 the general, with the officers of the Great General Staff, went to Saxony for their annual reconnaissance. During our stay at Dresden H.R.H. the Crown Prince Albert, now his Majesty the King of Saxony, took the greatest interest in our work, and the intimate relations then began between the Prince and the Chief of the General Staff and the officers which proved so beneficent in the wars of 1870-71. On this occasion the King gave a dinner in our honour in his palace. When it was over and we were going downstairs, the general suddenly stopped on the landing, saying in a reproachful tone to himself: "How thoughtless of me not to have put on a Saxon order to-day!" However, his aide-de-camp, Major de Claer, soon pacified him, remarking: "I should have taken the liberty of drawing your Excellency's attention to it, but you don't possess one." A contented smile passed over the general's face, but on the next landing he stopped again, saying with a certain bashfulness: "It is rather remarkable that I have yet no Saxon order."

When the Grand Cross of the Iron Cross was conferred on him, as he received the decoration he remarked: "It looks as if it were the cross for my grave." When anyone was to be invested with the highest distinctions, it always gave him the greatest delight to inform those concerned himself. The day before the grand entrance of the troops into Berlin when the decorations were conferred on the officers of the General Staff, he himself brought the Order of the House of Hohenzollern with swords to me at my own house. He also often wrote congratulations to officers who were promoted, informing them of the fact as soon as he had received the Royal Patents. When I and four other officers were promoted to the General Staff as captains, when we reported ourselves to him, he said the following words to us which have always remained in my memory: "Do not look upon this event as a reward but as a royal favour bestowed in advance upon services which it will be your duty to render and which his Majesty will expect from you."

A subject that interested him, often engrossed him so that he forgot people whom he might have been expected to remember. Soon after the war of 1866, travelling from Berlin to Potsdam, he met an officer who had been on his own staff, and asked him: "I forget where you were during the war!" Another time two brothers were at his house at an evening party, both were captains of the General Staff. The General came up to a group of gentlemen, one of whom was one of the brothers. After joining in the conversation, he asked the latter: "Just tell me who is that tall officer near the fire-place on the other side, I forget his name!"

"That's my brother, your Excellency," was the answer.

A smile stealing over the general's face suggested the idea that he had not obtained the information he wished. Some time after, the general went to another group of people and there joined the officer whose name he had inquired. Suddenly we saw him turning away, with the same winning, childlike smile on his face. Afterwards when we inquired from the young officer, what the general had asked him, he replied:

"He asked me who that officer was over there."

"And what did you say?"

"I said that he was my brother."

We had guessed this, but the general gave up inquiring any more the name of the two brothers who were at his evening party.

He had a surprisingly good memory for facts. Only a very short time before his death, he reminded me, when I was his neighbour at an imperial dinner, of some incidents of war which we had experienced together; they had entirely escaped my memory till he mentioned them.

His merriness was full of a childlike pathos, and showed itself in a peculiar way. On a military journey in the kingdom of Saxony we once had a banquet with the officers of the Saxon Cavalry who were manœuvring near the town which was our goal. We were all very lively and after dinner some amusing scenes took place. Amongst other things one of the gentlemen took a casque from the decorations of the hall, put it on his head and climbed up a pillar on which was a stuffed knight in full armour, from this place he made a very amusing speech, addressing the old knight. This scene became still more amusing when the visor of our comrade's helmet suddenly fell down, and out of the opening a rain of sparks from a cigar flew into the face of the knight. Moltke was highly amused; by the help of his long legs he had scrambled up on to a gallery that ran round the hall. He had just asked me to take a seat near him. But in spite of a run, I only succeeded in getting up just enough to lie helplessly across the barrier. This sight added to that of the pillar heightened the pleasure of the old gentleman to such a degree, that he showed it in a very peculiar way by incessantly clapping with his hand that part of my body which was just turned to him by my awkward position.

Another time at Ferrières, the General-Staff had decided to use the ample Liebesgaben[1] which had fallen

---

[1] Gifts of charity sent from their country.

to their share to give a dinner to which the Bundes-kanzler, the War Minister and other high officers were asked (with the request kindly to bring their own knives, forks, and spoons). One of our officers had just received a piece of poetry in honour of the day of Sedan by one of the most favourite poets. Filled with enthusiasm for this excellent and beautiful poem, the officer asked permission to recite it directly after the soup was served. But unluckily he made such a funny blunder of elocution in reading the verses, that all the listeners broke out into Homeric laughter, which only increased when a second attempt ended in the same manner. While we did not know what to do with our-selves with laughter, Moltke expressed his pleasure in throwing little pieces of bread which he had soaked in his wine, at the officer sitting opposite him.

He liked harmless jokes and often took part in them. For instance, he knew that I had a particular weakness for sweets, I especially liked macaroons such as we had at dessert at our dinners at Versailles. He therefore several times ordered quite secretly that these plates should be placed at the end of the table far away from me, or at another time they would all be collected before my place; it gave him great pleasure then to watch my astonished face.

His simplicity of diet in eating and drinking is well known; he would sometimes praise some very second-rate wine. At his house we once had some wine rather unlike French claret. When it was remarked upon, he said smilingly, that he had discovered too late that his Bordeaux had come to an end, but he had found some bottles of Aar-wine, and that he had hoped that the difference would not be noticed.

One of the first bulletins during the war of 1870 arrived under very ludicrous circumstances. It was at Mayence in the night of the 6th and 7th of August, when an aide-de-camp awoke one of the chiefs of the depart-ment, handing him a telegram from the Crown Prince which his Majesty had just received, but whose contents were not quite clear. (It was the second half of the telegram reporting about the battle of Wörth which had arrived before the first part.) The officer who was called, jumped up at once and sat down at the table upon which the maps lay, he wore nothing but his night-shirt and slippers. The talking awoke the second chief who slept in the next room, he entered in the same costume. Both seeing the importance of the news in spite of its mutilation, decided to inform the Quartermaster-General. Each of them had a candle in one hand, a map in the other, and so they proceeded to General von Podbielski who slept on the floor above them. Their continued conversation woke up the third chief as well as one of the aides-de-camp, and, if I am not mistaken, also the chief of the office, and this whole caravan now went to old Moltke, all in the same costume as described above, each of them carrying a light and maps. The sight of us as we entered the general's bedroom must have been very absurd, and while the general was awakening, he rose up in his bed without saying anything, only looking at us, probably wondering if he were awake or asleep. But for us also the long, thin figure of the gentleman who rose in his night-dress was rather ghostly, all the more as we saw him for the first time without his wig; the moonbeams seemed just at that moment concentrated on his classically shaped head. Under these circumstances and in these costumes we listened to the bulletin.

Another time the wig took a prominent part in an exciting event. It was at Meaux, during the night before the intended investment of Paris, when the chief of the division was called about 2 o'clock to the general, who had taken up his quarters in the Bishop's Palace, as important news had just arrived; after reading them himself, the general gave them to us to study. While we were engaged in looking at the maps on the table, the general, dressed in a long dressing gown, but again without the wig, walked meditatively up and down the spacious bed-room, in a recess of which stood his bed. The fire that had been quickly lit, was rather big, it threw out such heat that the perspiration ran down our faces. Suddenly one of us looked up to ask the general something, but when he beheld him, he stopped short, and drew our attention to what he had seen. The general, like ourselves, had wiped his forehead, but being completely lost in thought, as was his habit when engaged in serious considerations, he was not aware that he had picked up the wig instead of the handkerchief. This he continued to do until at last we plucked up courage to tell him. It was so ludicrous that we could hardly utter a word at first, but when at last he understood what he had done, he joined in our hearty laughter.

He was fond of quoting poets in moments of importance ; if he was disturbed in any recreation he often was heard to say, jokingly: " Meister muss sich immer plagen." [1]

He rightly deserved the appellation of the " great silent one," though in later years he had grown more communicative than he was in his younger days. One evening as we were playing at whist (we were then on reconnaissances in Silesia, I think it was in 1867) one of our comrades came in to read to us some lines from a comic paper. They referred to a remark made by General von Manteuffel about " seven feet of soil." Moltke listened seriously, then put the cards on the table, looked at us, raised his hands, and shaking his head said, from the bottom of his heart: ",I don't understand my friend Manteuffel !—why does the man speak ? "

On one of our reconnaissances we were most solemnly welcomed by the Mayor with a deputation before we entered the little town where we were to be quartered. When the Mayor's address became rather high

[1] Master must always be at work.—Schiller's " Song of the Bell."

flown, the general utterly confused the orator by the question: "Excuse me, but will you kindly tell me who you are?"

Another time during the war a Staff Officer of another Army Corps was dining with us. He was making some rather daring assertions about the way in which the war had been conducted when the general put this question to him: "Comrade, what are you in your civil employment?" (The gentleman addressed was neither an officer of the Reserve nor of the Militia, but was on the Active Service List.)

The general was a great lover of horses and fond of riding and driving. On his official journeys he liked to take the officers for drives with his own horses. On such occasions the wheels often came in collision with the stones instead of avoiding them. The more violent the jolt, the more pleased he was to say: "Do you see, I made a good hit," as if it were done intentionally.

He could be very amusing at a whist party; during the campaign he was by no means a good player. If, at any time, he thought he could win a trick by a so-called "fluke," he used to put down the cards and to fix his eye upon the next player, saying: "I must try to read in his face what sort of a hand he has." If he failed nevertheless he said with amusing seriousness: "I would have given my head, that he had not got that card. How he does deceive one."

One little incident at his expense amused him very much one day. When on reconnaissance in Silesia, after the war of 1866, we made a march on a Sunday. The general, availing himself of the opportunity to visit a friend who lived in the neighbourhood, entrusted the command to the eldest colonel. We marched in rank and file under a burning sun to a bare plateau in the hills. We could see from afar numbers of people on all sides streaming along the high road up to this place. At last when we arrived at the crowd, we found there must be about a

thousand people, amongst them all the schoolboys
of the neighbourhood with flowers, flags and
drums, under the guidance of their masters, one of
whom stepped up to the colonel (who, as he was leading us, was taken by everybody for Moltke), and made
a very patriotic address. The colonel listened attentively and then replied, without informing the people of
their error, what joy it must give everyone to hear their
patriotic sentiments expressed, and he hoped they would
always keep them in the future, and that it was especially
a teacher's duty to implant into the children's hearts a
love of their country. We then continued our ride,
followed by the "hurrahs" for Moltke, which were repeated as long as we were in sight. When our horses
were walking again, the colonel, perhaps having noticed
our surprise at his allowing people to think that General
Moltke had spoken to them, said : "How could I
disappoint the people whose enthusiasm had brought
them all the way to see Moltke by telling them, 'He
is not here at all.' Now every one thinks they have seen
him, and they will delight in it till their last day. My only
fear is that if a book hawker should ever come to their
villages with protraits of Moltke, he will not sell many
of them, for he would be told, 'Off with you, they are
not a bit good—he looks quite different, I have seen
him myself."

On the day after the battle of Gravelotte, on the 19th of
August, the General and Captain von Winterfeld drove
back with me in the afternoon from Rezonville to Pont
à Mousson. We crossed over that part of the battle-field
of Vionville where our extreme right wing had fought
on the 16th and where the victims of that day lay still
unburied. During our drive the general spoke but
three times. Once when he saw a Prussian non-commissioned officer lying on this field and grasping his
bayonet as if presenting arms amidst corpses of
French voltigeurs, he pointed at him saying: "He
was the bravest of the brave." And later, after he

had evidently pondered over the events of the day before : " Yesterday I learnt again that one can never be too strong on the battle-field," and at last when we saw the outlines of the buildings which stood on the hill towering over Pont à Mousson in the evening twilight, he said : " With what feelings we should have returned here to-day, if we had lost the battle."

During the end of the war the General Staff of the Head-quarters was worried by many external annoyances. We, thinking that we ought not to bear it, pressed the General to complain to his Majesty about it, and he gave us the memorable answer : " Gentlemen, in these troublous times his Majesty shall at least not hear from us any word of complaint ! "

I will give the following accounts of the Field-Marshal's work from the time between the last two great wars.

The Department of War History was then writing the campaign of 1866. As soon as a paragraph of the work was written, it was submitted to him, and he began to revise it most carefully. In many cases the paragraph was completely remodelled by his expressing the events in his classical style, omitting what seemed unimportant to him, cancelling any repetition, summing up the most essential points in short sentences, remarking : " An exact historical representation is the sharpest criticism."

Thus changed and revised, the work went back to the same department, where it was again looked through in order that each sentence might correspond exactly with the historical truth, and that important events should not slip into the background, or errors creep in through the compression of the material. If any cause was found for such criticism, the manuscript was returned again to the General, and this proceeding was continued till both parties were satisfied.

The General's private work, which he devoted principally, and as far as his time allowed, to historical events, always gave proof of the greatest care. Also the way in which it was revised, showed that he was not easily pleased with his own writing. He often tore up sheets of most laborious work which he had spent whole days in writing and that he re-wrote and re-modelled from beginning to end.

It was his habit, even with non-historical subjects, to make notes of what he had thoroughly thought over, and these notes he used as starting points for further developments. His critical reason was not satisfied till he had weighed all the possibilities and consequences of a given situation and saw them perfectly clearly. He used to think standing or walking about the room, his eyes fixed on the floor, that his attention might not be distracted by anything. If interrupted, he would look up with an expression which seemed to belong to another world. But this preoccupied meditation was so comprehensive and foreseeing that nothing took him by surprise in war time. Did any news necessitate a change of plans and other people seemed surprised, he would not need a moment for reflection, his eyes seemed to dilate, their wonderful expression became intensified, and at once he would explain precisely and briefly the course to be pursued now. Perhaps an exclamation of surprise would escape from his lips when the news showed that the adversary had made a wrong movement or had let an opportunity slip, which might have been to his advantage. But even the possible mistakes that the enemy might make, had generally been taken into consideration in the formation of his plans.

Y. VON VERDY.

General of the Infantry and Chief of the Infantry Regiment Count Schwerin (3rd Pommeranian) No. 14 (during the Franco-German war Lieutenant-Colonel and Chief of a division in the General Staff of the Head-quarters of his Majesty the King).

From the General Staff of the Head-quarters in the war of 1870 *to* 1871.

IN the campaign of 1870 to 1871 the Quartermaster-General, Lieutenant-General von Podbielski, was General von Moltke's coadjutor. There were on the Staff besides these two, three chiefs of the different divisions, three majors and six captains of the General Staff as well as two personal aides-de-camp.

The relations between the Quartermaster-General and the Chief of the General Staff were neither defined by general nor by special instructions for the coming war, but the matter was left to a practical development. By his rank the Quartermaster-General would expect to be initiated into the plans of the Chief of the General Staff, and to be, if necessary, his representative. He took the burden of minor cares from the Chief of the Staff, in conducting and superintending the business function of the Staff.

The right of independent arrangement, as regards the Commissariat and reconnaissances, was silently conceded him.

There were no special instructions concerning the division of work and the management of the service on the Staff. The three divisions of the Great General Staff remained just as they existed in time of peace, the chief posts were held by the same officers after the mobilization. The principal duty of the first Division (Lieutenant-Colonel Bronsart von Schellendorff) consisted in the arrangement of the forces, that of the second Division (Lieutenant-Colonel von Verdy du Vernois) in the Intelligence Department, the work of the third Division (Lieutenant-Colonel von Brandenstein) was the Commissariat and the Railways. Lieutenant-Colonel von Brandenstein was at the same time a military member of the Executive Railway Committee. The Staff officers and captains were dis-

tributed amongst the three Divisions. One of the
Staff Officers, however, overlooked the work of the
office, his special duty was to keep the register and
rolls and to give orders about the transport. The
personal and financial affairs of the General Staff were
worked as they were in time of peace by the principal
aides-de-camp.

When the General Staff of the Head-quarters arrived at
a fresh station, an office was at once established either
in a school-building or in any appropriate rooms, to
accomplish the necessary business without delay.
General von Moltke and his officers would be quartered
as near as possible to the office, which was the principal
meeting place for the officers on the General Staff;
during the day the greater number of them usually
assembled there. An officer, who was relieved every
twenty-four hours, was always on duty there, day and
night; which was very important in cases when the
head of the office was unavoidably absent. Letters,
telegrams, etc., were received by the head of the office,
who delivered them as they came in, or several at a
time according to their importance, to the Chief of the
General Staff and to the Quartermaster-General. They
were then handed over to the Chief of the respective
Divisions to be discussed or for consultation with his
Majesty. Telegrams which arrived during the night
were collected by the officer on duty and usually
delivered the next morning. In urgent or doubtful cases
he submitted them at once to the Chief of the respective
Divisions, who, if necessary, had the Quartermaster-
General and the other officers concerned called, and they
would refer the matter in such cases to General von
Moltke. Such occurrences were only frequent in times
of great suspense as to the progress of the war.

Metallographic maps of the seat of the war were kept
at the office; on these an officer used to mark the
positions of both armies every morning, so far as they
could be ascertained from the news that had been

received. Together with these General von Moltke particularly liked a Railway Map of Central Europe, which
with a pair of compasses and a magnifying glass were
always lying ready on his writing-table. Such simple
means of help with his knowledge were sufficient to keep
him completely cognizant with the whole position. The
whole time that the supreme direction of the Army was
in his hands, he made very little use of the large maps.

Every morning, sometimes several times during the
day, the Quartermaster-General and the Chiefs of the
Divisions met at General Moltke's to report. These
meetings were also attended by the Chief of the Office,
the first aide-de-camp, and also, as a rule, by the
Director-General (Lieutenant-General von Stosch) and
the Chief of the Telegraph Administration (Colonel
Meydam). On these occasions the position of the war
and the steps necessary to be taken were discussed ; but
these meetings had nothing of the character of a council
of war. General von Moltke stated his views and
intentions in the clear terse manner peculiar to him ;
and though he listened, and that always in a most
amiable manner, to any amendment, questions or even
doubts, the principal purpose of these meetings was
usually to assure himself that his plans were received
with a sympathetic comprehension by his comrades.

After such meetings General von Moltke, accompanied
by the Quartermaster-General, went to consult his
Majesty the King. If necessary, this happened even
at night. Though the General was perfectly conscious
of the responsibility he undertook in giving advice, he
felt most strongly that the decision and command rested
with the Sovereign alone. An account of the usual
proceedings at these consultations is given by the Field-
Marshal himself in the essay, " On the alleged Council
of War in the wars of King William I." [1]

After the consultation the orders which had usually
been prepared beforehand were filled in, ready to be

_____
[1] Compare " Moltke's Franco-German War," appendix.

despatched. Important orders of operation were frequently drawn up by the Chief of the General Staff himself, those sketched by others were submitted to him for a close inspection before making a fair copy.

These fair copies were done by officers of the General Staff, who were at all times pleased to do any work, even if it appeared inferior. Where the telegraph was available, it was constantly used for the transmission of orders, and was the natural means of communication between the Chief Command and the Army. The delivery of important letters at long distances was principally done by orderlies attached to Head-quarters.

They made their way, attended by two foot soldiers with loaded guns and requisition vehicles, often straight across the hostile territory. These riflemen deserve great praise for the faithfulness with which they fulfilled their dangerous tasks. The orders for operation were delivered by officers of the General Staff if the distance could be accomplished on horseback without a halt; letters of less importance were taken by cavalry orderlies. Now and then relays were formed for this purpose. The field-post, though it was an excellent way of communication for private business, was only used if a quick and safe forwarding was not of essential importance.[1]

If it were necessary that the orders should be explained by word of mouth to insure the concurrence of the Chief Commands with Head-quarters, a tried officer of the General Staff, usually the Chief of a Division, was sent. This was principally done on the battle-fields to keep the Commander-in-Chief informed of

---

[1] On one occasion some maps of the Côte d'or territory, sent off from Paris to Garibaldi in a balloon fell into our hands, and were sent on by post to General von Werder who could have made good use of them. But the field-post postillion was caught by the Garibaldians and in this wise the maps went to their original destination.

every occurrence in the more distant parts. But the Chief of the General Staff as well as the Quartermaster-General always remained during battle in the immediate vicinity of the king. Only once this rule was abandoned for a short time, and that was at the battle of Gravelotte—St. Privat. On this occasion General von Moltke led the attack of the Second Army Corps against the French left wing to the entrance of the Hohlweg north of Gravelotte, until the officers in his suite reminded him that his place was not under the enemy's fire. He then rode back to the king to Rezonville. There that same night, by the faint flicker of tallow candles, the orders were drawn up for the investment of the enemy's Army in Metz, and for the formation of the Meuse Army which, with the 3rd Army, was to march on Paris. Whether on duty or off duty, General von Moltke was always found in close connection with his Staff. He used to take a plain dinner at six o'clock with the Staff officers, unless he was commanded to attend the Royal dinner. His Round Table in the "Hôtel of the Réservoir" at Versailles has been much talked about. Here he dined for months almost daily with his officers at a small table which stood across the further end of the large dining-room. When he entered or left the room, he was respectfully greeted by the German princes, as well as by the officers and visitors who came and went and who took their seats at a long table which stood down one side, or at smaller tables placed about the room. Though he only joined in conversations that particularly interested him, he evidently enjoyed the merriment that generally surrounded him. It is well known that his table was extremely simple, it was immaterial to him what was put before him so long as he had sufficient to eat and drink. After dinner he used thoroughly to enjoy one or two cigars, at other times of the day he was hardly ever known to smoke. The moderation and regularity of his life, no doubt, contributed much to his always enjoying sound sleep. Yet if necessary he could even in his old age do with very little sleep without getting tired. On the contrary, if he had no urgent business he would enjoy a refreshing rest from eleven in the evening till seven in the morning in his simple camp-bed, even before decisive battles.

In an evening, after dinner, some officers of his Staff used to retire with him to his quarters for a game of whist. Very seldom, even at times of the greatest suspense, was this habit abandoned. The point was always five *pfennigs*, but the game was played with attention and interest; faults in playing or continued bad luck would vex the great strategist, even though he never gave vent to his annoyance in words.

While he was quartered at Versailles, in fine weather he used to drive after breakfast, accompanied by one or two officers of his Staff, in the neighbourhood of Paris, partly to enjoy the beautiful country and rich cultivation of the district, and also to acquaint himself with the position of the troops and their defensive operations, and after the opening of the artillery attack, to watch the cannonade. If within reach of the enemy's fire, he would leave his carriage and with astonishing agility and perseverance the general of seventy years would overcome the many obstacles of the country that might bar his way. Was the weather bad, he would pay a visit to the picture gallery at the Castle of Versailles. A lover of art and a connoisseur, he repaired there in defiance of all warnings and anonymous French threats, unattended, that he might enjoy the treat at leisure.

He never knew what it was to be afraid.

On Christmas Eve the officers of the Staff assembled in the office, under a Christmas-tree. Here too the General was in their midst, though only for a short time and quieter and graver than usual—it was the second anniversary of the death of his beloved wife.

During the whole campaign, which lasted more than

six months, not the faintest discord was ever heard in General von Moltke's Staff.

The members of the Staff formed a circle of friends each of whom endeavoured to do his utmost to fufil his duty in his own place, never envying his comrade.

Of course this was a happy circumstance in the formation of the Staff, but the real reason must be looked for principally in the charm which the personality of the great man at its head exercised. The superiority of his intellect left no room for rivalries. His sense of duty, his strict impartiality, his modesty and unselfishness, his dignified calmness, which never left him for a moment, not even under the most difficult circumstances, his kindness which never allowed even an impatient word to escape his lips,—these exemplary qualities brought into the brightest light by his historical successes—worked powerfully upon his surroundings. To be the assistant of such a man in a glorious time, was a fortune and an honour, for which everybody tried to make himself worthy by unselfish fulfilment of his duty and the suppression of all small feelings. In this sense, one may well say that Moltke's mind ruled his Staff.

VON BLUME.

Lieutenant-General and Commanding General of the 15th Army corps (during the Franco-German War, Major of the General Staff at the Head-quarters of His Majesty the King).

Recollections of an Officer of the General Staff.

ONE of the usual players at the "robber whist" (long whist) which the Field Marshal, as is well known, preferred, was an extremely good dealer. This skill was the General's great admiration, but he was also awaiting the moment when the quick dealer would make a mis-deal. For years this never happened, till

at last one evening, one card was over, and he had to
deal again. The General was rather triumphant, which,
however, he showed by a hardly perceptible smile round
his thin lips, so well known to us, and only said these
five words, " Bis dat, qui cito dat ! " The humour of
this dry remark had such an effect upon the dealer,
that he made a second mis-deal, but it must be said,
this was his last.

" I do not care for simple whist with three players.
I want recreation when I play in the evenings, not
excitement." Such was the opinion of the old gentleman, and so " robber whist," at one *pfennig* the point,
was the rule every evening,

The so-called " schwarze Dame " was for years the
General's favourite. On the General Staff journey in
1879 a rubber was sometimes played in the evenings,
though all the players, including the Field-Marshal, then
seventy-nine years old, had usually spent many hours in
the morning on horseback and besides this had worked
hard in their rooms. On one of such evenings, the
General was particularly lucky ; at his wish another
turn of the " schwarze Dame " was played, and another
and another, all of which he won. When the accounts
were settled, he was to receive more than two marks.
But the idea of having won the money from the other
gentlemen and chiefly because it was at his wish that
the game had been prolonged, seemed to make him feel
uncomfortable, and he said, " Gentlemen, but to-day
we have only played at half a *pfennig* the point ! "

It has already been shown that his celebrated silence
was only maintained under certain conditions. One
need only think of his excellent speeches in the Reichstag, which seemed to reach even more perfection in
clearness and beauty of language as the General grew
older. Needless to say that he despised empty gossip.
One of the most conscientious listeners in the Reichstag, he yet used to leave the hall without hesitation
when certain members spoke. On the other hand, it

was taken for a flattering, encouraging sign if the old gentleman went closer to the speaker that he might hear better.

The Field-Marshal seemed to make a rule of being very laconic in the few speeches that he had to make at banquets. On one occasion, on reconnoissance in 1881 in Holstein, when the naval officers had invited the General Staff to a most lively supper at the Casino, he gave out a longer toast, full of the most amiable humour.[1]

At the banquets which he used to give at his house in honour of the Emperor's birthday, and to which he invited the generals and Staff officers of the General Staff, his invariable toast was either "The health of His Majesty the Emperor and King," or, "His Majesty and King."

"What can I say about the Emperor in this circle? Everybody knows and feels the same as I do." These words give the clue to his brevity. The officers of the General Staff used to discuss among themselves the day before whether the toast would consist of eight or nine words; in 1884 the betting was nine words at most to an oyster breakfast; the Field-Marshal added, "Gentlemen!" by this one word the bet was lost.

But the unfortunate loser was of the opinion that "the Field-Marshal is getting old—he begins to be talkative."

Recollections of the last Staff journey of the Great General Staff under the command of the Field-Marshal written by a former officer of the Great General Staff.

THE reconnoissance of the Great General Staff in 1881 was the last made under the command of the Field-Marshal; the previous one, in 1880, had been

[1] Compare the following contribution.

conducted—for the first time—by Count Waldersee representing the Field-Marshal (Count Waldersee was then Chief of the Staff of the 10th Army Corps). Schleswig-Holstein was the scene of their operations, which were undertaken in the end of September and the beginning of October ; one of their objects was to investigate the fortifications on the land side of Kiel, a most important naval station.

We were all quartered at Kiel for several days ; and then the Field-Marshal, bearing in mind that the great object of these journeys was to enlarge the knowledge of the officers of the General Staff, in every direction and at every opportunity, frequently dispatched one of us to visit the fortifications of Sonderburg and the Düppeler Schanzen. The Navy placed one of their vessels at our disposal, and in it we left the harbour of Kiel at seven o'clock. At Sonderburg we disembarked and went, under Moltke's personal guidance, to the entrenchments, a distance of eight kilometres. Here one of the gentlemen explained the storming of the Düppeler Schanzen in 1864, the Field-Marshal on his part making some remarks and additions. We then inspected the lines of entrenchment more minutely, and marched back to Sonderburg, where, before re-embarking, we partook of a simple dinner to which the Field-Marshal had invited his officers and the dignitaries of the town. During the little voyage most of us enjoyed our well-deserved rest. But the old gentleman employed this time in making himself thoroughly acquainted with the arrangements of the interior of the vessel, which one of the Naval officers explained to him. We did not return to Kiel till darkness was coming on ; having just time enough left to dress for a friendly supper, to which we were asked by the Naval officers. The Field-Marshal made his appearance with military punctuality, and was so lively that no one would have thought that he had been on foot since early morning, and had marched 16 kilometres.

At table he rose to propose the toast for the Navy. He expressed himself in words something like the following :—" You, comrades, and gentlemen of the Navy, have the high calling and task of representing the honour of Germany in the wide world, and keeping up her reputation. Therefore it is only fair that, on your return home, you should find a comfortable nest where you can arm yourselves for new feats. And to prepare you such a snug nook the officers of the Great General Staff are endeavouring to-day.

" We of the Army do not see so much of the large world ; our boundaries are drawn for us. Sometimes, it is true, it does happen that we step into our neighbours' countries. . . ." At these last words, which were spoken by the General with a humorous smile, such applause broke out, that the ensuing words were not quite audible. This merry party was kept up till long after midnight, and the Field-Marshal was by no means the first who left.

P. A.

Recollections of a Member of the Reichstag.

IN all his doings, the Field-Marshal Count von Moltke showed an untiring devotion to duty, this also manifested itself in his political life. No member was more regular in attending the Reichstag than he, and none in the House excelled him in zeal and in the desire to obtain a clear insight of the questions under discussion. On December 2nd, 1885, the much honoured and aged president brought in his bill on " the alteration of the law of military pensions, passed on the 27th of June, 1871." The culminating point of this speech delivered in words that came straight from his heart were these :—

". . . . Is the army to attain her aims, will you see her strong, fresh and young, you must give her the pension law."

Count von Moltke won a glorious victory; when the bill was read for the third time on the 10th of April, 1886, it was unanimously accepted.

On the evening of this memorable day, I had left two family portraits at the Field-Marshal's house, according to a previous arrangement. One represented the Countess Friederike von der Gröben, née Countess von der Gröben of the Ponarien House, the other her husband, Count Ludwig of the Weslin House.[1] These portraits were drawn in pencil by the Court artist, Wilhelm Hensel, on the 9th of October, 1821, and on the 24th of June, 1822; "Von Moltke, Lieutenant in the 8th regiment," had copied them in July, 1826, for the family, and it was desired that the old hero should add a new signature to the original. While I was waiting to know when the portraits could be sent for, the Field-Marshal called me into his study, addressing me very kindly with these words, "What are you bringing me?" "Your Excellency," I answered, "the portraits of my wife's grandparents, of which I spoke to you the other day." "Let me see them." The Field-Marshal took the drawings nearer the lamp, examined them with great interest, and then much pleased said, "That is done excellently, excellently!" and turning to me quickly, "Who did them?" Rather amused, I replied, "Your Excellency did them yourself!" "I never in my life drew so well!" "I beg your pardon, your Excellency, there is your name in the corner at the bottom." The count took his square magnifying glass and then admitted it, but still was astonished.

[1] Oberburggraf of the kingdom of Prussia, Master of the Household of H.R.H. Prince Wilhelm, brother of H.M. King Frederick William III., born on the 23rd of December, 1765, died on the 16th of December, 1829; his wife was born on the 10th of June, 1780, died on the 18th of July, 1857. Both portraits are here reproduced.

" Yes, I wrote that, but I do not believe I ever drew as well as that ; " then he sat down at his writing table to the left of the three windows that were in the lofty room, and placing the movable lamp, which was fastened at his arm-chair, so that the light fell over his shoulder, he began to write,—

" Seen again on the 10th of April, 1886,
" COUNT MOLTKE,
" Field-Marshal."

When he had begun to write the second word, he stopped suddenly, saying, " The pencil is too soft, I must get another ; " he then went to the third window and chose another from a great number ; when he came back, I ventured to say, " It is a special joy for me that to-day's date will be written underneath ! " Moltke stopped, looked at me and asked, " To-day's date, why ? " " Because Your Excellency has to-day achieved another great action to the benefit of the army ! " The great thinker was silent, went to his seat, and while he continued the signature with a harder pencil, he said, in a tone which expressed the emotion of his true heart, " Many a one will be pleased." These simple words show the great soul of this eminent man.

COUNT V. SCHLIEFFEN.

Schlieffenberg, June, 1892.

Reminiscences of Count Eduard Bethusy-Huc of Bankau, the father of Countess Ella Moltke.

AS my intercourse with the General was principally of a private nature, I had frequent opportunities of admiring the affectionate disposition of our departed friend both in his and in my families, and also the strict faithfulness to duty which distinguished him in his family life.

I was introduced to Major-General von Moltke at Breslau in 1856, when he was in attendance on Prince Frederick William of Prussia. But it was not till after the marriage of my daughter Ella with his nephew Wilhelm that we came into close contact. In his family circle the appellation of the " great silent one " would hardly have been justified. For hours he would chat with my wife and my grown-up children, whom he regarded more as relations than connections. It was a delightful sight to watch his friendly expression as he played and joked with the younger ones and with the increasing number of my grandchildren, even those that were not connected with him.

His well-known love of horticulture and forestry often expressed itself in our grounds, and many a tree my wife had prevented my removing fell a victim to his authoritative opinion. His modesty and simplicity in private life was charming, it would have made him very unhappy when staying with his friends, to be the cause of any change in their habits. He knew that I was not an early riser, and when I entered his room on one occasion at seven o'clock, he declared to me that he would never be seen at Bankau again, if he saw me before half-past eight in the morning. If I went to his room about nine o'clock, I generally found that he had already spent some time in the garden, where he had discussed various things with my gardener, much to the benefit of the latter. He was particularly interested in our pine-apple growing, in which we were very successful, but it was rather an annoyance to him that he could not obtain any results at Creisau.

When asked if he wished to drive, ride or walk, he used to say that all three might be done—only, of course, one after the other. We usually went out riding for about three hours, and the pace he chose was certainly not suitable for an old man ; it was the exception to walk, as a rule we took a long trot in turns with a gallop, and if I had taken him to any ditch I am sure he would not have minded it at all. On one of these occasions we were accompanied by my daughter, who was not yet married. The Field-Marshal, by his and my carelessness, got on to boggy ground which threw his horse down. Fortunately no mischief happened, the ride was continued, and on our return an insignificant bruise was treated by myself with arnica, for we three had agreed to keep the accident secret.

"Now we shall see," the old gentleman remarked, "if little girls can be silent." Not till three years after was the occurrence revealed by the finding of a riding whip.

Another time we took a long drive in the afternoon, after having been on horseback almost all the morning. At a sharp descent of the road I was thrown from the box with the reins in my hands, the Field-Marshal with two of my daughters was in the carriage. It must have looked very dangerous, for the ladies screamed loudly, while the old gentleman remained quite calm and did not move a muscle. But later on he used to joke and speak smilingly about the "attempts on our lives at Bankau." After I had been dragged along some yards, I succeeded in stopping the horses, and we drove on without any further interruption. In the evening the hour for whist and music had almost gone by. The Field-Marshal, however, did not wish to lose either of these two amusements, so he proposed to have the whist-table taken into the music-room. Later in the evening, when the family were dancing, a gentleman was wanted for the quadrille—after the old fashion— I being unable to assist them on account of the bruises received in the afternoon; the old gentleman filled up the place, danced with the children, and became so lively, that at twelve o'clock he even danced a waltz with one of the girls.

Another day—it was on a Saturday in June—Frau von Moltke, my daughter's sister-in-law, who presided at the Field-Marshal's house, sent word that she would come to see us at Bankau. As we received her in the dimly lit entrance hall, we noticed a slim bent figure in the corner, with a large flappy hat suggesting the idea of an artist. To our astonishment the figure resolved itself into that of the Field-Marshal, who had come quite unexpectedly to take us by surprise. After he had taken off his summer overcoat, we saw that he was dressed in a black dress-coat with the linen cross of St. John's order on it. " Excuse," said he, " this state dress, but I have to be at the Rittertag (assembly of the knights) at Breslau the day after to-morrow, and on such occasions a dress-coat is obligatory."

The order with the ribbon and the white tie were in his breastpocket and were put on early on Monday at 7 o'clock before he left. What else the pockets contained, was not disclosed. There was no other luggage. The following day I asked the Field-Marshal to use one of my coats. While he was driving out with my wife it began to drizzle ; when she proposed having the carriage closed, he said with that humour peculiar to him, " Oh, please don't, it does not matter, it is not my coat."

I might quote many another anecdote in proof of the old gentleman's warm-heartedness and humour in private life amongst his friends.

Of the many interesting conversations on general subjects which I have had with him, I will at least mention two.

In the spring of 1867 we sat in the Constituent Reichstag ; the Luxemburg affair had come up again, and Benningsen's motion was on the Order of the Day for the next day but one. It was then that General von Moltke, in a conversation with me in the ante-rooms of the hall, spoke as follows : " After a war such as we have just had no one can really feel a desire to have another, and no one can be farther from cherishing such a desire than I am. And yet I cannot but wish that the occasion given for a war with France were taken advantage of ;

unhappily, I regard this war as absolutely unavoidable within the next five years, and within this period the now indisputable superiority of our organization and weapons will be equalled by France who is making great efforts, more and more to our disadvantage. The sooner, therefore, we come to blows, the better. The present occasion is good. It has a national character, and ought, therefore, to be taken advantage of." These words, convincing as they were in themselves, and coming from the lips of such an authority, seemed to me too weighty, despite their originally confidential character, not to be acted upon. I reported them to my Free Conservative Party, and was induced by it to ask the Chancellor his opinion, as the party justly shrank from binding itself in so important a question of foreign policy, without knowing the opinion of the Government.

Count Bismarck recognized the justice of Moltke's remarks, both from the political and the military point of view, but declared that he could never bear the responsibility of bringing the misery of a war upon his country, unless necessary (as in the case of the Austrian war), in defence of its vital interests or its honour. The personal conviction of a ruler or a statesman, however well founded, that war would eventually break out, could not justify its promotion. Unforeseen events might alter the situation and avert what seemed inevitable.

When I told the General this next day, he answered, " Bismarck's standpoint is unassailable, but it will cost us many human lives one day."

The date of the second conversation is about the middle of the eighties. A story was circulated at that time, not in the press, but in society, which could not but be disagreeable to the Field-Marshal, greatly though it seemed to do him honour. It was that in the evening of the day of Gravelotte King William had asked the Chief of the General Staff what was to be done if the enemy maintained his positions next day. Moltke, so ran the story, had answered, "Attack again, Your Majesty," and when the King replied that he had hardly the heart to do that after such painful losses, Moltke added, "Then I must tender Your Majesty my resignation."

Doubting the authenticity of this anecdote, I confidentially asked the Field-Marshal about it; he declared it to be a fable from beginning to end, without even an apparent basis in the occurrences of that evening. "I should never," he added, "least of all in time of war, have quitted my Sovereign abruptly, in face of the enemy. That is contrary, not only to discipline, but also to the honour of a soldier. The germ of such legends may, perhaps, have been the misinterpretation of what occurred more than once in the course of both the wars. The King, who, as is well known, acquainted himself exactly with all my plans before they were carried out, possessed, in a far higher degree than was known among the people and in the Army, a remarkably sharp eye for all the weak points, and sometimes demanded, with great tenacity, that his criticism, in itself well founded, should be taken into practical account. This was not always possible, at least in my opinion.

"Even in war there are many situations in which it is impossible to make any plan without a weak point, without trusting in the good fortune and valour of the troops. So, if the King could not be induced to yield theoretically, I was repeatedly compelled to declare, 'Then Your Majesty must graciously have the goodness to command yourself. My wisdom is at an end. I can make no other proposal.' After such a declaration, my advice was always followed."

I conclude these short statements with the joyful confession, that I shall always consider it a providential favour for myself and my family, that we were allowed to become so intimate with a man who was not only of undying historical fame, but was also, which is so seldom the case, the personification of a great, noble and pure man, whom we not only honoured but loved sincerely.

Reminiscences by Dr. von Kulmiz of Konradswaldau near Saarau.

WHEN during the eighties on a drive through the beautiful plantations at Schweidnitz which occupy the place of the former fortifications, the other occupant of the carriage remarked upon it, the Field-Marshal said, " If I meet Frederick the Great in heaven, I shall be in a difficult position, for having razed his favourite fortress Schweidnitz."

2. The former *Landrath* of the circuit of Schweidnitz once showed the Field-Marshal an old map of the camp at Bunzelwitz, situated in his circuit, asking him if the position had really been so excellent, whereupon the Field-Marshal remarked, " The strength of the camp lay in the presence of Frederick the Great."

3. On the 21st of October, 1889, Herr Wangemann, a collaborator of Mr. Edison, exhibited his phonograph at Creisau and the Field-Marshal spoke the following words into the apparatus, " The newest invention of Mr. Edison is indeed astonishing. The phonograph makes it possible for a man who has long been in his grave to raise his voice again and greet the present."

He then recited from the first part of Faust,—

" Ihr Instrumente spottet mein
 Mit Rad und Kämmen, Walz'und Bügel :
 Ich stand am Thor, ihr solltet Schlüssel sein ;
 Zwar euer Bart ist kraus, doch hebt ihr nicht die Riegel.

Geheimnissvoll am lichten Tag
Lässt sich Natur des Schleiers nicht berauben,
Und was sie deinem Geist nicht offenbaren mag.
Das zwingst du ihr nicht ab mit Hebeln und mit Schrauben." [1]

Then he added, " But human intellect places nature in a painful position. It forces her to lift many a veil by the torture of experiment, or at the risk of a revenge sometimes very severe."

He also recited some other lines of the first part of Faust,—

"Doch ist es jedem eingeboren.
Dass sein Gefühl hin auf und vorwärts dringt,
Denn über uns, im blauen Raum verloren,
Ihr schmetternd Lied die Lerche singt." [2]

4. At the country-seat of a niece of his who lived in the circuit of Schweidnitz near the Zobten mountain he proved his excellent skill as a landscape gardener, as he also did in his beautiful park at Creisau. With capital judgment he always chose the exact spot to make clearings or vistas, using the axe ruthlessly, even sacrificing beautiful old beeches, if necessary, to obtain a view over a piece of water. For years he argued with his niece and her husband about these trees, till at last he had his own way.

5. Once when he was on a visit there, and everybody was kept in the house on account of rain, he amused the children for about two hours with making soap bubbles. It was a charming sight to see the old

[1] " Ye instruments, forsooth, but jeer at me
With wheel and cog, and shapes uncouth of wonder;
I found the portal, you the keys should be;
Your wards are deftly wrought, but drive no bolts asunder!
Mysterious even in open day,
Nature retains her veil, despite our clamours :
That which she doth not willingly display
Cannot be wrenched from her with levers, screws, and hammers."

[2] " Yet in each soul is born the pleasure
Of yearning onward, upward and away.
When o'er our heads, lost in the vaulted azure,
The lark sends down his flickering lay."

gentleman, surrounded by a troop of children, one child on each knee, and to see how it delighted him to watch their pleasure.

He used to call himself "Opapa" when speaking to his great-nephews and great-nieces, and so they called him by that name.

6. Moltke was a noble benefactor, in the highest sense of the word ; as he liked to do good in a quiet way, many of his kind acts may never become known. I may mention one of them here. Once on a walk at Creisau he met an artisan and was struck with the man's sad expression ; when asked the cause of his trouble, he said that his son had been made a master workman, and that there was a good workshop to be sold not far off, but he had not sufficient money to buy it. The following day the Field-Marshal drove to the place which had been pointed out to him, and on learning that it would be a favourable bargain he enabled the artisan to buy it.

Only a few knew that the Field-Marshal spent considerable sums every year in charity ; this ought to be particularly mentioned, as he is often believed, especially by the nation at large, but quite erroneously, to have been rather stingy.

He only gained this reputation because his personal wants were extraordinarily few.

Baron von Magnus in Berlin sends the following account.

I ONLY had the honour of meeting the Field-Marshal three times. The first time in his study in the presence of Major Helmuth von Moltke, when I had about an hour's conversation with him. The second time at a special meeting at the *Herrenhaus.*

The third time again in his study on Tuesday afternoon before the Friday on which he died.

My endeavours to obtain for the working men, artisans, officials and country people, the power of acquiring house and landed property in a practical manner, led me to become acquainted with the Field-Marshal, whose warm interest in the welfare of the masses was well known to me. I was at that time on the committee of the German National Building Society, which has since then become a registered Association with limited liability.

My expectations, which were rather great before I went to the Field-Marshal, were far exceeded. I was allowed to report minutely on the aims and the organization of the German National Building Society, and on all three occasions our conversation was on the question of this society and on national economy at large. I was astonished at the penetration the Field-Marshal displayed, he grasped at once the principal point, which was that the security of the promissory notes on the ground was ensured by the landed property and life insurance. He knew how to give the right value to these questions ; he praised very highly the sound finance of this extensive and important undertaking, which was not only independent of charity and entitled those who had invested capital in the enterprise to the enjoyment of interest, but also made this interest a necessity. Every word revealed his interest in the public welfare, his tender heart for that class of the community which is only scantily provided with means, and his lively interest in all questions of political economy.

In short precise sentences he pronounced his delight at the new enterprise, and to my great joy signed on the day of our first meeting with his own hand, his name for 3000 marks (£150) for three shares in the German National Building Society.

The Field-Marshal was also present at the meeting in

the *Herrenhaus* when Privy Councillor Dr. Dernburg. Director Haas and myself reported on the Dwelling Houses and Settlement question with special reference to the National Building Society. He followed the transactions with great interest, as he afterwards took the opportunity of assuring me. Soon after I received the following letter the original of which I value like a precious jewel :—

Berlin, April 13th, 1891.

MUCH HONOURED BARON,—From the enclosed you will see that a Building and Savings Bank Society at Munich has acquired a plot of land for the purpose of building workmen's houses, but that it is in want of funds with which to build. They ask for my advice.

I am far too little acquainted with this matter to judge if this association with its ground could serve as a branch foundation.

Perhaps you would be kind enough for this good object to give me or the applicant the desired advice as you are an expert in the matter.

Faithfully yours,
COUNT MOLTKE, Field-Marshal.

It was on the Tuesday before the Field-Marshal's death that I was again allowed an audience to report on the business at Munich, which was mentioned in the above letter. He thanked me for having undertaken the matter for him. I also delivered a message from the select committee of the German National Building Society asking him to a committee meeting in the *Herrenhaus* on the following Saturday. He accepted the invitation very readily, and promised to attend the meeting in any case, inquired eagerly into the progress of the preliminaries, visibly pleased with the numerous drawings which had been sent in, and remarked that he himself would like to sign for a larger sum as soon as the society had been registered. Yes, his interest was

so warm that when he shook hands with me on my
taking leave, he said that he was overrun with requests
of all kinds, but that now he would refuse everything
to devote his remaining strength to the German
National Building Society, as he was thoroughly
convinced of its practicability and usefulness.

IN MEMORIAM.

Sermon at the Funeral Service of the Field-Marshal held on April 28th, 1891, by the Evangelical Field-Provost of the Army, D. Richter.[1]

PSALM xc. 2—6, 10, 12—14, 17.

HONOURED MOURNERS,

WE have heard the ancient psalm of Moses read from the old Field-Marshal's Bible which he used to read daily. This ninetieth psalm is suggestive of the life of this man of ninety, for the labour and sorrow of his life has made it precious, and his death is precious too, for he was always ready to meet it with this prayer constantly upon his lips, "So teach us to number our days, that we may apply our hearts unto wisdom."

Now the Lord has heard his prayer, now death has come as he desired. Yet he being dead, yet speaketh, as Moses, the patriarch, prophet and leader of his people did. "And Moses," so it is written (Deut. xxxiv. 7—9), "was an hundred and twenty years old when he died: his eye was not dim, nor his natural force abated.

"And the children of Israel wept for Moses.

"And Joshua, the son of Nun, was full of the spirit of wisdom; for Moses had laid his hands upon him."

We too stand by the bier of a patriarch of his people, a prophet of modern times, a leader in times of trouble to the glory of a new kingdom. Next to his own people who mourn the departed, the venerable head of their

[1] Here given by kind permission of Field-Provost D. Richter and Messrs. G. Strübing of Leipsic, the publishers of the sermon.

family, stands our Emperor as chief mourner, at the head of all Europe to do homage to the dead, the Emperor who has not only lost a most faithful servant but in him an Army. And with the Emperor mourn the German princes, the German army, the German nation; there is no division of rank or party, the whole nation mourns for him—all are united by one great grief and one desire to honour this great son of the Fatherland "our Moltke" also after death, and to thank God Almighty with all our hearts for having given him to us.

Let us, then, honour his memory and keep his legacy sacred!

Honour his memory! "His eye was not dim nor his natural power abated." What was the secret of this blessed life, what was the secret of the wonderful strength which did not leave him, though he was in his ninety-first year? Was it nature or was it the grace of God? Was it his rich deep mind or the iron energy of his will? The great work or his success in life? Was it the self-command or the unselfishness of his character? His many-sidedness or his reserved nature? One may well ask these questions: he was like a jewel that reflects on all sides—and he was a rare jewel.

All virtues had their influence on his life, but all of them were supported and harmoniously held together by the one great power in him: "His natural force was not abated." All the Field-Marshal did as battle-thinker and battle-guide with sword and pen, with deed and counsel as the servant of his Sovereigns and as citizen with the civic crown, as soldier or as savant—all will be indelibly engraved on the tables of history; the wreaths on his bier are proofs of that already, each one tells its own history, each one speaks its own language, silent and yet eloquent, like himself, the great silent one.

Not what he has done but what he has been, was his innermost strength.

"He was a man, take him for all in all,
I shall not look upon his like again."

He was a man, and let us add a Christian. There lay the secret of his strength. To be temperate even in overwhelming success, to remain modest and simple at the zenith of glory, to triumph and yet—to be silent, that is possible only to him whose strength is not of this earth; but who knows and has learnt something of Him who is called "Our refuge from one generation to another," and who has learnt to look, like Moses, on the holy land. All these thoughts seemed to shine like the morning dew of eternity on the brow of the departed, it appealed to us like a sermon cut in marble, like a revelation from a future world: the great silent one even on his death-bed is triumphant for the last time over the last enemy, whom he never feared because he could say, "Thanks be to God, who giveth us the victory through our Lord Jesus Christ."

And so we are standing here, deeply moved and yet comforted, at the bier of the great man, promising not only to honour his memory but to keep his legacy sacred for all time to come. That is a consoling thought for his relations, who took leave of his remains yesterday, but another thought for all of us—for he belonged to all of us,—a thought in particular for the Army. As Joshua was filled with the spirit of truth, because Moses had laid his hands on him, so let us, the younger generation, receive the legacy of the old Field-Marshal here at his bier and keep it sacred for ever, that his spirit, as the spirit of truth, may remain with us, and that his hands may be laid upon us as witness of his strength. As Cid so shall he lead the army on. And his greatness was shown in that he did not stand aloof at the zenith of his fame, but he gave to the Army and to the Nation his best, his own self, as the greatest organizer they have had. He lives amongst us, even in us, though he is gone away. He will live in the Army and in the Nation as the embodied spirit of truth and strength, discipline and temperance. His principle was "first to weigh and then to dare." He hated every low or mean thing, he was faithful in the unselfish fulfilment of his duty until death. And therefore, however deep the sorrow with which we again see one of the paladins who surrounded our old hero Emperor depart, it is one of the greatest and not the least of the old Field-Marshal's merits—that Germany is not only expected to bear but is able to bear the loss of one of her greatest sons and one of the greatest men of all times. The Emperor though he has lost an Army in him, may say so before all the world; for the Army will possess him for ever. About eighty years ago it went like the sound of a funeral dirge through the hearts of our fathers:

> " Deutsches Volk, du herrlichstes von allen
> Deine Eichen stehn, Du bist gefallen."

Now by God's grace this dirge has become a song of joy to our Nation :

> " Du stehst fest, ob deine Eichen fallen."

Let us, then, keep his memory and legacy to us in honour.

And now, in conclusion, let the great man speak to us once more, and let his legacy be remembered in thoughts which will go up into the unknown world. "I stand," so he wrote when he was 80 years old, eleven years ago, just after his birthday, "at the end of my earthly course. But with what a different measure will our earthly work be measured in the future world. Not the splendour of success, but the purity of our motives and the endurance in duty where the results were scarcely visible, will decide the value of a human life. What strange exchange of high and low will happen at the last great review. We are not even ourselves conscious of what we owe to ourselves, to others or to a higher will. It will be good not to attach too much importance to outward appearance."

Thus thinks a sage, so speaks a man, so confesses a Christian! He who dies thus, dies well. Amen.

Speech in Memory of General Field-Marshal Count Moltke, by Ernest Curtius,[1] at the public meeting of the Royal Academy of Science in Berlin, on the 2nd of July, 1891 (on the commemoration of Leibniz).

IT is an old custom on the Leibniz Day to remember those who have belonged to our circle, and on this anniversary a picture comes involuntarily into our minds, the picture of the man whom the Emperor and his allies laid to his last rest on April 28th, accompanied by the deepest sympathy of the German nation. The members of the Academy and their guests would rightly be astonished if any other person had been the subject of to-day's speech than the Field-Marshal Count Helmuth von Moltke, who has been honorary associate of this institution since the year 1860.

The Prussian Academy of Science, whose second founder was the Great King, does not only consist of experts, but, as its history shows, also men distinguished in the army and the science of strategy have become members. Without going back to the last century we can name Field-Marshal Baron von Müffling, the Generals von Rühle and Wilhelm von Scharnhorst as honorary members of the Academy.

Moltke's name was not only an ornament to the Academy that we may be proud of, he was, we can say, personally one of us.

Often and with pleasure has he sat with us at this table, taking an active part in the deliberations preparatory to the excavations of Nemrud-Dagh. He was not one of those who are chosen honorary members

---

[1] Here given by the kind permission of Privy Councillor Curtius.

of scientific associations merely to testify their interest in science or to give their patronage upon important occasions. Moltke stood on a height which towered above the limits of the different scientific vocations, and from inborn love for science he gave his rare mental powers to promote human knowledge ; a bold discoverer, he forced his way where men of science have gratefully followed him. An academical tribute to his memory must represent his position in regard to the scientific tendencies of his day, and this can but be a most welcome task to an academician ; for nothing gives greater pleasure, as our Ranke says in his "Tagebuch blätter," than to feel intellectually the pulse.

The Military Schools, in which the spirit of the Great King still lives, form the connecting link between the military world and the scientific life of the nation. It was his principle that a fully and freely developed education of the mind would raise military morality. By his orders first-class masters were appointed to the Academy of Cadets ; he founded, in 1765, the military Academy where young officers might have the opportunity of increasing their military knowledge.

In 1809 this Institution was further endowed and became the foundation of the General War School, called to-day the War Academy, to which Moltke belonged from 1823 to 1826, the memorable period when General von Clausewitz was the Director. He has largely shared in the blessings of this creation of Frederick the Great. The great advantage of this Institution consists not only in instructive lectures but in intimate intercourse with the most prominent men of all ranks of life ; it rouses men to take an interest in the intellectual movements of the day, it forms that tie between the profession of instructors and the military profession which is so highly valued in Prussia ; this influence of learned men on our military youths is vividly shown in the first decades of the century.

I first think of Karl Ritter. His special science was

closely connected with strategical studies; and full attention had to be paid to the new thoughts that might enrich this department.

And this attention was given in a very high degree by Ritter. For though geography and Ethnology formed a part of the ancient " historia " according to the method of the Greeks, it was still the custom to look upon the surface of the earth as a confused mass of countries which had by chance become the scene of this or that nation's history; for this reason the soil of the country remained a subject of indifference to the historian.

The discoveries of the clear-sighted and philosophic thinker Strabo, in regard to the connection between natural formations and intellectual development, found no followers; the geographical manuals remained nothing but dry summaries. Karl Ritter had the courage to unite two branches of the study of the world into one science; his " Geography in relation to Nature and History " was an epoch startling the intellectual world by the originality and grandeur of its conceptions; it was a new shoot from an old trunk which was welcomed with joy. In his books Ritter never mastered the matter which he treated; it was not as an author but principally as a teacher that he exercised a powerful influence over his time. With the military authorities it was of the highest importance that strict attention should be paid to the new flight in this branch of science; and Ritter was charged with the direction of the studies at the Academy for Cadets and appointed lecturer on History and Geography at the General War School.

Here the two men who will always live in the grateful memory of the German nation as an inseparable couple in age and vocation, Roon and Moltke, sat at Ritter's feet.

Both made their acquaintance with literature through him, and I know no more beautiful testimony

to the influence which united the War Academy with
the different professions, than the noble enthusiasm with
which Albrecht von Roon tried to make use of the new
progress in knowledge, and the unpretending modesty
with which he wished all he gave to be considered as a
legacy of his beloved master. It was like a personal
benefit to him to breathe the fresh air which had revived
the science of geography, which did away with chance,
revived dead material, and brought the mass of details
into one great whole.

He did not agree with military geography; the new
science was to him a fresh connecting link with all
thinking beings.

A still greater independence and a freer view was
taken by Moltke in this intellectual atmosphere; greedily
he absorbed all new ideas, which were offered in the
contemplation of nature and the history of the human
race. Leopold von Buch, who had paid special attention to Ritter's teaching of mountain ranges, threw
fresh light on the formation of the earth's surface;
Alexander von Humboldt, who had met Buch at the
foot of Vesuvius, brought back many new observations
from the new world. One of the most gifted of Buch's
pupils, Friedrich Hoffmann, investigated in 1827 the
conditions of the Roman soil, and was the first to prove
that the banks of the Tiber were of no less interest to
the geologist than to the historian.

Both ways of observation developed side by side,
supplementing each other. While the friends of
Archæology had formerly been content with revelling in
the sentimental realization of former times, or with
making an inventory of the remains of such times,
Niebuhr and Bunsen (who joined him in making
enthusiastic researches) raised the interest in historical
contemplations by bringing to light the growth of the
cities on their respective soils; statistics of ruins became
civic history. And what Ritter had drawn in big outlines was executed in detail for the first time at one of

the most important scenes of the history of the human race.

Those were events in the world of science without which the worth of Moltke's work would be unintelligible. They awakened his inquiring mind and showed the method to which he always remained faithful. As Ritter, Buch and Humboldt discovered a new link between nature and the history of the human race, so he, introduced by Professor Erman into the science of physics, learnt from them to practise his eye in both directions. As an artist loves and studies the human form, so he studied that of nature, which regulates the settler's choice of a dwelling-place. Born in a flat, monotonous country, he thirsted, as he tells us, for an undulating land, and under the accumulations of centuries he traced the original structure of the Seven Hills. As the sculptor manipulates his block of marble to reproduce the life-like features of the human head, it was his delight to learn from the earth's surface with the help of the plane-table and the compass the secret of its natural formation. He tried to understand the Campagna of Rome geologically. He had an observing eye for animate nature. Carefully he watched the *fauna* of the Dobrudja where the land, as he says, has been left to the animals after man had been dislodged from it by man; carefully he describes the varied piscine world which has given historical importance to the "Golden Horn," and like Ritter, who had a great preference for the study of the history of indigenous trees, he made investigations about the cypress in the East.

Geographical science, which burst its chains when Moltke was still a youth, has been reproached with trying to unite in a sentimental excess that which could not be comprised in the framework of one branch of science. The overflowing stream has again been divided into separate channels, and poles have been put up for divisions between the adjoining territories, which cannot be maintained. In my opinion we should only rejoice if the different branches of scientific investigation touch one another; for it is not in separation but in union of the many points of view that the living progress of human knowledge is based.

This was Moltke's point of view, and what gives him a unique position amongst his contemporaries, is the fact that he rose above the traditional separation of the branches of science with an independent spirit, devoting himself, without ever neglecting his vocation, to all the movements in the scientific world that came from Ritter, Buch, Humboldt and Niebuhr.

To this must be added the development of modern history.

An interest in public affairs was at an early age implanted in Moltke, partly owing to his parents' changeable home, near the German frontier. His first years were spent at Lubeck, and he himself said, in answer to the bestowal of the honorary citizenship of that city, that the many monuments testifying to the pride of the citizens when Lubeck stood at the head of the Hanseatic League whose fleets ruled the seas, its venerable town hall, the prominent spires, the protecting ramparts, with their shady avenues, the large vessels on the narrow streams had formed his earliest recollections, and had left an indelible impression upon him.

Here he made his first observations on the different historical epochs and the powers affecting them, and as he grew into a youth, a new connection of historical research had been indicated by Leopold Ranke. His writings drew Moltke's attention beyond the affairs of his fatherland to the contrast between the western and eastern countries, between Teutonic and Latin races. In the twenties came the "Servian revolution," an interesting exhibition of a tribe in its home aspect.

His political interest was awakened by the French Revolution of 1830. Moltke followed the fermenting movements on the frontier of his fatherland, not with the eye of a young officer who impatiently waits for the time when weapons must decide, but with that of a perfectly impartial, scrutinizing observer. Anarchy, in whatever shape, was despicable to him, and deeply rooted in his nature was the belief that violent insurrections are only justifiable when inalienable possessions are at stake. In regard to the events of his time, he was an earnest investigator who tried to understand the historical connection of everything. In consequence of the Belgian Revolution of 1831 the pamphlet about "Holland and Belgium and their relations to each other since their separation under Philip II." was published, and the following year the essay on Poland, which remained unnoticed for a long time, and in which the geographical formation of the Vistula Valley was discussed.

Moltke's intellectual superiority was fully appreciated in the Army. He soon saw that he would be principally employed on the General Staff; and he was all the more anxious to do everything in his power to enlarge his horizon and to satisfy his innate thirst for knowledge, so he acquired as early as possible a comprehensive knowledge of foreign countries, nations and languages.

In 1835 he received leave for a journey to Constantinople, Athens and Naples.

In Turkey the bloody overthrow of the Janissaries had broken the tradition to which the Osmans owed their victories. A fresh prop was sought for this Power, and the *Seraskier* thought he had found in the young captain, with his clear understanding and quiet seriousness, the man who could lend a helping hand to the remodelling of the army and the defence of the country. And so his journey, undertaken as a tourist, received a new turn, and became of historical value. The furlough was changed into a command to Turkey for the purpose of instructing and organizing the troops. Moltke visited the fortresses of the country in the suite of the Sultan. The growing confidence in his person was transferred to the army to which he then belonged, and in the year 1837 three other Prussian officers, Fischer, von Vincke and von Mühlbach, entered the Turkish Service as instructors.

It was impossible to change Turkey into a European military power. The battle of Nisib was a shameful defeat in spite of Moltke's presence, who, as appointed adviser to Hafiz Pasha, had given up all responsibility two days before the battle, after having in vain protested against Hafiz' disposal of the troops, and at the death of Mahmoud II. the Empire was perfectly defenceless even against her own vassals, so that it owed its preservation merely to the interference of the Great Powers.

If nothing of importance was gained by the political and military world, all the more was attained for the scientific. Moltke employed this sojourn in the Levant, which extended over several years, in promoting the science of geography, whose revival by Ritter he had so closely watched in his youthful days. And now let us consider his scientific work and its object.

One is accustomed to designate the science to which he devoted himself as Geography in general. The Greeks, from whom we derive our terminology, were more exact in their expression. For them "Geography" meant the conception of the earth as a whole, and consequently it would no more be correct to speak of the geography of Asia Minor than of the world's history of a state. The branch of geography which Moltke made his special study was "chorography," i.e. the description of a particular country with its characteristic peculiarities; this science has its indispensable supplement in topography, i.e. the fixing of the situation of places and monuments.

The discoveries made by means of these sciences are of two kinds. They are either of districts which come for the first time in contact with the world outside, or countries spoken of in ancient history, which have been forgotten, but whose re-discovery has enabled, us to understand the whole state of civilization which is found there.

This re-discovery of the countries of ancient civilization is the mission of our century in which scientists have been constantly engaged ever since Karsten Niebuhr recognized the old brick walls of Babylon in 1761. To this mission Moltke, a born topographer, with a gifted eye for the characteristics of every landscape, was introduced by a wonderfully happy providence. He was travelling by order of his Sovereign, who gave security as well as the necessary means; he worked with comrades who assisted each other in carrying out the common plan. In this way the roads which Alexander once paced off by his " bematists " from the Bosphorus to Babylon have been discovered; and one of the most important countries in the history of civilization, Asia Minor, this important central country, has been opened up for our benefit principally by Moltke. Asia Minor is a peninsula and at the same time a continent in itself, a bridge for the nations who penetrate into the Western countries from the East, a country of such eccentric configuration, that it stands in inseparable connection with the Syrian-Egyptian, Greek and Scythian worlds; by its streams which run into the Pontus and the Propontis, the Archipelago and the Mediterranean as well as the Persian Gulf, connected with all the civilized countries, it was the seat of the wars between the Shimites and the Arians, the Hellenes and the Barbarians, between Christendom and Islam. And with Asia Minor the land of the two rivers of Mesopotamia has been explored. Moltke was the first to take his plane-table to these countries, once the homes of the art of surveying. The banks of the Euphrates and the Tigris, the cradle of human history, were explored by him. On rafts like those of ancient times, made of inflated skins tied together—the only craft that can stand being knocked against the rocky cliffs, bending with the curves

but also turned by every current and easily swamped—
he, the boldest of navigators, dared to go through rapids
where no native was willing to follow him. His
journeys were campaigns which required presence of
mind, perseverance and courage. Moltke was quite
conscious that the sights he daily saw were remarkable, and he did not neglect the opportunity of making
notes in his lonely hours of leisure; they were not
intended for the public, but were communicated in letters
to his own people. That is the reason of his simplicity
of expression, when describing the charm of his
surroundings. His reports are a most natural reaction
of an overtaxed mind and body, enlivened by many
thoughts and remembrances of his early years. When
he wanders on to classic soil the spirits of the mighty
dead are with him, Hector and Achilles, Cyrus,
Alexander and Xenophon. The least *débris* of the old
Roman roads attracted his attention, and in astonishment
we stand with him for the first time before the rock-
buildings of Amascia. Much that is memorable he was
the first to see and to describe. At once he feels at
home in the dwelling-places of the ancient nations.
The locality was for him "a piece of reality which had
been handed down from a long-forgotten past"—that is
the appropriate remark of a genuine historian and a
thinking topographer.

Not considering details, what a complete picture he
puts before us of the life of these human races!

The state of affairs of an Eastern Empire, which is
kept together not by the power of a ruler nor by the
affection of the people, but by the indolent power of
habit, an Empire keeping up a continual fight with
her own subjects to enforce military service and
taxation! And then what touching pictures of the
ravages of time! The countries of ancient civilization,
upon whose mental harvests we are living even to-day,
the nursery of populous cities, are now nothing but
miles and miles of desert pasturages for roaming herds.

Nations whose histories belong to the most eventful
that the world possesses, have sunk back into pre-historic
conditions and are left to themselves, only free in so far
as they inhabit districts where no one else can live.

Traces of a kindred tribe of these desert-children,
showing them to be the bearers of Art and Science, were
found in the beautiful monuments discovered by Moltke
on Spanish soil. This fact drew his thoughts to the
different manner in which the nations of the West and
East have developed.

The Arabs succeeded in making themselves at home
on European soil and in attaining a civilization whose
decay is this very day considered as an irreparable loss.
They felt that forsaking European soil meant renouncing
their historical mission; they took the keys of their
houses at Seville with them, because of the firm
confidence they had in Allah the Just, that he would
bring their children back to the land of their glory.

The Osmans, on the other hand, build their tombs on
the other side of the Bosphorus, though they are still
in power at Byzantium, because they see the hour
approaching when they too will have to leave European
soil, and that not with the proud hopes with which the
Moors took leave of Granada.

Europe and Asia—that is the contrast which again
and again engages our attention, and which also forms
the principal subject of Moltke's letters. He takes us to
the scenes of the earliest foundations of states and science,
to the home of all the religions that have ever stirred the
world. With him we see the people of the East streaming over our continent to display their highest vital
powers here, and then to return to their own land or to
perish of enervation. Moltke's own personality shows
us the present contrast in a most striking manner.
Without the slightest affectation of superiority he stands
like a hero amongst beings of an inferior kind, in the
service of an Eastern country. A born ruler, he was
the only man of independent thought and action in sur-

roundings which, although partly in harmony with the higher aims of life, remained at the same time in bondage to superstition, love of pleasure and indolence.

Moltke is reserved in expressing the feelings that moved his mind most deeply, when he followed up the history of nations with a searching eye. Firm as a rock is his conviction that in Christendom alone, in which "one should not try to explain the inexplicable," as he expressed it, can be found the power necessary to preserve a state in existence. More self-assured than before, tempered to the full power of manhood, tried in dangers, privations, hardships of all kinds, rich in rare knowledge and incomparable recollections, but also prouder and fonder of his home, Moltke returned from the East to his Fatherland.

His notes, looked at in a superficial way, appear kaleidoscopic, but in reality they are one great unit. The various sights of the world that he had seen were reflected in his clear, calm and manly character; word and deed, description and disposition are united. Therefore his letters are not only a rich store-house of instructive observations, in style and matter, a classical work in which the educated of our nation may delight. but they are also a monument of the great man raised by himself at the most important period of his intellectual development. The language too, compared with his early writings, shows how Moltke had matured intellectually during his travels.

He also set on foot other imperishable works of scientific technique in the East.

The wonderful city on the Bosphorus, founded in the last ages of Ancient History, which, in comparison with Athens and Rome, might be called a city of old men, and which has never been the home of ardour or of the growth of vigour, yet which to this day, through her important position as a city on the converging lines of Eastern and Western interests, holds the world in suspense—

this city, with her incomparable surroundings, Moltke's master-hand has brought clearly before our eyes for the first time.

In addition a great work was achieved by the drawing of the maps (of Asia Minor and Turkish Armenia by von Vincke, Fischer, von Moltke and Kiepert); the first practical part taken by German research in a great work of our time. What Moltke did in the eastern highlands, in Mesopotamia and Kurdistan, his friends mapped out and supplemented, von Vincke in the western highlands, in the Halys Valley and Anti-Taurus, Fischer in the Taurus and its southern lowlands. These are the campaigns of our Prussian officers in times of peace; works of investigation, deeds indeed that do honour to the fatherland and its army. They give the first ground-work for a comprehensive and scientific representation of the continent of Asia Minor; they have been adopted, as a legacy of Moltke, by the Academy which regards the progressive conclusion of the work begun as one of her most important tasks.

In the sixth year after his return Moltke was again called to foreign lands by a new, unexpected cause. As personal Aide-de-camp to Prince Henry of Prussia, Rome was his residence, and he profited intellectually by this position! No sooner had he settled down to his life in Rome, than his scientific zeal was again awakened; he did not rest till he had drawn maps of the environs of Rome better than those in existence. In the winter of 1845 and 1846 he fixed the principal points; in February he began the open-air work. Early in the morning his carriage might be seen rolling through the sleeping city; freed from the narrow garden walls, when the sun was just rising from behind the Sabine hills, in the lonely country he began joyfully and diligently his modest work, which became a mental enjoyment to him in that the days of Ancient Rome were before his mind, and with the joy of a true friend of nature his eye roamed far and wide over the blue sea, and the land rich in historical events. He hardly allowed himself any rest even in the hottest time of summer ; it was very fortunate that he worked so incessantly, for his sojourn was shorter than was anticipated.

In July, 1846, the noble Prince in whose service he had found this precious leisure, died; on his second return home Moltke brought back the finished map of Rome and its environs, the treasure that has been enjoyed and valued by all who have since explored the Campagna.

From this time he could no longer be spared at home, but even in the most arduous official work his love for the soil of antiquity and his endeavours to promote its exploration, did not die. Athens, which he had hoped to see on his first journey abroad, was still unknown to him. In the spring of 1862 Emperor William, then Prince Regent, originated an enterprise, the object of which was to explore the antiquities of Athens, and to give to Karl Bötticher, the author of " Tectonic," an opportunity of examining the Acropolis ; This expedition is also remembered by most people, as having enabled Heinrich Strack to discover amidst the rubbish of Dionysius' theatre the marble seat of honour in their original places.

My object was, in the first place, to discover the plan of the Athenian fortifications, and remembering what we owed to the Chief of the Great General Staff in the province of ancient topography, I dared, without previously procuring a recommendation from the authorities, to bring forward my request in the Staff Building then in the *Behrenstrasse.* I asked for a topographer to accompany us, whose experienced military eye would be able to discover the locality and to map it out. The love of travel was awakened in Moltke. " I should like best to go with you myself," was his answer. Without making the least difficulty he granted the necessary technical support, and in 1865 the first connected map of the Athenian city walls could be laid before him.

Since then every research on classical soil has found encouragement in the Great General Staff. In 1872 the first topographical maps of Ancient Smyrna, Ephesus with the Artemision and the Royal city of Sardis were sketched. Two years later Kaupert, Inspector of Surveying, received a commission to make an exact survey of the valley of Athens. In 1866 Moltke had summoned him from Cassel, where he had achieved success at the topographical office of the Electoral Hessian General Staff, to make use of these results for the Prussian maps. This undertaking gained a larger significance with the foundation of the German Institute at Athens. Year by year young officers were sent out to continue the survey, and it is hoped that a general map of that country will be finished in a short time ; it will be the first safe foundation for historical local research, and also an indispensable beginning for geographical explorations.

The causes and connections to which we owe the scientific researches and maps of Byzantium, the Bosphorus, Asia Minor and Mesopotamia, Rome and the Campagna, Athens and Attica by Moltke himself and his friends, and partly under his directions by his officials and officers, may seem accidental, and yet they were all closely connected ; for it was the pleasure in research, and the gift for it, which made Moltke's life of such importance to the science of Geography.

Who can fully appreciate the intellectual activity of this great man in all its branches ? It would be presumption on my part to speak of his strategical works, the cause of his introduction into the academical circle, at the request of Pertz and Ranke after the death of Ritter. It would be a difficult task to describe him in his connection with men who have been great generals and also masters in the science of historiography. It requires the capacity of doing full justice to both sides. It is also impossible for the uninitiated to distinguish the different authors in the historical works of the General Staff, even though the grand and clear grasp of the political situation, as well as that of the seat of war introductory to the history of 1870, betray the master who by it obtained a lasting distinction recognized by everybody.

Since the wars of liberation, war history has also become a very different science. Strategy is no longer a speciality surrounded by secrets, using armies as the tools of an artificial mechanism. When armed strength is based upon the readiness of the whole people, strategy must become popular and war history must become part of the history of the people.

Moltke, whose life covers almost a century, grew up during the wars of liberation. As a boy he lived through the time of Germany's deepest humiliation; he saw his own home plundered by insolent enemies, and Blücher's corps laying down their arms.

So, when a young man, he joyfully watched the beginning of a new era, and in his letters of travel he speaks of defeats that may be the germ of an awakening of the nation. And so we understand what it was that brought the young officer from the Danish army to us; it was the home-feeling of the German mind, which wished to take part in the national development begun at Leipsic and Waterloo; and after he had worked indefatigably in educating himself for a General, and in perfecting military affairs during long years of peace, the task fell to him at the head of the General Staff of taking a personal share, and a very decisive one, for Germany in the promotion of those virtues whose beginning he had watched during the wars of liberation.

The law of compulsory service by which Prussia had

been regenerated must not remain at a standstill, as had been the case, to the disadvantage of the State, with the army of the Great King. The Emperor William I., when Regent, had seen the necessity of re-organization in the Army, so that it might stand perfectly ready for war in any serious crisis. It was natural that the greater demands on the revenues of the State should arouse displeasure, and that the organic improvement of the most popular of our State institutions should disturb the internal peace of the country; it was a time of severe trial for all the friends of the fatherland, insomuch that King William, seeing his good intentions, as father of the country, misunderstood, was thinking of abdicating.

At this crisis Moltke appeared, like a rescuing genius; the violent opposition was principally based upon the fact that judging by the experience of the last decades people did not believe in a realization of the reform. Then he, fully understanding Bismarck's politics and what was involved, knew as Chief of the Great General Staff, how to use the sword whetted by Roon, in such a way that the revived re-organization proved to be the greatest benefit, and was immediately acknowledged as such by all parties. That was a rare victory giving back to the people their King and to the country peace, and preparing the way for the State to take a new position in the world. Nobody has been able to render a greater service to this country.

Nothing is more characteristic of Moltke than the conciliating position he took in political life. For one can well say that in him all the friction and opposition between different classes and vocations that weak human nature is liable to, were lost in perfect harmony. A soldier in heart and soul, he always kept the welfare of his fatherland in view, and his military opinions were never anywhere separated from those of political life. He did not long to revenge the sufferings which the Germans had borne from the insolence of their neighbours in the time of humiliation, during his youth and before that, but he wished to make the return of such degradation impossible. His wish was to re-unite those compatriots that he had met in his travels, forsaken by their country, estranged from their homes, and to assemble the brethren who had fought against each other under one flag, never to be parted again. The banner which he carried as general, was in the mind of the highest sovereign principally a banner of peace.

Therefore, it was always his purpose, as representing the Army in Parliament, to make clear the inseparable connection between the interests of the Army and those of the State and of the people. Military service was called an unproductive occupation, he said, but its purpose and aim was the safety of the State, without which commerce and trade could not prosper ; it was for the rising generation the school of order, punctuality, cleanliness, obedience and faithfulness ; qualities which were surely not valueless for a productive occupation later on. His opinions, accompanied by the spirit of a gentle wisdom, were always founded on the basis of an irrefutable truth from whose impression no impartial hearer could escape. It was a necessity to him to base everything, even the highest art of strategy, on the simplest, well-known principles ; no soldier's virtue existed for him which did not rest on a moral foundation.

Though he was the most eminent master in warfare, he never felt the temptation of seeking for an opportunity to show off this mastership. If the decision of the battle-field was unavoidable, he had only one aim, which was, to obtain it as quickly and energetically as possible, to secure for the fatherland its highest, inalienable possessions, and quietly and modestly he retired to his peaceable employments after every success.

A man of superior mental gifts, he was never jealous of his personal power ; in every campaign he sedu-

lously endeavoured to leave to the leaders of the
different armies the greatest scope for their own
activity, after he had made a plan which would bring
matters to a point at a certain place and in a certain
hour.

At the height of favours with which the supreme
sovereign honoured the hero, who had had such a
large share in erecting the Imperial throne, in full
enjoyment of enthusiastic recognition by all Germans
at home and abroad, who felt again elevated and united
by his victories, admired by all contemporaries as one
of the most illustrious men of the century, he has
always remained humble, modest, plain and simple, as
if he had done nothing uncommon. A word, a look, a
gesture, which might have hurt an inferior, was impossible to him.

He possessed many qualities rarely found united in one
man. He was a man of action, who in his explorations
of Asia did not shrink from fear of endangering his life ;
a bold warrior, a strategist who dared to pass beyond the
outside lines of defence in reconnoitring, a man incessantly busy following with a sharp eye from the General
Staff Building all the armies of Europe, all the changes
of armament and technique of war, all the inventions
concerning the building of fortresses, all progress in the
means of communication, that he might turn every
experience to the immediate advantage of the military
forces of his country—and with this attitude of uninterrupted vigilance and efficiency maintained towards the
outer world, he always preserved the collected, thinking
mind, full of lively interest in art and science, to
which serious research was a necessity of life. Even in
ancient times it was a dispute which life was to be
preferred, the contemplative life of the sage, who sees
the events of the world pass before him with a calm
eye, or the practical life of the statesman and general—
Moltke has united both in himself and that in a rare

manner. He is an unequalled example that full development of the thinking power does not injure manly
energy. That a German should preserve this twofold
power up to his old age, is that for which we thank
God with all our hearts.

Moltke was a richly blessed man, as well during his
life as in the hour of his death. He thankfully appreciated the blessings which had accompanied his actions.
When he returned home from Königgrätz, he was
heard to say: " It is a beautiful thing when the Lord
brightens the evening of life as He has done that of
the King and many of his Generals; I too am now
sixty-six years old; for my work in this life I have
received a reward that is only given to few men. We
have had a campaign which is of immense importance
for Prussia, Germany and the world. God's grace has
rewarded our honest and active endeavours with
glorious victories. We old people, who have gone
through the Bohemian campaign, can boast whatever
hard fights we have had in our early years, of being the
favourites of fortune now."[1]

Thus he spoke then, not mentioning his own merits
even by a word. He knew well that it was not the
last fight; but he was thankful for the success gained
by the older generation, not thinking then that much
was still to be done by himself in unimpaired strength,
and that he was to become the chosen hero of the most
important century of our Fatherland's history, under
whose guidance the German nation felt herself invin-
cible.

The blessing for which Moltke was so grateful rests
on us and on our descendants. For it is not only
visible monuments that he has left us, in the German
unity, the German Empire which he helped to build
up so magnificently, but he is so dear to us, because
round him as round no other general the whole nation

[1] Compare Baron von Firk's " Feldmarschall Graf Moltke," p. 67.

has assembled in love and concord. He is the protector of this spiritual unity, who for centuries will ever be enthusiastically remembered by German hearts, an example of virtue which will keep our Fatherland on the heights to which he has led it, if we follow his motto :

Alle Zeit
Treu bereit
Für des Reiches Herrlichkeit !

THE END.